Totally Bound Publishing books by Tierney O'Malley:

Blue-Eyed Four
Passionate Bid

I0663093

The Blue-Eyed Four

PASSIONATE BID

TIERNEY O'MALLEY

Passionate Bid
ISBN # 978-1-78430-154-5
©Copyright Tierney O'Malley 2014
Cover Art by Posh Gosh ©Copyright July 2014
Interior text design by Claire Siemaszkiewicz
Totally Bound Publishing

Published in 2014 by Totally Bound Publishing, Newland House, The Point, Weaver Road, Lincoln, LN6 3QN, United Kingdom.

Dedication

To Tom, Francesca and Genevieve.
My sunshine.

PASSIONATE BID

Chapter One

Julian Ravenwood clenched his teeth so hard he thought they might crack from the pressure. But having cracked teeth was better than punching someone. He'd already humiliated his grandma and wouldn't do it again in front of people eager to hear more gossip.

Son of a bitch. Standing inside this church was the last place he wanted to be—wearing a tuxedo, polished shoes and about to get hitched.

Damn wedding. In his opinion, however fucking insignificant it might be, marrying a very young woman was a high price to pay for one mistake he barely remembered committing. Too bad his soon-to-be father-in-law thought otherwise, a thought that his grandma shared.

How could she pick Saint Claire's side? He couldn't believe it. His own grandma, who knew him since birth, agreed that he'd acted foolishly and should face his responsibility like an honorable man.

I am a fucking honorable man. Never tried pot, never cheated on any of my girlfriends, never cut in line. But, according to Saint Claire, I am the son of Satan who took advantage of his daughter's innocence. Innocent, my ass.

Julian had been drunk. Joanie sober. Wasn't it easy to see who'd taken advantage of whom? But no matter how hard he'd tried to explain that simple fact when the unthinkable had happened, they hadn't believed him. What he'd received was a hard slap on the face. It was the first time he'd seen his grandma that angry.

How could they not see that Joanie had been an accomplice and not a victim?

"Bro, you're scaring me with your fucking scowl."

Julian elbowed his friend, Nolan. "I bet you'd do more than scowl if you were the one getting married right now."

"Joanie's not that bad. I talked to her. She's cool."

"And fucking seventeen."

"Please, mind your language. You're inside the church."

Nolan turned around to grin at Father Keeley. "Sorry, Father, we have sinned — again."

Julian groaned and rolled his eyes as the pianist played the old universal wedding tune, *Here Comes the Bride*. It was a reminder that he'd fucked up his life. Big time. He looked to his left where the old lady in her bright pink sweater hunched low in front of the organ. Her body spoke of excitement. She was practically dancing. Well, at least someone appreciated the occasion because he, the stupid groom, definitely didn't care.

Yup, I don't give a damn about this wedding.

The handful of guests, including his two other friends, Trey and Henry, turned in their seats expecting the bride to appear at the door. A minute later, no bride appeared. Good. Maybe she and her father had come to their senses and realized that this whole thing was a mistake and they'd both gone home.

Perhaps to cue in Joanie to take the spot by the door where she should be, the organist pounded harder on the keys, repeating the music's intro, as she looked up and craned her neck.

Damn song. Here Comes Death would be an apt title for it, because this wedding was exactly that – a funeral. A string of curses fell from his mouth. Damn, he'd never been this angry. He should feel ecstatic or at least nervous. After all, today was his wedding day, the beginning of a new chapter in his life. Today was anything but.

Standing by the altar with ornery Father Keeley breathing down his neck was the last place on earth he thought he would be right now. He should be getting ready for the trip with his buddies in Florida, to enjoy the beach, beautiful women in their skimpy bikinis, and cans of cold Coors beer, not sealing his doom.

"You still going to join us in Florida?" Nolan whispered.

"Hell yeah."

"What about your bride?"

"What about her?" Julian flicked imaginary lint off his sleeve.

"What do you mean what about her? Tonight's gonna be the night, man."

"Shit, I'm not going to touch that girl with a ten-foot pole."

"Dude, so cliché. So you're just going to leave her?"

"Well, to start with, I'm going to Florida with you guys. What about you? Aren't you supposed to spend time with Gypsy?"

"Yeah. She's okay with me going to Florida, though."

"You should just kidnap her, take her to Reno and marry her. What do you think her dad'll do?"

"Gypsy will not agree to Reno. Her dad is hell bent on keeping her tucked in beside him all the time."

"Man, that sucks. When are we going to meet her?"

"Maybe after Florida."

"So she's going to play Rapunzel while you play Romeo and climb her trellis forever?"

"We'll make it work. I think you should too. Things happen for a reason. Give your marriage a chance. Don't worry, we're not going to replace your spot. Even married, you'll remain one of the Blue-Eyed Four. It's just you're the first one to fall. I wonder who's going to be next. Definitely not me. Not with Gypsy reluctant to leave her dad's side."

Julian met his friends' gazes. Two pairs of intense blue eyes looked back at him. Blue-Eyed Four. It was what Remy, the brusque bartender at the Old Cabin Bar in downtown Seattle, had yelled while pointing his finger at the four of them when the police had asked who was involved in the fight. Since then the name had stuck. Among the four of them, Nolan had a girlfriend, one whom Nolan swore owned his heart.

His friend was lucky to find a woman he considered the one. Unlike Julian, who had been saddled with a woman he only knew by name. Julian searched deep inside himself for any signs of excitement or giddiness, anything at all, but there was nothing. What he felt was the need to escape and hot-boiling anger for not being able to.

Goddamn it. He'd rather be anywhere but here.

Trey gave him a thumbs-up while Henry pretended to be licking an imaginary ice cream. They'd been trying to cheer him up. But so far, none of his friends' ridiculous behavior had worked.

Stomach sick, he kept his eyes focused on the church's stained-glass window just above the arched doorway. Through his peripheral view, a froth of white appeared. His heart sank low in his gut.

"Your bride, bro."

"Please don't remind me, Nolan. This is a fucking nightmare."

"She doesn't have a maid."

"Don't care. I need beer."

Nolan snickered. He shoved his friend, hard.

So the Saint Claires are still here. Fuckin' A. He kept his gaze glued on the rainbow-colored cross and ignored the hushed whispers that seemed to get louder every minute.

Father Keeley cleared his throat. The sound grated on Julian's nerves. The priest had been doing it all morning, as though Julian was a child being reminded to behave. Julian bet the father would have a real sore throat when the ceremony was over. This time though, he knew why the priest made an even louder ahem.

But he didn't need Father Keeley's reminder. He knew what he was supposed to do—look at Joanie Saint Claire, the part that he found hard to do. No, not that he didn't want to see her. He'd seen her around, and didn't find any problems with that. It was what she represented that he didn't like at all—a bride.

His bride.

Julian lowered his gaze to look at Joanie. *Oh. My. God.* He shuddered inwardly at the sight of his bride.

Joanie's face was pale, her eyes swollen, and her lips trembled the way one would when left out in the freezing cold. Shit, he'd never seen a bride who looked ready to cast up her stomach's contents. With Joanie's father at her side, she walked with the speed of a snail, unsmiling, and she looked on the verge of tears. She held her bouquet like a heavy basket dangling at her side. Her old man, who Julian often referred to as Saint Claire, held her other hand at the crook of his arm.

Saint Claire looked twice as bad as his daughter did. His face resembled a dark cloud during winter – heavy and thunderous, as if a mere poke would make him burst and shower everyone, particularly him, with his wrath. Julian bet that if Saint Claire could have his way, he'd blast him with his .38 Special to the center of the earth for what he had done to Joanie. Or what Saint Claire believed he'd done. When Saint Claire had requested – no, demanded – that he explain what had happened, why his daughter had ended up in his bedroom, Julian had told him everything to the best of his ability. The old man's sharp glance at Joanie, with his brows deeply furrowed, told Julian that he believed what had happened was consensual. However, Joanie was still seventeen, underage for legal consent, and Saint Claire had found a way to make him face the consequences – marriage.

One fucking mistake and his life had turned upside down.

Julian watched Joanie take baby steps. *Good.* The longer it took them to reach the altar the better. He needed every second to prolong his bachelorhood.

Change your mind, old man. Take your daughter back to your home, not to me.

But the aisle wasn't long enough to give Saint Claire time to think about the stupidity of their situation. To Julian's chagrin, Joanie and Saint Claire reached the altar.

Julian stole a quick glance at his grandma sitting on the front pew. Their gazes met. Grandma shook her head. A simple gesture, but it caused him a pain that wound its way to his heart. He didn't want to hurt her, but he had, and there was nothing he could do about it but apologize.

"*This is your fate, Julian. Accept it.*" Those were his grandma's words. He liked to believe her, but he knew the truth. They were all gathered in this cold, gray church because he'd consumed too much alcohol, and it had fucked with his brain.

Willing himself to focus on Saint Claire, the old man gave him a chilling look, sending him a silent warning. *Oh, yeah, I get the message in that look. It's the I-will-kill-you-if-you-hurt-my-daughter look.* Julian met the stare with his own hot glare. He would rather give Saint Claire an imprint of his knuckles, but the man carried a gun under his coat. Nah, he would never hurt an old man physically, but it felt just as nice to think about it. Besides, his grandma hadn't raised him to be a disrespectful ass.

Saint Claire, Julian noticed, had to pry Joanie's fingers off his arm. He heard the old man murmur, "It's going to be okay, poppet," before giving her a tight embrace that bespoke his unwillingness to give her away.

When Joanie finally let go of her father, Saint Claire turned to pierce him with eyes shiny from unshed tears.

Julian wanted to tell him, 'Hey, I'm not the only one to blame here.' But it wouldn't do any good since the other person to blame wasn't even considered an adult. Saint Claire broke eye contact and took his seat beside Julian's grandma. They greeted each other with a short nod.

With his spirits sinking even lower, he let out a deep sigh while waiting for Joanie to face the priest. Joanie's chin quivered and her eyes, like her father's, were bright with unshed tears. But when she focused her gaze on him, he saw something he couldn't exactly discern. Courage, anger, fear, maybe sadness? He couldn't tell. Whatever it was, he didn't care. All he wanted was to end this lunacy.

He acknowledged Joanie with a nod, which made her already flushed face deepen into crimson. She lowered her lashes and began chewing her lips.

Lord, this is why virgins are supposed to stay in convents.

He faced Father Keeley, who showed his displeasure openly by scowling. Fuck, why was everyone looking at him as if he'd sinfully offered Eve an apple and ruined the innocence and harmony in the Garden of Eden? This Eve, also known as his future wife Joanie, might be young, but innocent she wasn't.

Joanie had known what she was doing that night. Considering he hadn't had scratches on him or any sign that she'd fought him, showed what was obvious — she had willfully opened her legs to him.

She, Joanie Saint Claire, had done nothing to stop him from breaking her hymen, therefore making her a contributor to his impending doom. Their doom.

She should have screamed, clawed his face, and kicked his groin. But what had she done? Spread her legs wide then dug the soles of her feet into his ass. That last part he remembered well. Why? Who the fuck knows?

Maybe it was that good. "Hell." The word flew out of his mouth before he could stop himself. He heard Joanie breathe, a deep intake, but before he could apologize, Father Keeley reprimanded him in his nasally annoying tone.

"Watch your mouth, boy. You are in the house of God."

Nolan elbowed him. "Yeah, man. We're in the house of Allah," he added with a grin.

"Sorry, Father." Fine, he'd been acting like a jerk since he'd arrived this afternoon, but he had his reasons — he too was a victim in this mess. So whoever thought he was a jerk could go to hell.

Not knowing what to do with his hands, he clasped them in front of him. Father Keeley scowled, his nostrils flaring. Julian raised his brows in silent question. What? Was he supposed to hold hands with Joanie? He glanced at Joanie. Her head bowed while she picked the petals on her bouquet. Well, she wasn't complaining, so why offer his arm to his bride or even touch her fingers?

Besides, touching Joanie had been his downfall. Doing it again would be plain stupid. No way would he hold his unwanted bride's hand. It wasn't going to happen again, not in this fucking lifetime. Never. There wasn't much he could do to prevent the wedding from happening, but at least he could show Saint Claire he opposed it. Old man Saint Claire was probably seething right now, thinking about his gun and wishing he could shoot him. But Julian knew better. The man was hell-bent on seeing this wedding done and tightly sealed. To save Joanie's reputation.

What's up with that? Losing one's virginity in the twenty-first century wasn't a big deal anymore. Even girls in middle school let their boyfriends finger fuck or have sex with them. Virginity wasn't that precious and important. Not to him. *Obviously to some it was.* Like Saint Claire and yeah, his grandma, who still valued morals.

Christ, who would have thought, in this modern age, a woman who wasn't promiscuous still existed? And he'd fucked her. He'd often wondered what it was like to deflower a tight, untried woman. Now that he'd finally experienced it, he could only remember parts of the deed.

Joanie had been a virgin, but for fuck's sake, he'd been so drunk he couldn't tell how he'd broken her hymen. Had he been rough, gentle? Had she cried like his friends told him virgins always did when they lost their precious maidenhead?

He avoided looking at Joanie, giving his attention to the wooden crucifix dangling from Father Keeley's hand. He tried to think of something, anything, just to block out the priest's droning voice.

Without a doubt, Julian was beyond pissed, and truth be told, nervous. How could he not be? In a few minutes, he'd be a freaking married man because he'd got fucking drunk at a party and his wife would be...the town's clumsy, untidy nerd. Again, he glanced at Joanie Saint Claire and quickly assessed her from head to toe.

Joanie was still looking down at her bouquet, scrunching up her nose with her lips moving from side to side as if something bothered her. Seeing her bouquet's condition, he thought any bride would be making faces too. The bunch of white orchids looked as wilted as she did. Julian's eyes widened when he noticed her paint-stained cuticles. It looked like Joanie hadn't prepared for this wedding at all. And if she had, damn, she'd totally failed. She wasn't wearing earrings or a necklace, no bracelets or rings...not even lipstick. The white silk ribbon holding her hair was already undone. Brown ringlets escaped her lopsided bun and a few curling wisps dangled down her temple and nape. He'd seen her with her hair down before. The shade resembled a thick mop dipped in caramel and milk chocolate.

Joanie reminded him of a beer diluted with ice—
bland. The first time he'd gone to Joanie's house to
face Saint Claire's accusations and hear the
consequences if he didn't accept his condition, Joanie
had sat on a chair wearing a pair of faded, paint-
stained blue jeans and sneakers with their laces
untied. He'd assumed she'd looked that way because
Saint Claire had failed to inform her about his visit.
Today, she'd proved his assumption wrong. On her
freaking wedding day, Joanie looked like a crumpled
bed sheet. She couldn't even keep the ribbon in her
hair.

Had she dragged her ass here the way he had with
his own ass this morning? Yeah, he had to force
himself to come here too. But unlike Joanie, who
looked like a bride who had just rolled out of bed, at
least he'd buffed his shoes. He hated this wedding,
but at least he'd tried. Fuckin' A!

Joanie moved her head to look at the priest
thumbing the pages of his Bible. The simple
movement shifted the flower-shaped hairclip on the
side of her head. He plucked the antique-looking
ornament when it began to slip down. Joanie looked at
him and frowned. He showed her the ornament.

"Oh, that thing never stays in my hair. Could you
hang onto it, please? I don't have a pocket," she
whispered.

Seeing her hands were full, he nodded and shoved
the clip in his pocket. Something else caught his
eyes—her white ribbon. The slip of material dangled
on her nape. Without thinking, he reached to retie the
irritating useless material. "Your ribbon was undone."
What an unraveling bride. *And she'll be mine. Shit.*

"Thank you."

Father Keeley cleared his throat then looked at Julian with his thick eyebrows arched so high they touched his hairline.

Christ, even the priest had forgotten to trim his brows.

Fuck the fates for putting him in this situation. Yes, he'd thought of having his own family someday. But not this soon. Not this year. Not at the age of twenty-three. And definitely not with his soon-to-be father-in-law sitting on the front pew with a concealed weapon beneath his suit jacket, which should be freaking illegal.

He wanted to marry when he was ready and with the woman he loved. Not like this — by force and against his freaking will.

Joanie's thick wired-framed glasses slid down the tip of her nose. She pushed them back up with her forefinger and sniffed. She turned her head to the left then to the right. "Could I borrow your hankie?"

Sighing, he pulled out the white handkerchief from his suit pocket and handed it to her. "Here."

Well, if she was sad, that made the two of them. Getting married wasn't his idea.

Joanie accepted his pristine white handkerchief, then gave him a wan smile, allowing him to notice the metal in her mouth.

Braces? Aw, fuck. He didn't know Joanie wore braces. Come to think of it, there was lots he didn't know about his bride. Like her middle name, favorite color, if she had a habit of grinding her teeth, whether she snored at night, or if her jaw clicked when she chewed her food.

Good God, he needed a miraculous intervention here. If he could get out of this situation, he promised never to drink or touch virgins again. "Shit," he said low but loud enough for the priest to hear.

Father Keeley looked up and glowered at him. The way his thick, brown eyebrows joined together reminded Julian of a long, hairy caterpillar.

Julian scowled back. Father Keeley shook his head at him, then continued reading where he had left off.

He wouldn't be here if he had followed his head instead of his dick. What had happened that night during his party was a blur. But waking up the next day with a cold barrel of a gun poking against his ribs and Joanie sitting on his bed wrapped in a blanket with her shoulders exposed and hair wildly mussed was as clear as bottled spring water.

Now, here he was standing by the altar with Joanie waiting for the priest to finish reading verses from his worn, leather-bound Bible.

He'd heard about brides fainting during their wedding. Maybe he should start the trend of grooms fainting at the altar. If he hit his head on the marble steps and split his skull open, Joanie's father might change his mind about filing a rape case against him if he didn't marry his daughter. Seventeen? No way on earth would he have guessed her age. Yes, she looked young, but not that young. Her boobs made her look like a nineteen or twenty-year-old chick. And whenever he saw her with his grandma, she carried herself with the confidence and composure of an intelligent woman. She even moved and acted like a mature person, and his grandma talked constantly about Joanie being a responsible girl who offered her services as a reader.

When Grandma had told him that someone had replied to the ad about an afternoon reader she'd placed in the local newspaper, he'd thought a college student had answered it. Not once had she mentioned she was only seventeen. All she had said was that the reader was nice and could really use the money to help her dad. He'd never asked anything more about Joanie. Now he realized he should have.

This Joanie standing beside him looked totally different. Her composure, the self-confidence he'd glimpsed in the past were gone. All he could see was a young girl who wanted her daddy and not a husband.

Seventeen and a virgin. Fuckin' A. But how could a man know about a woman's virginity unless he fucked her? It wasn't fair. He supposed life wasn't treating her well, since she didn't want to be in this church either, but goddamn it, she should have at least told him her age. Now they were both paying for it with something they obviously didn't want. Why couldn't Saint Claire see his point? A teenager like Joanie should be enjoying jumping on a trampoline, watching movies, shopping. Not preparing for a married life. Seventeen.

Julian pinched the bridge of his nose. What would he do with a seventeen-year-old bride? Worse, one he didn't want? How would a marriage founded on anger, regret, grief and a quick tumble in bed survive? Because of a brief moment of insanity, he now stood at this altar listening to the priest seal his doom.

Feeling helpless, he looked back at his friends again. They, too, seemed shocked to see his bride.

Father Keeley mentioned his name. Julian realized it was time to take his vows. *Here we go. Doomsday.* His head began to throb.

Chapter Two

Four years later

Julian ran his fingers over the most beautiful ass he had ever laid his eyes on. As a professional model, Georgina not only possessed a beautiful face but a perfectly sculpted body his dick throbbed for all the time. He'd never seen her with smudged makeup, chipped nail polish or wearing anything wrinkled. Georgina was the embodiment of perfection.

He'd been searching for a woman like her. One who would read to his grandma in the afternoon, who liked his job as a veterinarian, and one who matched him thrust for thrust in bed.

Sadly, he wasn't the perfect candidate for the likes of Georgina Myers. A married man like him meant troubles, problems. Especially when his estranged wife refused to sign the damn divorce papers.

Like a skin lesion, his current marital status served as a sign of disease, a stigma to the single, beautiful and smart women he dated, warning them to stay away. Georgina, however, hadn't run out of his door like a rock propelled from a slingshot when he'd told her the truth about his marriage. Instead, she'd remained sitting on the bed while she'd cried — calmly at first, then she'd thrown a tantrum that had surprised the bejesus out of him. She'd picked up a pillow and hit him until the pillowcase had ripped. She'd called him all kinds of names until froth had formed around her mouth. When she'd finally calmed down, she had smiled and said, "I'm sorry, Julian. You surprised me. Sweetheart, this is not going to work."

That had been two months ago. And yet, she had remained, which told him he still had a shot at keeping her, although she never failed to express how much she hated his marital status.

If he could just remove the part of his life that drove women out of his bed in a hurry, everything would be...peachy. As peachy as Georgina's bottom.

He really must get rid of his estranged wife.

Holding his hard shaft, he rubbed the head of his dick up and down Georgina's thighs, smearing the clear liquid that emerged from its tip. "So beautiful," he whispered on her neck.

Georgina stirred and rolled onto her back, stretching her long, slender limbs. Her naked body still held a pink glow from their last lovemaking. "Hello, Doctor. Inspecting my body again?"

"Of course. Got to make sure everything is good and functioning." He lowered his head to capture one erect nipple. "Hmm... This one is good. Let me try the other one." He licked the other nipple and watched it harden.

Georgina moaned.

"Is that one good too?"

"Uh-huh. No problem on that one." Georgina spread her legs when he moved on top of her. With deliberate slowness, he snaked his hand between their bodies. Inch by inch he lowered his hand until he reached her still-wet pussy.

Georgina wrapped her legs around his ass. "I love it when you touch me there."

Julian pressed the pad of his thumb on her slippery clit. "Should I continue?"

"You'd better, Dr Ravenwood. I think my temperature is rising."

"Hang on a sec." He reached for his Trojan and tore the wrapping. "You hangin' there okay?"

"Yes. But hurry."

Julian unrolled the rubber onto his throbbing cock and positioned himself over her. "I'm ready, beautiful."

"Good." Georgina tightened her hold and pulled him closer, her heels digging hard into his skin.

Closing his fingers around his cock, he rubbed himself up and down against her clit before pointing the swollen head at her wet pussy. "Sweetheart, I know how to cure your problem—with a bit of slow penetration." He pushed the tip of his dick inside her slippery passage. "Then go deeper like this." He pressed harder until his full shaft was buried inside her then pulled out slowly, only to thrust again. "Once inside, thrust repeatedly like this." He groaned at the sheer pleasure of having her walls throb around him. "Your condition will get better."

"Ooohh, I love your cure. What do you call this prescription?"

"Fucking a beautiful woman." He thrust harder and ground his hips to go as deep as he could.

"Love it. Don't stop. Do it again."

"I won't stop. Georgina. Hmm... Lift your ass, yes." Georgina writhed underneath him. "Yeah, come for me. I want to feel you contract while I'm fucking you like this."

"Hmm... I love it. Talk dirty to me. Suck my nipple. Yes. Oh, Julian. You are so long and thick."

"And you love my dick."

"Of course. No other dick can fuck me this good. Oh, yeah..."

"Got that right. Now lift your ass."

Georgina lowered her feet on the bed and raised her ass. "Fuck me hard and fast. Faster. Now."

He licked one erect nipple and gripped her hips. "Hang on, Georgina. You're going for a good fucking ride." He surged inside her repeatedly.

His control was quickly slipping, but he waited. Feeling Georgina come with his dick buried deep inside her was as pleasurable as releasing his own orgasm. The plush bed squeaked as he pumped his hips. Hard and deep, he took her. This was how Georgina liked sex—rough. Julian didn't stop pumping until Georgina screamed his name.

"Fuck! Yes, scream for me." Julian leaned back on his heels, placed his hands at the back of Georgina's knees to spread her legs wide then looked down where their bodies joined. The sight of his cock shiny from their mixed juices and her plump pussy had him pulsing. "Oh, yeah. Fuck me, baby."

He thrust his hips and watched himself go in and out of her warm pussy. Unable to take it anymore, he quickened his pace.

Georgina screamed as he rammed her hard. "More, Julian. I'm coming!"

"You want more, I'll give you more." He pressed his thumb on her clit while keeping up his fast tempo.

"Yes..."

When he felt Georgina's thighs and butt muscles contract, he released his own orgasm. Spent, he collapsed on top of her. He was still trying to catch his breath when Georgina pushed her soft hands against his shoulders.

"You're crushing me."

"Sorry." He rolled to lie on his back. "Please stay, Georgie. Stay forever."

Georgina smiled. "Forever. Such a romantic. I already told you—married men are on my long list of men to avoid. I'm only here because you have such a great ass. But it's time for me to go."

"I won't be married soon."

"Still, you'll be divorced. And divorced men are second on my list."

"So I'm in a no-win situation then."

"Don't blame me. You shouldn't have married your wife."

"I married her against my wishes. Joanie's father forced me. It was almost like a shotgun wedding. She was underage at the time so it was either marry her or go to jail."

"Her father probably wanted to saddle her with a rich man and he spotted you as a great candidate."

Julian doubted it. Since he'd left, he'd never heard from either Joanie or her father. They hadn't demanded anything from him. "So this is it for us then. Are you sure you don't want to stay? Grandma will miss you. She enjoys your company, Georgie. And I will miss you."

"I'm sorry, sweetheart. Just think. What if your wife shows up here and starts pulling my hair? I've had horrible experiences with wives threatening to shave my head if I don't leave their husbands alone. One wife from Texas even dumped a spit bucket on my car."

"That's gross.

"Hell, yes. I don't want trouble, Julian. And your wife—if she refused to sign your divorce papers—is trouble. Try to understand my situation."

"I understand."

Georgina traced Julian's ear. "You know, I thought... I was hoping you'd be the last..."

"I will be if you give me a chance." Julian buried his face between Georgina's breasts and inhaled her sweet perfume.

"I already did. I stayed this long. But I'm not comfortable with this. It's not your fault. You're a victim of your wife and her father. Are you really going to see her?"

"Yes. She kept sending the papers back unsigned. If I go see her, then I can hand her the papers and have her sign them. Three days. Give me three days and I promise you, I'll be back a single man. Georgina, I want you here on this spot—naked, wet and ready for me."

"Wow, you are so romantic." Georgina hit Julian's shoulder playfully. "Julian, I enjoyed being with you. But I'm afraid of your wife."

"She's just a little critter. A foot shorter than you. Nothing to be afraid of."

"You really think she'll sign the papers if you meet her in person?"

"I'll make sure of it."

Georgina pursed her lips. "I don't know, Julian. I can tell she's going to be trouble. She refuses to sign them because, and believe me on this, she wants something from you. Money, I'm sure. Don't give her anything more than what she deserves."

"I don't know Joanie's reasons, but I'll find out."

Georgina made a good point. Why would Joanie keep sending the divorce papers back unsigned if she didn't want something in exchange? He'd find out what it was. If her demands were reasonable—he'd give them to her just to earn his freedom. "My trip to Bend, Oregon will set things right between Joanie and me."

"Then go and do it."

Julian smiled. Oh, yeah. He could tell she was reconsidering his desire for her to stay. "Will you be here when I get back?"

"I like you, Julian. I really thought we had something going here. But... You have a wife."

"She won't be when I come back."

"Are you sure?"

"I'll make sure of it."

"Good. Well, go see your wife, make her sign the papers and see to it that she's not going to knock on your door for the rest of your life. When you accomplish all that, call me. Then we'll talk. You know where to find me." Georgina cupped his sac, massaged him gently before wrapping her long fingers around his shaft.

"You don't have to go back to your apartment. Stay here with Grandma."

"Oh, I love Grandma and I like it here. But like I said, until you find yourself a free man, I'll have to worry about Joanie coming behind me with a pair of scissors to cut my hair. Angry wives and soccer moms are horrible. I can't and I don't want to deal with scorned wives. Gosh, I can't believe she wouldn't set you free. I'll be in my own apartment. I'll miss you, of course, and your sweet grandma. She bugs me with her requests to read her favorite book from ancient places as if I'm a news reporter, but I like her."

"Grandma bugs you?" Damn, why did he think that Georgina would warm up to his grandma the way Joanie did?

"I don't mean that in a bad way. But yeah, she bugs me, especially when she asks me to read her boring books. Still, I try to read them because she's sweet. Tell her that I'll visit her all the time."

An image of Joanie reading to his grandma formed in his head as if it had only happened yesterday. The first time he'd met her, Joanie was sitting on a chair, back straight, feet together, reading his grandma's favorite book. She had read as though she'd been reading to others all her life. He had actually been impressed with the obvious confidence that had seemed to surround her. He remembered liking her melodic and soft voice. Listening to Joanie had been almost like listening to books on tape. She had read with emotion and proper diction.

He remembered he'd been watching her for quite some time before she'd finally noticed him. When she'd looked up, he had greeted her with a wink. He remembered Joanie's face turning beet red, her jaw slackening as she'd dropped the book. Her dark green eyes had grown even bigger behind her glasses as she'd stared at him. He had chuckled so loudly at her reaction he'd woken his grandma up. After that day, whenever they had seen each other or he'd found her reading to Grandma, she'd reacted the same way with or without him winking—bright red spots had painted her cheeks and she'd stumbled on the words she was reading.

His presence, he'd realized, had made her uncomfortable so he had tried to make himself unnoticeable whenever she came to read to Grandma in the afternoon. He couldn't understand her reaction to him. But whatever her reason had been, he didn't give a fuck. To his grandma, who suffered from macular degeneration, Joanie was a godsend. To him, she was a big mistake.

"*Sonnets from the Portuguese* by Elizabeth Barrett Browning."

"Who?"

"Elizabeth Barrett Browning. Grandma loves her poems. The book was a gift from my grandfather. Grandma is a romantic at heart."

"Just like you. Well, Julian. I love you, sweetheart. But I don't like sharing anything with anyone, especially a greedy wife. Yours is obviously greedy because she won't let you go free."

"All I ask is for three days. I'll be back a free man, and we'll continue with what we have right now."

"You mean our endless humping?"

Julian cupped her mound, dipping the tip of his middle finger inside her entrance. "Yes."

"Hmm… I like us too."

"But I'm married. I know."

"Yes."

He untangled himself from Georgina's long limbs and got up to use the bathroom. He chucked his used condom in the toilet, flushed it down then grabbed a washcloth. After washing himself, he brought the towel back to bed with him.

Georgina eyed him like a hungry lioness. Her arms stretched above her head and one leg bent, moving from side to side.

"You're like a beautiful canvas," Julian said. "I couldn't get enough of your beauty if I tried."

"Come here, Leonardo."

Julian grinned. "I wish I could paint like him."

"Don't care if you can't paint because you can really fuck good."

As soon as he stretched his body beside her, Georgina rolled on top of him and started kissing her way down. She stopped when her mouth was right above his hard cock. "I'm going to miss you. So when are you leaving?"

Without waiting for an answer, Georgina began sucking the tip of his cock.

* * * *

Leaning against the cab's passenger door, Georgina watched Julian put her travel bags in the trunk. Moving out of Julian's apartment without Julian's knowledge had been his lawyer's idea. Rick had said that Julian wouldn't think that she was after his money and that Julian would chase after her if she played her cards well. She really hoped this ploy would work.

She'd had enough sleeping with old and young men who wanted nothing but to have her mouth around their dicks. It was time to stop. Julian fit the description of the man of her dreams. Someone who would put a ring on her finger and give her a comfortable life. Love would come next for sure, but for now, she must think about securing her future first.

Georgina kept her gaze on Julian. She could really see herself married to him. So fucking what if she had to read to his blind grandma? Whatever it took to win his affections, she'd do it. No matter how boring the job would be.

She noticed the women who walked by them ogling Julian like a delicious dessert on a table. Who could blame them? Julian could rival the models she'd worked with. Being a recipient of his gaze alone could make any woman sigh with pleasure.

"Keep looking at me like that and we'll end up back inside where I can have my way with you." He stood in front of her, his hands on her waist.

Laughing, she wrapped her arms around his neck. "Go to Oregon and rid yourself of that baggage you call 'wife' then come to me."

"That's the plan."

"By the way, don't worry about your grandma. I will still come over to keep her company."

"I'd appreciate that."

"Me moving out doesn't mean I'm totally giving up on you, you know." Keeping a blind old woman company, talking about her cooking and dead husband, had been the most boring thing Georgina had ever done. But it made Julian happy, so fuck it. She'd visit the old bat. Her time spent with the grandma would be worth it, once she married Julian.

"Glad to hear that."

"By the way, I'll bug your lawyer to take me out to dinner every night."

Julian asked, "Every night?"

"Yes. You pay him enough. He should make himself useful." *I let that scum fuck me in exchange for a promise that he'll do everything to make you mine.*

"Rick has his good uses." Pulling her against him, Julian planted a kiss on her temple. "This is not a goodbye."

No. Just a ruse to make you want me more. "No. Let me know when you're single again then we'll talk."

"Will do."

After a hot kiss that made *her* want for more, she got in the cab. While waving back at Julian standing on the curb with his hands in his pockets, Georgina couldn't help but wonder if she had just made the biggest mistake of her life.

Chapter Three

Joanie opened the Subaru's back passenger door then reached in to unbuckle Sam's car seat. Her daughter blinked her sleepy eyes then leaned forward to look around, most likely looking for her papa.

"Hey there, little bug. Get a good nap?"

"I want Papa." Sam's lips thrust out, her chin quivering as she rubbed her eyes on the head of the doll she always carried tucked under her armpit. "I want Papa," she repeated.

That makes the two of us.

Sam's trembling tiny voice gripped Joanie's heart. Her chest hurt so badly it was almost impossible to breathe. She desperately needed her own father, to cling to him. Like Sam, she wanted her dad too. If only she could make Sam's wish come true. Tamping her emotions down, she forced a smile and tickled Sam's chin.

"Bug, remember what I told you? Papa's in the big ship now, sailing away." She told Sam this little white lie many times. Still, Sam would ask and look for her papa as soon as she woke up from a nap, but especially when she was tired.

"Yeah, but I want the ship to come back." Sam's big, sleepy blue eyes brightened with tears.

Poor thing. They both missed her papa, but nothing in this world could make the ship come back. "I miss him, too, bug." A big lump formed in her throat as her heart ached with pain. *I'm not going to cry. I'm not going to cry. Not in front of Sam.* She hated lying to her little baby, but it was the best thing she could do right now. Sam wouldn't understand anyway. Pasting a smile on her face, she tried to divert Sam's attention the only way she knew how. "Hey, how about we go for a walk in the woods and visit the bridge Papa had built for you?"

Wiping her tears with the back of her hand, Sam asked, "Can I bring my net?"

"Of course."

"And the tank?"

"And the tank."

"I'm gonna catch a big butterfly."

"And what will you do after you caught it?"

"Release him again."

"What a good bug." Joanie felt her shoulders sag from relief and thanked her stars her daughter was easily entertained. Working at the bar and taking care of Sam was finally taking a toll on her. She was tired all the time and felt irritable, and Sam's constant questions about her papa weren't helping her disposition. Lucky for her, Sam's melancholy about missing her papa could pass as quickly as a butterfly flapping its wings.

Walking and playing in the property Sam called Sam's Woods always helped divert Sam's mind off her papa, at least for a short time, while she chased small insects and anything that flittered or jumped. Thank God for little mercies.

Joanie lifted Sam off her seat and put her down on the ground. "You know what, bug?"

"What, Mama?"

"I think, this time, we should leave Dolly home."

"Noooo. She'll be sad without me." Sam hugged her doll like a lifeline before smoothing the braided cotton hair. "Uh-huh, she's gonna be sad. Right, Dolly?"

Joanie wasn't in the mood to argue with her three-year-old daughter. Not today, not with her feet screaming for a good rub. "Fine. But you will be sad if you lose her."

"I won't lose her, Mama. Promise."

We shall see. Dana, her best friend, had said a walk in the woods would be good for Sam's spirit, and she was right. Joanie had noticed that in the woods, Sam's attention always focused on things adults never paid attention to, like how a leaf resembled a wing of a dragon or how mud stuck to the soles of her shoes. Watching Sam run around the spacious property with her net catching butterflies and harmless bugs, giggling, her eyes shiny from laughter, eased her pain a bit, and she was sure Sam's loneliness as well. The woods, like a therapeutic medicine, helped relieve the ache caused by Joanie's father's death. Not to mention the fresh air helped Sam's lungs as well. As long as they had the backpack with them, she felt comfortable letting Sam spend time in her woods.

Sam's Woods.

Nauseating despair enveloped Joanie's whole body like a thick, heavy cloak smothering her. The small property wouldn't be Sam's for long. What would she tell her when the new owner started building up a fence around the property?

Just like the housing market, divorce lawyers and every business around the country, she too had suffered from the worldwide economic meltdown. Her Garden Gate Studio had taken a nosedive lately, and she hadn't been able to afford to pay the rent anymore.

A day after she'd buried her father, she'd had to close her gallery. There was nothing more terrifying than the thought of not having food or shelter for her daughter, and worse, no business meant no insurance. So last week, she had made a decision to put the property up for sale. The money she'd make would pay for Sam's medication and the loan her father had taken from the bank. She could pay off the credit card company too.

With the power of the Internet, more than a handful of interested buyers had called. Two days ago, one—a horse trainer—had shown sincere interest in buying the property. It was amazing how ads spread like fire over the World Wide Web. Maybe she should take photos of her paintings and post them on the Internet. She might sell them quicker that way.

Carmen Smith, a real estate agent with raven dark hair piled high like Amy Winehouse, had come by the day before and taken additional pictures of the property. She'd said her client was in Dublin, Ireland, closing another deal. It would take five days before he could come and look at the property in person. But he liked the property and agreed with the offer based on the digital pictures. He would finalize his decision this week. Once he'd signed the papers, he wanted to remove the barbed wire fence and replace it with concrete walls, so Joanie would have to rush to remove whatever she had stored in the property.

Her dad had had his old truck parked in the woods, but he had given it to his friend, a mechanic, who had hauled it to his shop and gutted it. Her dad had said he wanted the woods clean for Sam.

Carmen's news should have sent her into a state of extreme happiness, but she felt the opposite. For her, losing the woods would be like Sam losing Dolly. But she had to sell it. They needed food more than a place to catch butterflies.

Joanie opened the front door and let Sam in first. "Go get your net."

"Yippee!" Sam took off, her little feet making slapping sounds on the floor.

If only she could find a way to keep the woods... God, she knew how important that place was for her daughter, but she didn't have a choice. They needed the money as badly as she needed air to breathe.

Stepping into the house, she made an assessment. As soon as the buyer cut the check, she'd call Paul, the neighborhood carpenter.

Last time Paul had looked in the attic, he'd found lots of moisture, most likely from the leaky roof that had caused mold to form and spread in their bathroom and into the kitchen ceiling. A problem like that would cost her hand and foot. She must replace the roof and the ceiling. He'd added that the cracked windows should be replaced too. Not only were they foggy, they were useless at stopping the cold draft from coming in.

Mold and cold draft—two things that would make Sam real sick.

Yes, they needed new windows and the leaky roof must go. Next, she'd look for a smaller place to rent or buy—if she could afford it—to use as a shop. Waitressing and dancing at the local bar helped pay the bills, but she couldn't stomach the way customers treated her. She would quit the job once the money was secure in the bank, and she knew for sure that they would have food on the table.

Good Lord, Sam's heart would shatter in pieces if she lost the woods. But she'd rather give it up than see Sam suffer again.

"Mama, I'm ready." Sam's striking blue eyes shined from the afternoon sun's reflective light. She had the eyes of her father.

Joanie closed her eyes and imagined anything other than the man who haunted her dreams. "Give me a sec, bug. I'll pack your snacks. Did you have fun at school?"

"Yup. Marcus ate his crayons again. He said the red fire engine crayon tasted yummier than the yellow banana one. He wants me to try it too."

"Did you?"

"No. Papa said only food goes in my mouth."

"What a good bug." Joanie sighed as the scattered canvases caught her eyes. She loved the smell of paint, but she couldn't have them around. First, there wasn't enough room to store them all in the house. Second, there was Sam's health to consider. What a mess. If her dad were still around, they would work together on this problem, and she wouldn't have to dance at the bar because he would still be working as a mechanic. God! As caring as he was, she couldn't believe her dad didn't have a life insurance policy. Now that she thought about it, she didn't have life insurance either. If something happened to her, her daughter would get nothing.

Her throat constricted. She missed her dad so much. It had been two weeks since they had buried him, but the pain was as fresh as the night the medic had pronounced him dead. Joanie stood in the middle of the room wishing for her father's familiar voice to disturb the quietness of the house. Nothing. Their first night without her father had cut her deeply, but watching Sam run around the house looking for her papa until she'd exhausted herself and fell asleep on her papa's worn black recliner had broken her heart into little pieces.

Her dad, Sam's 'Papa', had been her rock and a solid wall she'd leaned on. Even during her darkest times, he had always stood beside her.

How many times had he said, "Remember, poppet. The sun will keep on shining even to those who believe it's the end of the world." Together they'd faced the degrading, hurtful gossips who had tittered about her having a husband for one day. Not once had her dad blamed her for what had happened. Nothing had changed between them. In fact, their bond had become stronger than ever. He'd doted on her, had held her hair while she'd bent over the toilet bowl throwing up from her morning sickness, fetched her water to drink, fed her fruit almost nonstop, and showered her with books to read. And when she'd delivered Sam, one would have thought she had given birth to nobility. Her dad had procured the whole ad page of the local paper to announce the birth of Sam, including her first picture. He'd bought plush toys — all US made from the local store — given Sam her first bath and had built a bridge in the woods so his dear Sam could cross the stream without getting wet.

Now he was gone, leaving her and Sam, the house and the small wooded property they would soon lose. Her shop would have been enough to support Sam if the economy had remained strong — not anymore. It was gone.

Too bad waitressing and dancing at the Pink Mermaid was the only job that fit her schedule. She could work while Sam stayed at the Hurray for Me School, a preschool that offered daycare in the afternoon.

"Mama, will you carry the tank this time?"

"Sure, bug." Joanie turned around to hide her tears from Sam and busied herself by opening the cupboards. She took the boxes of Cheez-Its and Froot Loops and put them in the Hello Kitty backpack sitting on the kitchen counter. Opening the refrigerator, she grabbed a carton of apple juice and a can of Diet Coke and dropped them in the backpack also. Out of habit, she unzipped the small pocket on the outside of the bag to make sure Sam's Epinephrine and inhaler were there. "Okay, little forest ranger, are you ready to trek into the woods?"

"Yes, I got my binocs, tank, jungle hat and net."

Joanie smiled at Sam's getup. She wore pink shorts and sandals, the heavy black, outmoded binoculars her papa had given her hung from her neck, and a green plastic toy soldier hat with a shoelace for a string tied tight below her chin. She didn't look like a forest ranger at all.

Joanie had made fifty-five dollars in tips today and a good two hundred fifty from dancing last night. Tomorrow, she'd go to Walmart and see if she could find a small pair of khaki shorts and boots. If her budget allowed it, she'd find Sam a khaki vest with big pockets on the front to complete her ensemble. Her baby would be four in two weeks. She could wear the clothes for her birthday party. Sam would look nice in them.

With Sam leading the way, Joanie followed into the woods. Her heart slowly slithered down to her belly while listening to Sam jabbering in her tiny toddler voice about catching a big butterfly today. How could she explain it to her that her favorite place would no longer be hers? Joanie kicked a small rock.

Life is so freaking unfair.

Chapter Four

A month after Georgina had left Julian's apartment, he found himself staring at the Saint Claires' house. Since he had failed to convince Georgina to stay, he hadn't rushed to Joanie's. Facing the Saint Claires was comparable to having a root canal. If he could avoid it, he'd do it. But, like his lawyer said, his connection with Joanie had been the cause of his failed relationship with Georgina. It was time to do something about it — in person. He didn't want to face either one of the Saint Claires, but this was the only way to make Joanie sign his forms. Damn, he should have said yes to Trey's offer of coming with him. Trey could face Saint Claire with his own gun and badge.

Julian parked his car beside an old Subaru wagon and just sat there. *I must do this.* He got out of his car and looked at the wagon. The car must have been red when it was new, but now, the color resembled rust. Man, look at those tires. Telltale signs of excessive wear showed on the front and back tires — bulges, cracks around the bead and the crown, tread depth, damage. It looked like hazardous material shaped like a car. *If I saw this on the road, I'd steer clear just in case it burst into flames.*

The house in front of him was in no better shape. Pine needles and moss covered the roof, the porch looked in need of a new paint and the glass windows were all fogged up. The house was located in a beautiful lot tucked under the canopy of the cedar trees. The front yard was big and behind it was a wooded area. What an ideal place for pets. Julian imagined a golden retriever running around freely, barking, and chasing a ball or a little boy...and girl. Someday, he'd buy a house with a yard like this.

He looked at the small piece of paper where he'd written Joanie's address. Man, this can't be the Saint Claires' house.

He pressed the button on his tiny black remote attached to his key ring. His rental car, a silver Crown Victoria, beeped. Tucking his hands in his pockets, he made a three-sixty. What a place.

Instead of high-rise buildings, huge cedar trees stood everywhere. Their branches rustled with the gentle breeze. The air was clean and smelled like wood smoke with a hint of baked bread. And something else was missing—noise. No vendors. No yellow taxis honking and people walking as fast as if the devil himself was after them. So far, he'd only seen a couple of people, and they'd waved at him. Unlike the crowded streets of fast-paced Manhattan, the roads were open and there were no tollbooths to deal with. He probably didn't even have to lock his car here.

Julian took a deep breath and let it out in a whoosh. Saint Claire had picked a good place to move—not that their house in Seattle had been in a bad location. It had sat on an equally beautiful area with a view of the Puget Sound and Olympic Mountains, close to civilization and Starbucks coffee shops. So why had the Saint Claires moved here, and more to the point, this house?

I don't give a rip. Where they lived was no concern of his. What he wanted right now was to convince his present wife to agree to end their marriage. And the sooner he talked to the Saint Claires, the sooner he could get back to Manhattan, contact Georgina and show her the papers. He'd bet she'd come back to his apartment, his bed.

Seeing no one coming out of the house, he walked toward the front porch. A pink tricycle with a matching pink basket hanging in front of the handlebars caught his attention. A kid lived here, too? In this shack? Whose kid? Joanie's?

A squirrel scurrying from a tree branch brought his attention back to why he stood in front of the Saint Claire's house. He wondered if Saint Claire was inside peering through the foggy glass windows, watching him approach his house, ready to shoot him. Julian winced as he touched his side where the older Saint Claire had pressed the barrel of his gun. Man, Saint Claire had succeeded in shrinking his nuts to the size of gumballs when he'd pointed his gun on him that day. Just thinking about the incident made his testicles turn into little prunes. Well, not really, but kind of.

He admired Saint Claire's guts, though. The man had been so protective of his daughter's reputation he had threatened to send Julian to hell himself if he'd refused to marry Joanie. Thinking about it, he'd probably have done the same thing if he'd been in Saint Claire's shoes.

It had been about four years since he and Joanie had tied the knot. The whole ceremony was just a memory, one that he would soon forget. It would quickly happen if he disconnected anything that tied him with Joanie. He wished the dratted woman would have just signed the divorce papers instead of sending him stupid notes.

The first note she'd written had been, "Come back. See the precious soul you left behind." And the second one, "You left someone who is rightfully yours. Come back. Don't be a fool." A fool? Jesus, why did she think he'd left her? Because he hadn't wanted to claim what was rightfully his. The woman with curly, light brown hair that shined almost gold in the sun, wore braces and thick wired-framed glasses, with a body... Damn, he couldn't remember her body because he had been so fucking drunk when he'd had sex with her. Since that night, he had never touched her again, not even after the wedding. Hopefully, this would be the last time he laid eyes on her.

Rick Mason, his lawyer, had said meeting her in person would be good. Apologize and smooth her ruffled feathers and he might be able to avoid a time consuming battle in court if Joanie decided to do that. Damn it, what did Joanie want? A settlement perhaps? *But I never received anything from her other than stupid notes. What's her purpose? Whatever she wants, I don't care.*

All he wanted was to speak with Joanie as soon as possible without a long-winded discussion and without the hysterics and the crying.

For some odd reason, women used tears as a weapon to make men surrender to their wishes. Georgina was one of them.

Georgina. He liked her a lot. More so than the other women he had dated in the past. She was great in bed and showed tolerance and interest to his blind grandma. Perhaps, he'd be able to get her back and give their relationship another chance. He was tired of looking, of hopping from one woman to the next only to find his bed empty again after a week or a day because of his marital status and grandma. He felt like a deformed freak.

The front steps creaked from his weight. He hoped his foot wouldn't go through the rotten boards. Peering through the foggy window, he didn't see anyone inside. *Fuck!* The hotel where he would be staying tonight was five miles away. If the Saint Claires weren't home, that would mean coming back again tomorrow.

He wanted this meeting to be quick. In, sign the papers, and out. He looked for a doorbell but found none, so he opened the screen door and knocked. No answer. Where the hell were they?

"You might find them in the woods, on the bridge."

Julian turned around. A woman standing across the street pushing a stroller waved at him.

"In the woods?"

"Yeah. Just follow the dirt path right there on the west side of the house and you'll find them."

Julian thanked the woman and quickly headed toward the side of the house.

He found the dirt path easily. Worn and clear of grass, the path was obviously a well-traveled one. He could see two sets of footprints on the soft dirt. One set looked like it belonged to a grown-up and the other was that of a child. Was the child Joanie's? Had she found another man after he'd left? If she was involved with another, why the hell had she returned the papers without her signatures on the line? *Damn, so many questions and no freaking answers.*

The woman had also said something about a bridge. Julian kept following the path until the sound of a child's laughter reached his ears. He must be getting closer to them.

Realizing he was only a few steps away from seeing Joanie, an invisible punch in the gut made him hold his breath. Weird. It was understandable, he supposed. Seeing her again was like seeing an old classmate or a friend or an enemy. Except, she was neither of the first two and most likely the latter. Yeah, that was it. His curiosity about what would happen when they met was affecting his nerves. After all, this person he was about to see was Joanie, the wife he'd left the day after their wedding.

One thing about their wedding day he couldn't get rid of was the image of Joanie's cheeks, rubbed red from her constant wiping to remove traces of her tears. Her sad face was forever etched in his mind. Yeah, she had cried silently the day he'd stood in her room, removed his wedding ring and placed it on the dresser. He remembered not giving a fuck about it. What he'd cared about that night was keeping his distance as far away as possible from her and Saint Claire.

To this day, nothing had changed. He still didn't want to be around the Saint Claires. Not because he'd remained a stupid young man blaming others for his mistakes, but because… Well, they'd both tried to trap him, forcing him to shed his bachelor title against his will.

He wondered what Joanie looked like now. Still a scraggly painter, maybe? He hoped she wouldn't scream at him like the abandoned wife she was, or throw stuff and hit him with her slippers—or worse, point her father's gun at him. *Shit, the gun. What if Saint Claire is around carrying his gun? Fuck.*

* * * *

Joanie tried to hide her irritation. She'd known this would happen, and couldn't blame her daughter, only herself. It was her fault that Dolly had gone missing again. If she had insisted that Sam had left the doll, they would be heading home right now. She should have learned a lesson after the Walmart drama. She had been furious at herself that day, too, blaming her stupidity for Dolly's disappearance.

She remembered sitting for hours inside the Walmart manager's office waiting for a Good Samaritan to return Sam's doll. Sam, sitting on her lap, had cried until she'd suffered a hiccupping attack.

If Joanie had paid attention to the little doll, Sam wouldn't have cried her eyes out and she wouldn't have had to deal with the Walmart manager's not so subtle advances. The fat tub of lard had patted Sam's knee then squeezed Joanie's while licking his chops. Luckily, after three cans of Diet Coke and a box of Kleenex, someone had turned the doll in to the Lost and Found.

Dad had given Dolly to Sam the day she was born and they'd been together since then. Losing Dolly would be comparable to losing a limb. *Lordy, they'll have a hell of a night if they can't find that rag limb.*

"Do you remember where you set her down, bug?" This would be the last time she would let her take the doll outside of the house. "Sam, look at me. Do you remember if you left her on the bridge?"

"Don't know, Mama." Sam's tiny fists rubbed her eyes, her lower lip thrust low. "I want Dolly."

"Okay, come on. Let's check the bridge."

"I wanna go home."

"You want Dolly or not?" Sam nodded, then let out a long yawn. Of course she wanted her doll. What a stupid question. Joanie looked at her daughter and felt horrible for keeping her in the woods for hours. Sam's eyes were droopy. Poor thing was tired. It was a good sign though. Tired, Sam would go to bed without a fuss. No whining and crying about her papa. "Okay, let's go back and look for Dolly."

"I want to stay here with Nigel."

"Nigel?"

"My frog. See?" Sam lifted the tank and showed a tiny frog she had caught in the water.

"Bug, you know you'll have to release the—Nigel, right?" Why did she have to name the damn frog? Naming an animal would only make the letting-go part harder. Joanie watched her daughter tap her tank. "How about a piggy ride? Let's go."

"No. Nigel wants to stay here."

Good Lord. She was tired from working all day. Starting an argument with her daughter was the last thing she wanted right now.

The wind blew, rustling the tree branches. It would rain tonight, she thought. She looked back where they had been. The bridge was only a few yards away from them. It would be easier if she went back alone. She could run and see if the doll was there.

"Sam, I'll get Dolly. Stay here. Don't move, okay?"

"Okay."

"I can see you, bug." Joanie walked backward, her eyes on Sam. She'd be okay. It was safe here in the woods. They'd never seen a trespasser before and with the barbed wire fence, no wild animals had wandered into this area. She waved at Sam, whose shoulders were already sagging. As soon as they got home, she'd give her dinner and a quick bath. Sam slept better at night after a warm bath.

She jogged backward and looked behind her. About thirty-five feet more and she'd be on the bridge. With one last look at Sam, she turned around and ran. Her eyes darted left and right, scanning the path for Dolly. Where are you, Dolly? If the doll wasn't on the path, then that would leave the bridge.

Except for the leaves Sam had picked and scattered on the bridge, there was no sign of the rag doll. If Sam had dropped Dolly in the water, she'd be downstream by now. She looked back at Sam talking to the frog. Good bug. On her knees, she scanned the area below. Ferns, rhododendrons, and sticker bushes lined both sides of the stream. But where the heck was the doll? She went down on all fours, crawled to check the other side of the bridge. "I told her not to bring Dolly, but nooo. She had to insist. Now, she's gone. Damn it." Where the heck is she? Joanie thought for a moment. Could it be that Dolly was underneath? Glad to see Sam was still standing where she should be, Joanie lay down on her belly and hung her head over the side of the bridge to peek.

* * * *

Julian couldn't believe it. A little girl stood on the path all by herself. He looked around for a sign of Joanie, gun toting Saint Claire, or anybody. No one was around.

The girl must have sensed him coming. She turned around to look at him.

Pretty girl, Julian thought. She wore pink shorts, white top with butterflies printed on the front. Her sandals, also pink, showed her tiny little toes. But her green hat was interesting. It looked like a soldier's hat a boy would wear. Whose child was she? If she was Joanie's, the woman wasn't fit to be a mother. Didn't she know how dangerous it was to leave a child alone?

Little fingers waved at him. He waved back. "Hey there. Lost your mommy?

"No. I lost Dolly."

"Need help finding her?"

"No, thank you. Mama's looking for her."

Julian scoffed and shook his head. Unbelievable, he mused. He'd seen and heard enough stories about parents losing their children because they'd left them alone only for a few minutes to grab a cup of coffee, get a car key, or shop for a loaf of bread. Parents who thought they could do any of those things without keeping an eye on their children had no common sense and shouldn't be allowed to have children.

"I'm Julian. What's your name?"

"Papa said I can't talk to strangers." The little girl ended her last word with a yawn, then rubbed her eyes.

"And he's right." He took a few steps to close their gap, then squatted in front of the girl. She was more than a pretty girl. She was a beauty with big, bluer-than-blue eyes, plump rosy lips and thick black locks. If her hair were golden, she could have been Goldilocks. Someday, this girl would break many hearts. The girl's eyes were not Joanie's. One thing he remembered clearly about Joanie was her green eyes behind her thick glasses. "Where's your mama?"

"Mama's getting Dolly."

"Where?"

"There on the bridge." The girl pointed her little chubby finger toward the bridge.

Julian saw the bridge but no one was there. "Should we go there?"

"Mama said stay here. Do you like butterflies?"

"Yeah, I do. Are they your favorites?"

"Uh-huh. But we didn't catch one today. Only Nigel. See?" She lifted her tank and tapped on it. A tiny frog jumped into the corner of the tank. "Yesterday I got a big butterfly. But I let it out. You know why?"

"No. Why?"

"'Causssse," she sighed. "I have to go to sleep."

"Ah, I see."

"You did?"

"Did what?"

"See me let go of the butterfly."

"No. 'I see' is just an expression."

"Mama said the butterfly needs to go home."

"And she's right. Are you going to let Nigel out, too?"

The little girl bit her lower lip. "Maybe. I painted the butterfly. Wanna see it?"

"Sure. But first I need to talk to your mama." As an afterthought, he asked for her mother's name. "What is your mama's name?"

"Sam." Julian stood up and looked at the woman who had bellowed the girl's name as if the world was about to end. "Bug, come here. Now."

"Mama, you found Dolly." Sam ran toward her mother.

"I told you I'd find her."

The significance of the mother's simple gesture didn't escape Julian. She looked Sam over from head to toe, as if making sure the girl wasn't hurt, before pushing Sam behind her in an obviously protective move.

Shit, if he were a predator, he would have been gone by now, with her daughter. Julian returned the woman's stare. She stood straight, holding a dripping doll in one hand and a small pack in the other, her expression unreadable. Leaves clung to her hair as if she'd had a good roll on the ground. Dirt and mud ruined the front of her white blouse and her shoes were wet. What the heck had she been doing? Who in the world was she? She might have looked unkempt, but this wasn't Joanie.

"Hello," he greeted and waved his hand in the air.

It could have been the light, but the color of the woman's face turned paler by the minute. She licked her lips repeatedly and held the child behind her away from his view. The way she slowly moved backward, dragging her daughter with her, one would think she wanted to bolt and run away from him.

"Hello," he repeated. "I come in peace." His joke didn't earn a laugh or smile.

"You're trespassing."

"Sorry. I met a lady and she told me to come here."

Sam peeked from behind the woman and waved her little hand at him again. He waved back, making Sam giggle.

"Why are you here?"

"My name is Julian Ravenwood. I'm here to see the Saint Claires, but nobody answered their door. Do you know if…?"

The woman shook her head slowly back and forth as if she were seeing a ghost. Her eyes were big and her mouth slightly open.

"Do you know if…?" he started again. But he couldn't finish his question. This woman looked oddly familiar. No way. Impossible. She couldn't be his wife. She couldn't be Joanie. Could she?

"Do I know what?" she asked.

"I'm looking for Joanie Saint Claire. Do you know her?"

Sam tugged at her mother's hand. "Mama, your name is Joanie Saint Claire."

Joanie groaned, but he'd heard Sam's words as clear as the bright sun in Hawaii during summer. "Joanie?"

It didn't escape him when Joanie rolled her eyes. Julian couldn't believe he was facing the same woman he'd left crying four years ago. Gone were her glasses, braces, and ugly paint-stained clothes he'd seen her wear many times before. Her hair still had a wild look, but her jeans rode low on her hips, her shirt, barely meeting them, showed the flatness of her stomach. Joanie, the untidy nerd. Who would have thought she'd turn out to be a hottie?

Holy crap, he'd married a beautiful wife after all. How about that? His friend, Trey, had predicted that Joanie would make his cock hard. Well, his prediction hadn't happened yet, but kind of close.

Calm the fuck down, Julian. She's just another woman.
I've seen better.

All this time, he'd expected to see the same Joanie he'd left behind. This was a pleasant surprise. Beauty or not, however, he must tread carefully. Joanie had what he needed and what better way to get it than to be nice to her? He took a few steps forward and extended his hand.

"Good to see you again, Joanie. You look great." She continued staring at him and ignored his hand. "I see you're a mama to a beautiful girl with a beautiful name, Sam."

"I'm Sam," Sam piped up.

"Hello, Sam. I'm Dr Julian Ravenwood. Kids call me Dr Julian. How do you do?"

"I do drawings and catch butterflies. I like hopping, running, and my friend Marcus likes to eat crayons and bugs. Not me."

Julian laughed at Sam's innocent, honest reply. He liked this little girl.

"What are you doing here?" Joanie didn't wait for his answer. In a brisk tone, she asked Sam to pick up her net. "Bug, let's go."

Joanie grabbed Sam's hand and walked past him. He got a whiff of her perfume... No, it wasn't perfume — soap. She smelled of soap and something else.

"We need to talk, Joanie." He followed behind, his gaze focused on her well-rounded ass. *Nice.*

"Are you going to see my drawing?" Sam looked back, her little feet trying to catch up with her mother's long stride.

"Sure, bug."

"Stop!" Joanie turned around so fast he nearly collided with her. "Her name is Sam. You, Dr Julian Ravenwood, have no right to call her bug."

"My papa called me bug," Sam piped in.

So Joanie had indeed found another man. He looked at the child. Man, she didn't waste time replacing me. "My mistake. Sam, I would like to see your drawing. But first, I need to talk to your mother."

"I'm busy. We're busy. Sam is tired. She needs her dinner and bath. I am tired and have tons of cleaning to do. Come back when we are available."

"It'll take only a minute."

"I don't have a minute or a second. You need to leave. Write me a letter or something. Call me on the phone. But you have to leave."

"I will as soon as you give me a minute."

"Fine. Why don't you tell me whatever it is you want to say and leave?"

"Mama, he said he wants to see my drawing. The big butterfly."

He looked at Sam. Her little quivering voice tugged at his heart. "On second thought, it'll take more than a minute or two to say what I want and maybe half a minute for you to sign the papers. While—"

"What papers? I signed them all."

"No, you didn't. At least not the papers that I mailed to you twice but came back twice." The only paper she'd signed had been their marriage certificate. Was she talking about those? But he'd kept the certificate.

"I like papers. I like to draw," Sam said.

"What came back twice? Julian, I have no idea what you're talking about."

"Joanie, I'm talking about the divorce papers."

"I got to go poo-poo," Sam announced with a hint of urgency in her voice. Joanie dropped the net on the ground, picked up her daughter and ran.

Chapter Five

Images of Julian had been her constant companions over the years. More than a handful of times, she had thought about seeing him again and how she would feel if she did. Now she knew. Choked. Breathless. Mixtures of indescribable emotions danced around her heart, making it impossible to breathe.

When she'd spotted him talking to Sam she'd felt joyous, almost like crying. But the feeling had been short-lived. Panic associated with questions about Julian's sudden reappearance had torn through her. Was he here for Sam? How had he found out? Why now? It was only when he'd mentioned his reason for coming that she'd began to breathe, albeit shakily, again.

So he was here to serve her with divorce papers. She'd known this would happen. For a while, she'd waited for this time to come. Whenever the phone had rung, she'd jumped. Afraid to answer, thinking it was Julian on the other line waiting to give her the final blow, her stomach had clenched. But it had been years since he'd left his wedding ring on her dresser and the call or letter from him hadn't come. Now, he showed up, looking indescribably handsome and wanting a divorce.

What had taken him so long? What was he blabbering about divorce papers she'd returned and hadn't signed? What about the papers she'd sent him? He didn't say anything about those. Didn't he get them? Well, maybe not because he'd brought his own papers for her to sign. So what the heck had happened to her papers? Lost in the mail, most likely.

Gah. Everything was turning into one of those convoluted stories Sam would sometimes tell her.

She stole a glance at him. Julian, with his arms crossed against his chest, leaned his shoulder against the doorjamb while quietly observing Sam sitting at the kitchen table and tapping her fingers on the tank. He looked every bit as good as the last time she'd seen him. Joanie took advantage and began to assess him. His dark, wavy hair, cut unevenly, gave him a rock-star look. The strong outlines of his shoulders strained against the long-sleeved shirt he wore. His casual stance showed the length of his thighs and slimness of his waist. What a man. Tall, handsome, with a well-proportioned body, and eyes so unusual with their dark blue hue and even darker rims. Julian was one of the Blue-Eyed Four. The other guys, whom she'd seen only a handful of times, possessed the same dark blue eyes that women went gaga over. Just like her — when she'd been a silly seventeen-year-old. Julian reminded her of a model on a book cover that she'd seen the other day. He had that warrior type build but not in the freaky, bulky, Mister Universe way. Come to think of it, he looked even yummier compared to the model.

Yummy? Damn it. Stop it, Joanie. You shouldn't see the man who left you like a discarded rag as yummy. He left you, remember?

"Right."

Julian looked up. "Did you say something?"

Joanie cleared her thought. Dumb move, Joanie. Stop talking aloud. "No. Do you mind if I feed Sam first before we talk about your papers?"

"I don't mind. I'll wait in the living room while you take care of Sam. And, Joanie, just call me Julian."

Joanie nodded her head without any intentions of calling him by his first name again. First name basis wasn't for strangers, and he'd been one since he'd left. It should stay that way. "Sam, wash your hands, please. I already put Dolly in the washer. She'll be clean, too, when she comes out."

"Okay, Mama."

"I'll make your dinner."

"Hotdogs! I'm getting hotdogs, Mama?" Sam clapped her hands, her eyes big.

"Well, I know it's Friday, bug, but—"

"Do you like hotdogs? Wanna have some?" Sam asked Julian.

Julian smiled at Sam, then looked at Joanie. "I do. Hotdogs are my favorite. But I am not invited for dinner, Sam."

"Why? Do you spill ketchup on the table? Marcus does it a lot. Papa said he's a messy-messy boy. He can't have a hotdog with ketchup, nah-uh."

Julian surprised Joanie when he picked up Sam and sat her on the edge of the kitchen sink. He helped wash her hands. Joanie noticed he washed Sam's forearms and feet too. Sam squealed from getting tickled. "I don't spill food on the table, Sam, but your mama didn't invite me for dinner."

"Mama, can he eat hotdogs with us?"

Sheez. What was she supposed to say? No? "Sure. He can stay for dinner."

"Ooh, you can stay."

Friday was always a hotdog and chips night at the Saint Claire household. But with her aching feet and back, she'd thought about breaking the tradition and eating microwavable lasagna tonight instead. Thanks to Sam putting her on the spot, now she would have to grill the stinking frozen hotdogs.

She handed the towel to Julian to dry Sam's hands and feet. "What do you say to Dr Ravenwood, Sam?"

"Mama, he said call him Dr Julian." To Julian, Sam said, "Thank you, Dr Julian, for washing me."

"You're welcome, Sam." Julian lowered her back onto the floor.

"Sam, why don't you show him your butterfly drawings while waiting for dinner?"

"Okay, Mama."

Without Sam in the room, the air suddenly became humid and thick. Joanie's nervousness whenever Julian was around revisited, making it impossible to steady her erratic pulse. "Can, can I offer you something to drink? Diet Coke? Wine? Coors beer?"

"Coors is fine. You have a charming home." He pulled out a chair and sat down.

"Thanks." Joanie watched him roll his water-splattered sleeves, showing his arms sprinkled with dark hair. Images of him on top of her, naked and warm, quickly formed in her memory. She could see him again staring down at her, moving on top of her, thrusting his hips, breathing hard as he filled...

Oh, my God. Joanie turned around to dispel the images and opened the refrigerator to grab a can of beer. "Do you need a glass for your beer?"

"Nah, the can is good." Instead of handing the can to Julian, she placed it on the table. "Thanks. Got rid of your glasses, huh?"

"Yeah." He noticed? "When I broke my last pair, I decided to use contacts instead."

"Your glasses were fine but without them, I can see the real shape of your eyes better."

"Because they're not magnified or look like an owl's anymore?"

"Who said you had owl's eyes?"

Joanie stared at him for a moment. Debating whether to tell him the truth or not. She decided to tell the truth. "You."

His jaw dropped as if he lost his face muscles. "I did?"

She chuckled at Julian's reaction. "It was a long time ago."

"I'm sorry. Damn, I don't remember ever saying you have owl's eyes."

"Forget it. Glad I got rid of the glasses. My friend told me it'll be hard to find Mr Right with a pair of magnifiers for glasses sitting on the bridge of my nose."

Julian took a swig of his Coors. "Are you saying Sam's papa is Mr Wrong?"

"You could say that."

"Sam's papa has blue eyes."

Joanie's heart banged in her chest. "How did you know?"

"You have green eyes, Sam's are blue. Really beautiful, by the way. They remind me of a sparkling ocean. So extraordinary."

Oh, God, why did they have to talk about eyes? Feeling uncomfortable, she tried to change the topic.

"Don't you have friends with blue eyes? They're not that extraordinary. Beautiful but not extraordinary."

"You think yours are?"

"Didn't say that."

"You have to agree, though, that Sam's eyes are like her father's."

"Oh, yeah. Sam shares the same features as him." Good God, Joanie. Calm down, she mentally told herself. Julian was here to talk about their divorce, not Sam. *My secret is safe.*

"She's a beautiful child."

"Thanks."

"How old is Sam?"

"Old enough to keep me busy. She's crazy about going into the woods to chase butterflies and find all kinds bugs."

"Why did you move? Innis Arden, your old neighborhood in Seattle, is nice. You had a great view of the Puget Sound and Olympic Mountains."

The neighborhood in Seattle might have been nice, but the gossip that had swirled around her had been worse than the Pacific Northwest's harsh winter wind that had overshadowed the beauty of their surroundings. "It was nice until... Dad grew up here and he thought it was time to come home to roost. Besides, we have a bigger property here, which turned out to be great. Sam loves the woods."

"I agree. Kids need places like this to run around. You should give her a pet. A golden retriever is good with kids. Very gentle."

Joanie nodded. A dog sounded great. But with Sam's asthma and allergy to animal dander, they couldn't have any pet around. She took out her last pack of Ball Park hotdogs from the freezer and grabbed the bags of chips from the pantry. "Hotdogs are frozen. It'll take a while."

"Need help?"

Maybe start the grill because I surely don't know how. "No, thank you." Last Friday, instead of hotdogs, she'd made spaghetti and Sam had complained. Now, she wanted hotdogs again. Ugh. She could do this. How hard could it be to start a grill? Her dad had used this thing many times. Surely, it wasn't that hard. There must be a starter around somewhere.

"Is your dad going to be here soon?"

I wish. "No. Why?"

"I just want to be ready when he does."

"Afraid he'd point his gun at you again?"

"The man could frighten an ox, you know."

Dad could be as gentle as a butterfly, she silently thought. "Don't worry. He won't do it again."

"Did he finally get rid of his gun?"

"No. I think it's upstairs hidden somewhere collecting dust."

"Where is Saint Claire?"

Joanie looked away, her eyes focused on the foggy window. "Bend," she whispered. "Bend Cemetery. He's been there for two weeks."

"Cem...cemetery?" Julian cursed under his breath, but loud enough for her to hear. "I'm sorry, Joanie."

"It's okay. Just don't say anything about Dad in front of Sam."

"How did it happen?"

"Aneurism. Dad went to bed and didn't come down the next day."

Sam came back in the kitchen, carrying her scrapbook. "I'll show you my biggest butterfly."

"Bug, Dr Ravenwood wants to see the drawing you made last night, not your whole scrapbook."

"It's okay. Wow, you have a scrapbook." Julian picked up Sam and sat her on his lap. "What do you have here? What a collection. Did you draw all these?"

"Yup."

"Really cool. And you're only how old?"

"Am gonna be four on my birthday. This many." Sam bent her thumb and showed Julian four fingers.

"I'm going to be twenty-seven on my birthday."

"You're oooold. Like Papa."

"I'm not that old." Julian turned a page. "You like bugs."

"Uh-huh. They're cute."

"I like bugs and all kinds of animals too. That's why I became a veterinarian. I help them feel better when they're sick."

"I want to be a vetri...arr...unn..."

"...narian. Vet-uh-ri-narian," Julian supplied.

"Yeah, like you. I will make animals feel better. Like cats, dogs, bunnies, horsies, sheeps, dragons, dinos, buff-aloooes... But they will stay outside. You know why?"

"No."

"Because they can't stay here."

"She's asthmatic and highly allergic to animal dander. On top of that, she's allergic to cashew nuts," Joanie explained.

Julian furrowed his brows at her, then rubbed the top of Sam's head with his hand. "Poor baby. If the animals make you real sick, you could be an entomologist instead of a veterinarian."

"I can feed the animals?"

Joanie couldn't take her eyes off Julian's hand gently rubbing Sam's head. The simple action touched the very core of her heart.

"Honey, entomologists study insects or bugs. You like bugs, right?"

"Yeah. But I don't eat them. Tommy and Marcus ate ants with dirty feet. They can be the en-o-ogist."

"Hmm, maybe some entomologists eat bugs, but what they do is learn about insects. You'll know about insect anatomy, metamorphosis, and —"

"Unicorns are magical creatures! They are sparkly and can fly."

Joanie burst out laughing. When Julian raised his brows at her, she raised a hand on top of her head and made a cutting motion. She mouthed, "Over her head," then laughed again.

Julian grinned and shook his head. "Let's see this drawing. You drew this guy also. Who's he?"

"That's Marcus. He's my best friend. I punched him today because he chewed my hair."

Joanie groaned. She'd call Mark and Dana to apologize. Her dad had taught Sam to punch anyone who touched her without asking permission first. God, she had already talked to five different parents because Sam had socked their children in the chest for sitting too close to her. Okay, her teacher had said it was more like a tiny shove and the kids had ignored Sam after she'd told them to please move. Still, Sam must learn to keep her hands to herself.

"You know how to punch?"

"Uh-huh? Papa showed me how to. Like this." She punched his chest. Julian pretended to wince and fall back on the chair.

"Wow, you're strong. Now, who's this one?"

"My papa. He's in a big ship sailing away."

"Ah. I see."

"You said it again. A expression."

"You've got good memory. Did you know that elephants have good memories?"

"I'm a giiirrllll. Not a elephant."

"I know, hon. I know," Julian said.

Sam and Julian, in her kitchen—finally, an old dream coming true. Joanie watched her daughter talk to the father she didn't know. She had dreamed about this, the three of them in one room, happy—but that dream died after Sam had turned one. It was also the same year she'd finally stopped crying every night. She still thought about Julian, the what-could-have-beens, the what-ifs and buts. She had been playing different scenarios in her head practically every night, but without crying.

Sam giggled at something Julian said.

Joanie watched. In two weeks, Sam would turn four. Too young to remember Julian. He was here only to serve his divorce papers, then he'd be gone from their lives forever. She could hardly wait to hear him explain about the papers he'd said he'd mailed twice but were returned to him without her signature.

Unsigned papers. Odd. Something didn't add up here. Something was wrong.

Duh. Since the first day Julian had expressed clearly that he hadn't wanted to be a part of her life, nothing had been right.

Joanie took a deep breath. Julian was here to snip the last thin thread binding them together. She'd known this time would come, but why did it feel like the very foundation beneath her was turning into a quicksand?

She stole a glance at Julian. Cheek pressed against Sam's temple, he moved Sam's hair off her face with his fingers while they looked at the doodles. He held Sam as if he'd been doing it for years. Sam didn't hide behind her the way she normally would when meeting strangers. Her daughter had liked Julian at first glance. Was it possible Sam felt an invincible connection to her father? And what about Julian?

Sam raised her hand and touched Julian's cheek. Julian slightly turned his head to lean on Sam's hand. *Oh, my God!* Quickly Joanie turned around, grabbed the buns and her last pack of hotdogs she'd set on the counter to thaw, then hurried out to the backyard.

She shouldn't watch them. The image would only burn in her mind. Not good. But like metal to a magnet, her eyes drifted back to Sam and Julian again. Through the cracked glass window, she watched. This time catching Julian's gaze.

Then he winked.

"Oh my God," she squeaked. Lord, she was blushing. She could feel it. Good God, she was acting like a seventeen-year-old again. Joanie lifted the grill's lid to hide her face. She concentrated on what she should be doing and forced her mind to think about vile things to paint out Julian's image. Sadly, it was Julian's image gently caressing his daughter's soft cheek and Sam giggling at his touch that formed in her head.

Lord, I'm doomed.

After a couple of tries, Joanie managed to start the grill. She lined all of the hotdogs on the grill the way her dad had done and closed the lid. Tapping the tongs on the side of the grill, she watched the smoke seep through the space between the grill and the lid. *Much better. Just watch the hazy smoke and I'll be fine. Forget about the gorgeous man in my kitchen.* For some annoying reason, she wanted to look at Julian again, so she did.

Julian was busy talking to Sam. Sam must have said something funny because he laughed and rubbed his chin on top of Sam's head. If she could only capture the moment. If she could only —

She smelled something burning. "Shoot." Lifting the lid, her jaw dropped. Her hotdogs were black. "Damn it." One side of the hotdogs was black but the other side still showed a bit of brown. They weren't as juicy looking as her dad's used to be, but they would do. She transferred the burnt, pathetic hotdogs onto the plate to make room for the buns on the grill. Sam liked hers browned and warm. What about Julian? Well, his would be warmed too. She placed the buns on the grill face down, counted to twenty, and took them out to avoid ending their having the same fate as the hotdogs.

Joanie decided to set the table first before putting the plate of burnt hotdogs in the middle of the table.

The moment Sam spotted the hotdogs, she scrunched up her nose. "Eeww. Black hotdogs."

Great, bug. Way to embarrass your mama.

Julian, thankfully, didn't say a word. He simply moved Sam onto another chair and smiled at her.

"You don't have to eat the hotdogs to be polite."

"But I like them well done."

Joanie couldn't tell if Julian really liked his hotdogs well done or he was just starving. But he ate three hotdogs in a bun, half a bag of chips, and drank two cans of Coors. Sam, who insisted she sit on Julian's lap, finished half of her skinned hotdog and a glass of apple juice before her eyes started drooping.

"Sam, you can't go to sleep yet. You need a bath."

"I'm tired, Mama. And I want my papa." She shifted her small body to face Julian, then tucked her chubby arms under his armpits.

"I'll bring you upstairs." Julian rose from his chair. "Let me carry her, Joanie."

"You don't have to. I can—"

"I know. But my little friend here is as heavy as an elephant. You can't carry her.

Sam giggled. "I'm not a elephant. I'm a girl."

"Of course you are not." Julian kissed the top of Sam's dark head. "You're as light as a butterfly princess with big blue eyes like... Kind of like my grandma's."

"Your eyes are blue. I like blue snow cones."

"Yup, we have the same eyes."

"I'll tell Marcus you're a butterfly prince."

Julian kissed Sam's nose. "Thanks for inviting me to dinner, Sam. I've haven't had a hotdog in a bun and chips for dinner in a long time."

"I love hotdogs." Sam yawned and snuggled deeper in the crook of Julian's arm.

Joanie watched the whole scene until her chest felt like bursting. She knew, after today, her life would never be the same again. Someday, she'd tell Sam about this, how her father unknowingly showed his love to his daughter.

"Lead the way, Joanie."

Joanie blinked back her tears then quickly looked away. "Wait, I need to get her doll." Joanie took the doll from the dryer. "Bug, here's Dolly."

"She's warm."

"Yup. And clean." She walked ahead of Julian in a hurry and went straight into Sam's room. "In here. She'll just have her bath tomorrow." She turned the bed down and waited for Julian to lower Sam on the bed. "Thanks for washing her feet. Could you please get her pajamas? Behind the door. Thanks."

"Can't she sleep in her clothes?" Julian handed her the pair of pink pajamas with pigs printed all over it.

"She'll be miserable if her allergies act up. We walked in the woods today. You never know what she got stuck on her clothes. I should have given her a bath right away. Bug, sit up."

Sam yawned. "Mama, I'm sleepy."

"Here, I'll hold her up."

"Thanks." Julian kept Sam sitting up until Joanie had finished changing her clothes. "Sam, say goodnight to Dr Ravenwood. He's leaving now."

"Night-night, Dr Julian."

"Night, Sam. Thanks for sharing your pictures with me."

"Uh-huh. Come to my party. Come, okay?"

"Okay."

"Mama, sing me My Sunshine." Sam rolled on her side and hugged her doll.

"I'll wait downstairs, Joanie." Joanie waited until Julian was gone before she started singing *You Are My Sunshine*. It was their nightly anthem. While rubbing Sam's back, she sang their song. When she'd finished, she kissed Sam goodnight and turned off the lights, leaving only her firefly nightlight on. "I love you, bug."

Stomach cramping at having to face Julian alone, she went downstairs.

* * * *

The furniture had seen better days and the rugs were threadbare. But the spectacular paintings, mostly landscapes, that hung on the wall made up for what the house lacked in furnishings. Julian also noticed there were paintings stacked up in every corner of the room as if Joanie had just moved in. Or was she in the process of moving out? All paintings were initialed

J.S.C. — Joanie Saint Claire. He wondered if she used Ravenwood at all.

Pictures of Sam in various stages lined up on the mantel above the fireplace. In all of Sam's pictures, she wore a silver necklace with a ring for a pendant. He'd briefly seen the necklace when Joanie had changed Sam's clothes, but hadn't got a chance to get a better look. His gaze went back to the picture of Saint Claire and Sam sitting on the edge of the low bridge, laughing. The two were holding fishing poles. Damn, he couldn't believe the man was gone. It seemed all the men in Joanie's life were gone. First him, then Sam's papa, and now, even her father was gone.

Other than Joanie and old Saint Claire, he didn't see anyone in the picture that could be Sam's papa. Where was Mr Wrong?

He'd been admiring an oil painting of a little girl walking barefoot on a well-worn path surrounded by tall green grasses when he heard the floorboards creak. He looked toward the stairs. Joanie was coming down the steps. She must have tied her hair in a hurry because she'd missed a few locks that hung along her nape and ears. In that area, she hadn't changed. Her hair still looked as wild as ever.

This time, though, he didn't see her as an untidy woman, but a very seductive one. *Yeah, very seductive.* Why had he noticed? Well, who wouldn't? Those jeans of hers molded onto her hips and thighs like a second skin, showing her nice curves, and her tight shirt—well, only a blind man wouldn't see her beautiful body.

The day they'd got married, she had worn her hair up with a silk ribbon to hold it, but the darn ribbon had kept slipping off her hair. When the wedding was over, he remembered pulling the thin material and tucking it in his pocket. Only a few days ago, when he had been getting ready to come here, he'd found the ribbon and a flower clip which had adorned her hair, still inside his desk drawer. Why he had kept them, he had no clue.

"Thanks for entertaining Sam. She's been moody since Dad passed away."

"That's understandable."

"Don't worry about her invitation. Tomorrow she won't remember that she asked you. She probably won't even remember you on her birthday."

"You think so?"

"She's too young to remember things."

"Sam told me her papa sailed away."

"Yes. In a matter of speaking."

"Is he in the Navy, a seaman or a fisherman?"

"Please sit down. Would you like a cup of coffee or tea or another Coors?"

The change of subject was quick, but not subtle enough. If she didn't want to talk about her man, so be it. Her love life wasn't his concern. "Coffee sounds good."

"I'll be right back."

Joanie disappeared into the kitchen in a hurry. He noticed how Joanie kept tucking her hair behind her ear and avoided looking at him. Without a doubt, he'd made her nervous. She probably didn't want to be around him, but for an abandoned wife, Joanie was acting cool. Was it because she didn't care about what happened and was, in fact, happy he'd left her? If that were the case, then maybe he'd be able to leave with her signature. She had a lovely daughter now. She'd obviously moved on. So she should end their marriage.

When he'd initially left Joanie without looking back, guilt had nagged at him. It had lasted for months until he'd finally convinced himself that his decision to leave had been the best move for both of them. Well, hell. Now he found out Joanie had moved on before him. She'd even got herself a child.

A myriad of emotions had played on Joanie's face when she'd seen him. After her initial shock had passed, she'd looked about ready to cry. Then the look in her eyes had turned furious. He supposed it was only natural. He'd surprised her with his unannounced visit, but she'd surprised him too. She'd changed. Without her thick magnifying glasses, he could see the real shape of her eyes. They were still big, but beautiful like the deep green forest. She had full lips like Sam's and a nose that was perfect for her oval-shaped face. She was twenty-one now and a mother, but her body didn't bear any sign that she'd had a child. Slim, with a flat stomach and a nicely rounded butt. He'd noticed her shapely legs too. With her package, he wasn't surprised she'd found a man.

A bright flash lit the room followed by loud thunder. Damn, he hoped it wouldn't rain too much. He planned to drive back to Portland airport tomorrow to catch his plane—if Joanie signed the papers tonight.

The soft pattering of footsteps sounded from upstairs. Sam. Thunder must have woken her up. Without waiting for Joanie, he met Sam halfway down the steps and scooped her up by the armpits. "Hey there. You okay?" Sam wrapped her chubby arms around his neck.

"I'm scared." She sniffed and rubbed her cold nose against his shoulder.

"Don't worry, love. I won't let the thunder get you."

"Promise?"

"I promise."

"Papa said he won't let thunder get me."

Julian sat down on the couch, holding Sam on his lap. The little girl felt soft and good against him. She smelled of soap like her mother. He adjusted Sam's position so she was lying across his lap. The crook of his arm pillowed her head. "I always keep my promises, love."

"Okay."

Sam sighed and buried her face against his chest. Seconds later, she was fast asleep. He noticed she was still wearing her silver necklace. Jesus, didn't Joanie know it wasn't safe for Sam to wear her necklace when she went to bed? It could choke her to death in her sleep.

He lifted the chain and pulled it out of her pajama top. The pendant, a silver ring, shined from the reflected light from the lamp. The simple band was too familiar. His heart thudded—hard. If the ring was what he thought it was, then there should be an inscription…

"What are you doing?" Joanie asked. She was holding two steamy mugs. "Why is Sam down here?"

"The thunder scared her and she came down here. Did you know she's scared of thunder?"

"Yes. But her papa always tucked… Shit. I'm sorry. I heard the thunder but—"

"You forgot her papa is gone."

"I was— My mind was off somewhere… Yeah, I forgot. Why don't I take Sam back to her bedroom?" Another loud crack of thunder made Joanie jump.

"She'll just wake up again. It's better if she stays here. Joanie, she can't go to sleep wearing her necklace. It's not safe. Do you know how many kids die every year because of a simple string?"

"She's been wearing her necklace since the first day she was born. She's attached to it."

"Well, it's time she should take it off. She's too young to be wearing a necklace like this. If it gets snagged, it'll hurt her."

Joanie became quiet. She just stood looking down at Sam still holding the two coffee mugs. "I gave her the necklace because it was the right thing to do. Hurting her was the last thing in my mind."

"Give it to her when she's older."

She set down the mugs on the coffee table. "You're right. It's time to take it off. There is no use hanging onto it." She splayed a hand on her chest and nodded.

Somehow, Julian had a feeling he had struck a sensitive spot. "It is for her own safety, Joanie."

Joanie looked into the mugs. Across her pale and beautiful face, a melancholy frown flitted. "I know. You show great care for a child you just met."

"I'd do and say the same thing to any mother who has no sense about what's dangerous to her child."

Sadness gone, her face flushed with anger. "Are you saying I am stupid and senseless?"

"I found Sam alone on the path and you let her wear a necklace to bed. What am I supposed to think?"

"You don't know shit about me. Now, are those the papers you were talking about?"

Julian took a brief look at the manila envelope he'd placed on the table. "Yes."

Joanie nodded. As if someone had blown out the light within her, her face turned utterly sad and her eyes shined from unshed tears. "The divorce papers."

"Yeah." Damn, why was she crying? She'd already found another man. Their divorce shouldn't make her sad. They'd been separated for years. He was just here to legalize their separation so he could be with another and start his own family. This meeting was just a formality. The thought, for the first time, made him feel, guilty. *I'll be damned.*

After tonight, he most likely would never see her again. Tonight would be the best time to make amends. "I owe you and your father an apology."

Joanie turned her head away to wipe her eyes. "For what?"

"For everything. For leaving you the day after our wedding, for the grief, and I'm sure, the humiliation."

"I understand why you left. Any man would probably have done the same thing. You loathed me and the idea of us getting married."

"Joanie, I don't loathe you, but you are right. I didn't want to get married."

"But Dad forced and threatened you. It was wrong of him to point his gun at you. But at the time, he was just trying to save me."

"You were underage." He cleared his throat. "Your dad acted the way a father would to protect his daughter. I'd most likely do the same thing if it happened to my own daughter." It had been her first damn time too. He had seen the proof of her virginity on the bed sheet. "I'm sure your dad saw red when I left."

"Dad's anger about you leaving me lasted over a month. After that, he actually felt happy that you didn't stick around. We stopped talking about you as if the wedding never happened. Then we talked about you again when... I... Well, everything happened a long time ago. Can we talk about your papers now? You said you wanted to leave right away, right? Do you have a pen?"

"Eager to be free of me, huh?" Why had she returned the papers unsigned if she was as eager as him to get a divorce? He couldn't understand why, but her coolness somehow irritated him. She should be screaming at him, throwing things, swearing, or demanding support. He'd feel a lot better if she slapped him. He deserved it. Not this.

Joanie was slighted. A woman he'd treated with scorn, she deserved to be mad. So why was Joanie acting so calm? Okay, she didn't care about him and probably would be ecstatic as soon as he was out the door, which again raised the question — why had she returned the papers unsigned?

"This is what you wanted from the start," Joanie said, her eyes focused on Sam.

"Then why didn't you sign the papers, Joanie?"

"The divorce papers, right? These?" She pointed at the manila envelope.

"Yes, these. The same ones that I sent you two times."

"I didn't sign the papers because I never got them."

"You never got them?"

"No. Did you send this to our old address? Because we left a month after our wedding."

"No. I mailed it here. And I know you received the envelope. Come on, Joanie. There is nothing wrong with admitting the truth."

"Are you accusing me of lying and pretending? I'm not stupid, you know. Maybe I acted stupid when I had," she glanced at sleeping Sam, "S-E-X with you, but that doesn't mean I remained stupid."

"Look at the address on the envelope. Isn't that your address here?"

"Yes."

"Then you received these. You even wrote the — didn't you write a note when you returned these to me?"

"A note? You're saying you sent these papers to me, but I sent them back unsigned and with a note attached to them?"

"Yes, twice in fact."

Joanie stared at him. Lines of concentration deepened along her brow. She appeared to be deep in thought, or maybe she was good at pretending. But if she were telling the truth, then who returned the mail? Saint Claire? Impossible. The man had hated him so much he would probably have been the first to suggest a divorce, demand support for Joanie, and testify in court that he, Julian Ravenwood, had been a rotten husband. In fact, during his first months in Manhattan, he'd expected the man to show up on his doorstep with his gun cocked and ready to fire. After what he'd done to Joanie, Saint Claire would have been glad to see him gone from Joanie's life forever. And didn't she say that a month after he'd left, Saint Claire had been happy that he was out of Joanie's life? So who'd returned the papers? Sam's papa?

"What was on the note?"

He leaned forward, careful not to disturb Sam, then opened the manila envelope to retrieve the small sticky notes.

Joanie flashed him a look of confusion, blinking as if she were trying to rid herself of something stuck in her eyes.

"Who wrote these notes if you didn't, Joanie?"

"I don't know. Let me see."

"You don't know?"

"No I don't. Let me see the notes." Joanie looked at Sam and her eyes turned even sadder. Her green eyes lost their sparkle.

"Well, I have an idea. Maybe Sam's papa opened the envelope and wrote the note inside without telling you. Maybe he saw an opportunity for extortion, blackmail, to make money."

"What? He would never do such a thing." Joanie grabbed the notes from him and the envelope. She pulled the papers out so fast he was surprised she didn't rip them apart.

He watched her, saw her eyes grow even bigger as she read the notes. "Well?"

Her lips moved, but no sound came out. Shaking her head, she looked at him. "Well, maybe you're right."

"Right about Sam's papa's plan for extortion? Why? You're not telling me everything."

"Does it matter?" Joanie looked away and focused her eyes on Sam again.

"Yes, it matters to me. Look at me and tell me you don't know why Sam's papa secretly wrote the damn notes."

"I told you, I don't."

"Those notes are like clues, with indirect meanings. Have you any idea what he's trying to tell me? Do you know?"

"Dr Ravenwood, you're here because you want my signature. Whatever his reason for writing the note and for returning the papers is irrelevant. You're here. I am here. Give me a pen and I'll sign your damn papers." Joanie stood up so fast her knee bumped the side of the coffee table. Coffee from the two mugs sloshed and spilled on the little white doily sitting in the middle of the table. "Damn it," she mumbled but he heard her clear enough.

"What the fu...dge are you talking about? The note is irrelevant? Don't you see? There is a reason why your man, whatever the hell his name is, wrote those—"

"Why do you care? Why do you want to know?"

"Joanie, if your man intends to extort money from me, of course I have to know. With him not telling you about it raises a flag. He might end up hurting you and Sam. The least I could do is to stop that from happening. I want to help. Besides, if someone said to you, I have a secret to tell, then that person changed his mind and decided to keep the secret to himself, how would it make you feel?" Sam moaned and kicked her legs. He looked down at the little girl. "She misses her papa. When is he coming back?"

"You're not here to talk about Sam's papa. Let's get this over with so you can go back to where ever you live now."

"Manhattan."

"Fine. Go back to Manhattan. Where's the pen?"

Sam rubbed her legs together. "How long did you two play in the woods? Her legs must be hurting." Julian gently massaged Sam's legs.

"Dr Ravenwood, I should take Sam back to her room. She'd be more comfortable."

Joanie had been hedging the topic about Sam's papa. Sam had said her papa had sailed away. He looked at the child in his arms. Even when sleeping, she was beautiful. Sam's lashes were long and dark just like his and her blue eyes...

A little girl, soon to be four years old, with sharp blue eyes that reminded him of his baby pictures. Holy hell.

"What is Sam's full name?"

"What?"

"Sam's full name, Joanie."

"Samantha Rose."

"And her last name?"

"What's this questioning about? Julian, let me put her back in bed then I'll sign the forms. We need to hurry if you have to fly back to Manhattan tonight."

She'd done it again. With his suspicion gnawing his insides, he stood up. "I'll take her. Clean up the spill on the table before it ruins the wood."

"Julian! Damn it, what are you doing?"

"Clean up the mess, Joanie." He made it back to Sam's room in a hurry. He looked around to see if there were any signs that another man had fathered Sam. Butterfly and animal paintings decorated the pink walls. Saint Claire's framed picture sat on her bedside table. There were stacks of books on the headboard, but no picture of a man he could pin as Sam's papa. Goddamn it. Lowering Sam on the bed, he stared at the sleeping little girl. "Sam, honey. I just want to see your necklace."

Chapter Six

Joanie read the two notes over and over. The handwriting was definitely her father's — bold strokes and inconsistent with his upper and lowercase letters. What had her father done? Why? He'd hated Julian for leaving her. Dad had called him a coward and said he didn't deserve her and Sam at all. So why lead him here to see Sam?

The memory of all the nights she and her dad had sat in the kitchen talking about Julian swirled in her mind. For the past six months, her dad had talked about contacting Julian, to let him know about his responsibility, which had really surprised her. Her dad had said the bastard should help pay Sam's bills. He'd insisted Julian was the only one who could help give Sam a better life, education, and health insurance. Sam's last trip to the hospital had forced them to borrow money from the bank.

She'd refused. It was enough that Julian had been saddled with a woman he didn't love or care for. Forcing him to face another responsibility, which he would likely hate, would be too much. Julian had walked away from her and Sam. She'd wanted it to stay that way. She loved him, had loved him since she was sixteen, but Julian had reciprocated with an antipathy that had doubled when Dad had forced him to marry her. And she'd told all of this to Dad.

Frustrations, financial instability and Sam's health had made her dad bring up Julian's name in their discussion. But she'd never suspected that he was serious.

Oh, my God. Could it be that her dad had gone against her wish of keeping Julian uninformed about his daughter because he was thinking about Sam? Had her dad died that night worrying about her and Sam's future? Had she caused his death?

Joanie wiped the tears off her face with the heels of her hands. There was no other explanation for her dad's action. Her dad had written the notes to Julian despite his dislike for him. He'd done it for his granddaughter.

"She's mine."

Joanie whirled around and found herself facing Julian. He was holding Sam's necklace and he looked about ready to throttle her.

"What?"

"Sam. She's my daughter."

"No."

"No? Then explain why she's wearing a necklace with my wedding ring for a pendant."

More tears rolled down her cheeks. Her whole body shook from controlling her anger. If Sam hadn't been in the house, she'd have screamed at him. "The ring is not yours."

"Is that right? Joanie, I stared at this ring for hours after we got married. I know this ring. Our initials are engraved inside. This ring is mine."

"No. Not anymore. When you removed and left the ring the night of our wedding, you relinquished your right to it. It now belongs to Sam." God, she wanted to stomp her foot. "I gave it to her because it proved that you indeed existed. You know, you were right when you said she shouldn't wear it. The ring would only hurt her. I'm so stupid not to think about that. You want it. Take it. Pawn it, sell it, throw it, melt it, or give it to a homeless person you see. Do whatever you want with it. Sam will ask me tomorrow about the necklace, and I'll tell her she lost it in the woods."

Julian pocketed the necklace. "Where's yours?"

She straightened her body to ease the pain in her shoulders. Crap, it felt like she'd been carrying a sack of flour for hours. "Why?" What did he care about what happened to her ring?

"It's a simple question. Where is your ring? Sold it?"

"Somewhere." She waved her hand the way a queen would when dismissing her subject. It was the truth. Well, partly. Her friend Dana had been keeping the ring. So it was somewhere in her house.

"You should have told me about Sam, Joanie. I have the right to know."

Right? What right was he talking about? "Stop. When you left me, you gave up your rights. And aren't you here to sever the last remaining connection you have with me?"

"When I left I didn't know you were with child."

"Would you have been happy if you'd found out you'd got me pregnant? Would the baby have stopped you from leaving me? Back in Manhattan, if you'd heard I was pregnant with your baby, would you have come running back here? I don't think so. You'd probably move to Antarctica just to get away from me, from us. Don't be such a hypocrite. You're here

84

because you want me to sign your damn divorce papers that you insist I returned twice. Why don't we just talk about that, huh?" She ignored Julian's hand motioning for her to stop. "Forget about Sam. You don't need us. We don't need you. We lived and survived without you. I survived. Damn it, Julian. You're not supposed to know."

"Calm down, Joanie. You'll wake up Sam."

"I am calm!" She smacked her palm on her forehead. *I don't need this aggravation. I just want to sit down and rest my damn feet.*

"When Sam said her papa sailed, is that what you told her about me? Or, there is really another man she thought to be her father?"

"There is no other man, Dr Ravenwood. Sam's papa is Dad, my dad, and he's dead. Sailing on a ship is the only way I could explain to Sam why Dad's not here anymore."

"Then who wrote the notes?"

"Dad. He wrote them. He shouldn't have let you in on Sam. It was a mistake."

Julian looked down at the crumpled envelope in Joanie's hands. "Your dad? You're saying it was Saint Claire who wrote the notes."

"Yes. I recognized his writing."

"But he didn't like me."

"He didn't. But he thought you deserved to know."

Julian shook his head. "Smart. Well, he made a smart move. Hardheaded, but smart. What he did wasn't a mistake. He wrote the note with a good purpose. Although I thought he was talking about you."

Yes, Dad had had a good reason—Sam. Her dad had gone through all the trouble of sending Julian the notes for Sam's sake. It must have pained him to do it, but he'd done it anyway. He'd loved Sam so much that he was willing to share her with the man he'd despised.

A good purpose. Nodding to herself, she looked Julian straight in the eye. "The papers. I will sign them. On one condition."

"If it's within the bounds of reason, I will accept it."

Arrogant... Handsome beast. "One hundred thousand for your freedom." The amount would be enough for what she needed. She'd be able to fix the house and maybe have enough to buy a small shop. And she could keep the property—Sam's woods.

"Quite a big amount, don't you think?"

"Not if you won't hear from me and Sam ever again. You'll be free to remarry and be free of us. You don't have to worry about child support, alimony, or anything."

"If I give you that money, you'll sign the divorce papers, and I won't hear from you again?"

"Yes."

"Do you think demanding money was Saint Claire's reason for writing the notes?"

"No. Dad would never lower himself that way. He was an honest and hardworking man. He'd eat slugs before he'd beg for money or use extortion. This is my decision."

"So, this is why I didn't hear from you for four years. You were waiting for me to make the first move so you could make demands?"

He was wrong, but Joanie didn't feel it necessary to explain why. "Think about it. You won't have to support Sam. Give me the money and we'll be off your hands. This way when you remarry, you'll start with a clean slate. Your wife-to-be wouldn't have to know about us."

"Damn it, Joanie. Do you honestly think, now that I learned about Sam, that I could just forget about her? That I'd turn my back on her?"

"You already did, Julian. What's the difference of turning your back again tomorrow as soon as you settle with my condition?"

"There's a fucking difference. When I left, I thought I was only leaving you."

"And you would have stuck around if you knew I was pregnant?"

Julian didn't know the answer her question. As far as he knew, when he'd left he hadn't wanted to be saddled with Joanie. But Sam was different. She was his.

"Joanie, I'm not giving up Sam."

"Julian, I will not sign your papers."

Toe to toe, he stood facing her. All these years, he'd thought she was one timid little nerd. He was wrong. "Don't be difficult. I don't mind sending you alimony or child support, but I'd mind if you cut my connection with Sam. She's my daughter."

"Don't be stupid. Give me the money and I'll sign your papers, Julian. Go back to your bachelor's life. No wife. No kid. Don't look back. If you're truly concerned, don't worry, we'll be fine. So, what's your answer?"

"Your condition is absurd."

"Whoever you're marrying next would think otherwise."

Joanie was right. With him free from any obligations, his life would be less complicated. He'd live like a single man. If he agreed with Joanie's condition, chances were, he wouldn't see Sam again. Sam would grow up not knowing him, and if Joanie remarried, her husband would raise Sam.

Freedom, the very thing that he'd had in mind when he'd left Manhattan. Inside his pocket, he rubbed the ring. He leveled his gaze with Joanie. Unfuckingbelievable. They'd had a daughter together. Joanie was surprised by his sudden visit and mad at his audacity to claim Sam. That was understandable considering he'd been gone from their lives for years. Joanie had the right to think him a cad, but he could prove he could be a good dad.

Dad. Good God, he was a dad. The idea was overwhelming and...damn, uplifting.

It had been true when he'd said he wouldn't give up Sam. From the first time he had laid his eyes on the child, he'd felt his connection with her. Considering the way Sam had wrapped her chubby arms around him, he was sure the child had felt the same way toward him. They'd both felt connected to one another. He was sure of it. Damn amazing.

"Okay."

"Okay what?" Joanie asked.

"I agree with your condition."

"But what?" Joanie's brow arched high. With only a half a foot distance between them, he could see how long and thick her lashes were. Now that he was truly looking at her, he noticed the unusual shade of her eyes—mossy green. Earlier, the color had resembled the evergreen cedar trees. Must be the result of lighting. And her lips, they were naturally pink and lipstick free.

On their wedding day, he remembered kissing her on the cheek instead of her lips. He wondered if he'd kissed her the night he'd taken her virginity.

"But?" Joanie repeated.

"Huh? Yeah, I have my own condition."

Joanie straightened her posture and licked her lips. Obviously, she didn't like him throwing demands back at her. She began chewing her lower lip. The simple action sent heated blood down his cock. What the fuck was wrong with him? He hadn't had sex since Georgina had left him. It had been a month. That must be it. He was just fucking horny.

"If your condition is within the bounds of reason, I'll accept it."

He smiled at her mimicking his words. "Touché."

"What's your condition?"

"I'll stay here until Sam's birthday."

"But her birthday is not for two weeks."

"Exactly. I want Sam to get to know me, her real dad."

"Why? You won't be part of her life. So what's the point?"

"You're right. I won't be here to play the part because that's your condition. I will stay as far away as possible from the both of you. But I will send her cards, birthday money, and graduation money. I'll even purchase her first car. For her college, I will set up a trust fund. I will talk to her online and we'll see each other on the webcam. While growing up, I want her to know me, not as Dr Ravenwood, but as her dad. And when she's old enough, I will tell her the truth about us. She can then decide for herself if she wants me in her life or not. Those are my conditions. I'll give you the money in exchange for my two weeks with Sam, Joanie."

"For a doctor, you sound so stupid."

"And if you're not stupid like you said you are, you'll accept my condition. Listen, Joanie, I am not asking to split the week with Sam. Two weeks with her and occasional cards every year will be my only

connection with her. I just want her to know I exist."
He chose not to press the issue of his seeing Sam more
often at this point in time.

"Two weeks. What should I tell her when you're
gone? Oh, your dad is not coming back, bug. He just
wanted two weeks with you. Yeah, right. Her papa is
gone forever and you will be gone after your dream
two weeks with her is over. Have you any idea what
the impact of your stupid selfishness will be on her?
What is she going to tell her friends? That she had her
dad with her for two weeks? I had a husband for
merely a day. You don't know what it was like, Julian.
You can't just play with people's lives. This isn't a
game."

Julian pinched the bridge of his nose. *Fuck.* He'd
thought his meeting with her would be easy. He'd
underestimated her. She was right about the
repercussions of his selfish idea, but she was being
unreasonable too. Why couldn't she just sign the
papers and talk about how he could help raise Sam?
Vindictive, beautiful wench. He didn't think she'd be
one.

Just let her sign the papers, cut her a check, then
leave. Simple. Walk away. Take your freedom, and
you might get lucky. Georgina will come back to you,
Julian. Don't be a moron.

But what about Sam? Yes, his demand of two weeks
with Sam would probably hurt her, but not having
him in her life would hurt her even more. She was
already the product of a broken home. As it was, they
would have a long distance relationship, but she'd
have a dad around. No, disappearing from her life
was out of the question. He met Joanie's stare. "My
condition still stands. Two weeks for a hundred
thousand dollars."

A loud crack of thunder boomed and he swore he felt the whole house shake. Sam's ear-piercing scream followed.

Damn it. Taking two steps at a time, he beat Joanie to Sam's room. Sam was already off her bed.

"Hey, love. Thunder scared you again, huh?" Julian asked.

"Uh-huh."

"Don't you worry, I am here now. Wanna go back to bed? I'll lie down with you."

"Okay. Promise you won't leave."

"I promise, love. I won't leave." Hugging Sam tight against his chest, he lowered himself onto the bed. The single bed dipped from his weight. Sam snuggled up against him, her little rump pressed against his stomach. She said something but he caught only the words butterfly, purple dragon, and butter.

Julian pressed his nose to the back of Sam's hair and inhaled her scent. Something inexplicable wrapped around him, like a blanket that made him snuggle tighter with Sam and caused heaviness in his chest.

When he'd seen the ring, wave after wave of shock had slapped him. The revelation had actually stunned him. He'd not been able to react. No, he hadn't known how to react. How does one act when he learned he'd fathered a beautiful child?

He slid his hand beneath Sam's and looked at how tiny it was compared to his. Hers was soft with dimples instead of knuckles showing. He rubbed the chubby part. At that moment, he knew he would fight for his rights as her father.

If what I feel right now is love, then yes, I love my little girl.

God, how could he love Sam when he barely knew her? "Yes. I love you, baby." He kissed the back of her head, trying to fight the emotions that were locked in his chest, but were now finally out and assaulting him. What had he done and what was he going to do? Two weeks with Sam. What a fucked up deal.

Sam jerked in her sleep. "Come, okay?"

"Yes, baby. I'll come to your party." Twice now, he had made a promise to her. He hoped to God that he'd be able to keep his words.

Chapter Seven

Downstairs, the old grandfather clock struck eleven, which meant Joanie had been lying on her bed staring at the dark ceiling for hours. Normally, the sound of rain pelting against the glass window lulled her to sleep. Not this time. Her mind and body were wide-awake, attuned to the man lying in the tiny bed in the room across from hers.

Two weeks of staying with them. What an idiotic idea. Had he any clue how awkward that would be?

Outside the wind howled. The tree branches creaked and whipped the side of the house. Damn it. They'd be screwed if a branch broke and landed on her paper-thin house. She threw her bed covers back and got up. She stood by the window and peered outside, but it was too dark to see.

Cold air seeped through the sealants around the window. Joanie picked at the old putty. She had work to do around the house, most of which involved money that she didn't have. At least, not right now. If Julian agreed with her, she could have the money she needed. Then she could start with the important repairs. Feeling the cold draft, she grabbed her robe and walked out to peek into Sam's bedroom.

Julian was on his back with his eyes closed, his feet flat on the floor. Sam's belly was pressed against his side and her leg draped around his hip. He looked uncomfortable lying on the tiny bed, but the look on his face said otherwise.

He must have sensed her. Slowly, he opened his eyes and looked at her. For a moment, she let herself meet his gaze. She stared wordlessly across at him, her heart pounding.

Lordy, he's one fine-looking man. So pleasing to look at.

Their eye contact broke when Sam shifted. Her foot jerked, kicking Julian right on the groin.

"Oomphh." He bucked and grabbed Sam's foot.

"Are you okay?" Joanie mouthed in sympathy.

Julian nodded. Slowly, he scooted to the side of the bed. He adjusted the cover around Sam and kissed her forehead.

Joanie watched him as he rose to his feet. Julian tucked his hands deep into his pockets and stood silently.

Frozen, Joanie remained standing in the doorway.

"Meet me downstairs, Joanie." With one last look at Sam, he squeezed by her and left the room.

* * * *

Joanie watched Julian pace in the living room while raking his hair with his fingers, leaving it standing on end. Obviously, finding out he had a daughter was too stressful for him. Did the unexpected news put a kink in his present plans? A plan to remarry? Joanie wondered. An invisible punch hit her in the gut. Lordy, why did that thought never fail to hurt her?

Hadn't she moved on already, or had she only made herself believe that? Whatever her feelings were, they didn't matter anymore. Sam mattered.

"I accept your condition to stay until Sam's birthday. But you'll have to agree with mine, of course."

Julian stopped pacing and pierced her with a look that made her want to bolt and lock herself in a room. His fists were opening and closing. Joanie could imagine him thinking he was gripping her neck. She took a step back, just a tiny bit and raised her chin. She wouldn't be intimidated in her own home, especially by him.

"When do you need the money?" He practically spat the last word.

Soon. Right now. Pronto. It would be great if she could get the money soon. At least she could inform the buyer that the property was no longer for sale, and she could call the carpenter again for an estimate on the repair. "How soon can you give it to me?"

"Eager, huh? Care to tell me what you'll do with it."

She hated the sarcasm in his words. He said them as if she was a gold-digging, money-grabbing bitch. "No. It's none of your business what I'll do with the money."

"On Sam's birthday, I'll give you the money."

"Fine." Two weeks. She could handle that. "I'll sign your papers when you hand me the money."

Julian nodded, his stare unwavering. Damn his blue eyes. If she continued with this stare-down, she'd find herself on the floor like Sam's melted ice cream on a hot sunny day. Good grief, after all these years, he still had that same effect on her — he mushed her brains.

The memory of him naked, standing in front of her, flashed in her mind like a bolt of lightning.

Julian's grandma had thrown a party to celebrate his college graduation. Alcohol flowed like Niagara Falls and Julian was drinking that night, perhaps more than what his body and mind could take. She had been standing beside a potted fern trying to blend in and not get noticed by Julian's boozy friend who had started harassing her, urging her to go outside and see what he had in the trunk of his car. He had been pulling her arm when Julian had appeared and yanked the guy away, shoving him against the fern. The guy had fallen backward and remained on the floor unmoving. She'd guessed the guy had fallen asleep, because those who'd witnessed what had happened had just laughed. Julian had asked if she were okay. He hadn't waited for her answer but grabbed her arm and told her to go upstairs where she should stay until the party was over. She'd said fine. Julian had insisted on escorting her to make sure no filthy scumbag grabbed her again. But he hadn't been able to find the stairs and had swayed like a bamboo blown by a strong wind.

At that moment, she'd thought it was Julian who should have been in his room to sleep off his drunken state before he passed out on the floor and hurt himself. Without second thought, she'd taken his arm and anchored it around her shoulder as she'd guided him upstairs.

"You smell good," he had said. *"Like vanilla ice cream. I like vanilla flavor."*

"You smell like beer. I don't like beer."

He leaned heavily against her. "I know what you like. To read. To paint. To blend on the wall like some wallpaper."

"You mean a wallflower."

"This is not a place for someone like you."

"*Your grandma invited me to come.*"

"*Don't know why. This isn't your crowd. You won't find another Browning fan here.*" They reached his room, and she was about to help him get to bed when he tightened his hold on her shoulder and asked the most absurd question, "*Would you like me to kiss you?*"

"*What?*"

"*You like me, don't you?*"

"*Yes, but —* "

He kissed her, his mouth hot and his tongue probing. She tasted beer and something unique. Julian brushed his fingers against her breast and broke the kiss. They looked at each other and before she could say good grief, Julian lifted her blouse over her head and unhooked her bra with cunning familiarity. His stare — like an afternoon sun kissing her exposed skin — warmed her whole body. Thrilled to be receiving his attention for the first time, she stood in the middle of the room while Julian took off his clothes. His ripped body, protruding dick, and wicked smile were exposed for her to gawk at. When he molded her breasts with his palms, she closed her eyes.

Julian breathed hard and fast while his hands traced her body from her shoulders down to her thighs and in between her legs. Then he cupped her pussy. Heat rippled under her skin as her body recognized the sexual desire she'd felt more than once, while tangled in the web of an erotic dream. Julian chuckled when she shivered from delight as his fingers pressed on to find her clitoris. While he teased her, he massaged her breast lightly with his other hand.

"*Perfect,*" he said then he lowered his head to suck her nipple.

The intense feeling of his mouth wrapped around her hard nipple nearly lifted her off her feet. She remembered tiptoeing, grabbing a handful of Julian's hair, pulling him even closer to her breasts. It was delicious. But not enough. She wanted more. Her pussy throbbed for more.

"Open your legs, Joanie. That's it. Fuck, you taste so good." With the pad of his thumb, he continued to fondle her clitoris. But there was more. Julian dipped his finger in her wet vagina before penetrating her fully.

At that moment, she thought she'd lost her mind.

"You're dripping wet, Joanie. Tight and fucking wet. Have you been fucked before?"

The word 'fuck' heightened her pleasure. She wanted to fuck, had dreamed about it since she'd met him, and it was finally happening.

"You can fuck me, if you want," she said. She felt bold and embarrassed at the same time, but the moment was too good to pass up. Julian had finally paid attention to her. It was her chance.

"And that's what you want, right? For me to fuck you?"

"Yes," she replied, enjoying the feel of Julian's finger moving in and out of her. Probing, rotating. Oh, it was so good she didn't want the feeling to end. For the first time, she felt what it was like to get finger fucked. It was beyond what she had expected. She moaned and spread her legs wider. *"Yes. I want this. You."*

"Good." Julian hiccupped the word, then walked her backward until the back of her knees touched his bed. He lowered her slowly, then covered her body with his. The length of his cock felt wonderful pressed against her pussy. She raised her hips, seeking more pressure.

He must have known what it was she needed, because he lifted himself a bit to move his cock into position.

She didn't have to wait long before his engorged cockhead touched her wet opening. It was sweet and delightful, at least until she felt the sting when he pushed the tip of his dick deeper.

"Damn, you're so tight. Spread your legs wider. I'm going to fuck you good. Real good," he said then surged forward, breaking her hymen. Pleasure quickly dulled the pain as he started moving in and out of her.

Finally, her dream came had come true — Julian in bed with her, his cock sliding deliciously in her untried passage. She remembered smiling up at him, loving each and every slide of his hard dick deep inside her womb. Opening her legs wider, she welcomed his invasion. She loved the feel of him inside her. Each time he thrust, she clenched her muscles to grip him tighter.

She watched him lick his fingers and wondered what he would do, then he placed his fingers in between their bodies to touch her clitoris. She knew then what he intended to do — to please her. Julian rubbed her clitoris, masturbated her until she felt feverish. The erotic motion sped up the pleasure building up inside her. It didn't take long before she reached her first orgasm.

A distant rumble of thunder made Joanie jump, pulling her out of her musings, bringing her back to where she was — standing in front of Julian. Joanie blinked fast. Julian was watching her, grinning as if he had seen what she had just imagined. Her face burned, embarrassed at the possibility. God, she was nuts. Why couldn't she get rid of that image? And what an idiotic time to think about it, too — standing in front of Julian.

"What the heck is so funny?"

"You. You look like you just had an orgasm while standing there."

Joanie felt like she was standing in front of a bonfire. Her face heated so much she actually began to fan herself with her hand. "I didn't have an...an orgasm."

"I didn't say you did. I said you looked like you had one. Two different things." His grin widened.

"Don't talk to me like I'm a trollop."

"A trollop? Haven't heard of that word since I was in college."

"Whatever. Your two weeks with Sam will start tomorrow. Come back at nine. I'll have her ready by then."

"I'm thinking it's best if I stay here."

"Not going to happen. That's not part of the deal."

"Yes it is. My two weeks means twenty-four hours a day, times fourteen days with Sam. I'll get to know my daughter better this way, don't you agree?"

"This is inappropriate."

"We're married, Joanie."

"Only on paper." Rain tapped on the glass windows. Damn rain.

"It's raining like crazy and I'm not familiar with the roads here. I'd appreciate it if you let me stay."

She wasn't cold-hearted enough to send him outside in weather like this. She was about to say that he could use her dad's room, but changed her mind. Her dad's things were still where he had left them, and she wanted the room to stay that way—for a while at least. There was also an extra room upstairs that could be used as a guest room, but she had never thought to convert it into one. "Fine. Stay if you want. You can use the couch. Bathroom's upstairs. You know where the kitchen is. Do you have an overnight bag? You can store it in that coat closet. If you need a toothbrush, I have an extra one upstairs. Goodnight."

Julian looked at the worn man-eating couch then looked back at her. "I'll take the toothbrush offer."

"Be right back." Joanie marched up the steps, keeping her head from craning back to see if Julian was watching and still smiling. When she reached her room, it was only then that she allowed herself to look back.

A long time ago, she had wished for this moment, for them to stay under the same roof together. Finally it had happened, but under totally different circumstances.

The clock struck twelve. "Damn it, I have to get up in six hours." She thought about letting Julian sleep on the most uncomfortable couch in all of Oregon without a pillow or blanket, hoping he'd leave tomorrow and stay in a hotel somewhere. But her father hadn't raised her to be inhospitable to anyone. She walked over to her closet, pushed the sliding door to the side and grabbed her spare blanket and a flat pillow.

* * * *

He knew she was still up. Not only was she stomping like a heavy elephant, the sound of the creaking floorboards gave her away. Was she still searching for the toothbrush?

Thinking Joanie had forgotten about the toothbrush, he turned off the kitchen light and the lamp in the living room then stretched his body on the couch. It felt like hours had passed before he heard Joanie coming down the creakiest stairs he'd ever heard. He supposed that was good. At least, Joanie would know if an intruder were going up the stairs.

He didn't move from his position on the couch. He kept his eyes half closed so he could watch her. The light from upstairs shined behind Joanie, outlining the contours of her hips and long shapely legs through her thin robe. His little wife had changed. Joanie stood beside him. She was so close that he could smell her clean, fresh scent. His finger itched to lift the hem of her robe to know if she smelled like soap all over, if she felt as smooth as she looked. He decided to shut his eyes instead.

Fuckin A. Joanie was tempting, too tempting for his own peace of mind. He felt the weight of the blanket as it covered him from neck to ankles. Nice. At least she didn't cover him with bricks. Joanie's soft hands lifted his head gingerly before she slipped the pillow under him. So his unwanted wife had felt sorry for him and brought him a pillow. It was as flat as a board but better than nothing.

He opened his eyes and found Joanie staring down at him. For a moment, he just looked at her. Something deep inside him that resembled regret stirred. He regretted hurting her and not knowing they had a beautiful child together, but he didn't regret leaving her. Nope, he didn't.

"Thank you."

"You're welcome. Here is your toothbrush. Goodnight."

He took the toothbrush from her outstretched hand. "Goodnight. Don't let the bed bugs bite."

"There is only one bug here. She's asleep and she's as harmless as an angel is. See you tomorrow morning."

He watched her go back up the steps, noticing the gentle sway of her hips. Suddenly, he didn't think the idea of staying with her in the same house was a good idea at all. Joanie, he admitted, was a temptation. Yes, Joanie didn't possess the regal posture and height models like Georgina boasted about. She was about five feet three, or four, inches, with skin obviously exposed to the sun a lot. She walked as if trying to beat every tick of the clock, and served burned hotdogs. Still, there was something about her only a man would notice in a woman. Sex appeal.

Julian sighed. His thoughts were rambling. He looked at his new toothbrush. The handle felt too small. Peering closely at it, he burst out laughing. The label on the handle showed it was a Dora the Explorer toothbrush. Neat. He could hardly wait to use it. Maybe he and Sam could brush their teeth together.

He adjusted his position to something more comfortable, but the couch's cushions were too thin, and he could feel the frame poking into his back. Fuck, lying on this couch was worse than being in a hammock. His legs were too long and dangled off the end. He tried a fetal position, but his neck bent at an odd angle and he was sure he'd have a hell of a kink to deal with in the morning. Releasing a frustrated sigh, he stretched on his back again and crossed his arms on his chest.

The floorboard upstairs creaked again. He closed his eyes and tried to imagine Georgina's face and what they could be doing if they were still together.

But as hard as he tried, it was Joanie's face that stared back at him. *Hell.*

Chapter Eight

The sound of banging pots and pans woke Julian up. Disoriented, he opened his eyes. It took him a long, full minute before he remembered where he was. Groaning, he tried to get off the couch, but his lower back screamed from a bad kink. He should have made a pallet on the floor instead of sleeping on this couch. The last time he'd felt like this was when he'd had a fight in a bar over a woman. A fist had made contact with his spleen and the pain had lasted for two weeks. This time though, his lower back hurt as if someone had beaten him with a baseball bat. He straightened his back and heard it pop. "Ahh... That's better."

Joanie's laughter made him look toward the kitchen. His dear wife was up and must be cooking breakfast. He sniffed the air, caught the smell of bacon, and freshly brewed coffee. Nice. He'd almost forgotten how the aroma of breakfast affected one's head in the morning. What a wonderful way to welcome a new day.

But he found that it was even more wonderful to watch Joanie move in the kitchen. There was something about a woman and a kitchen that he found so appealing. Before his grandma had suffered from macular degeneration, he remembered watching her hum while cooking in her kitchen too. He had enjoyed every minute of it. Was it because he knew there'd be food when a woman worked in the kitchen?

Joanie was facing the stove. He heard eggs crack followed by the sizzling sound. She looked so domesticated. Julian leaned against the doorjamb and watched Joanie work. With her back toward him, he had the opportunity to assess her.

For a woman who'd already borne a child, she looked fit. Even in the checkered red dress she wore, that reminded him of his grandma's picnic tablecloth, he could see her well-rounded ass and small waistline. The backs of her knees were exposed and no signs of varicose veins. Like yesterday, she had tied her hair in a bun, exposing her long neck. A few short hair strands coiled at her nape. She looked delicious from behind. Julian wondered what her front looked like this morning. There was only one way to find out.

"Good morning."

"Eeek!" Joanie jumped and whirled around. Her eyes were round and registered shock, at least until she realized it was just him, then the look in her eyes turned murderous. "You scared me."

"Didn't mean to. Sorry." His eyes immediately focused on the V shape of her neckline. Damn, the dress barely covered her breasts. Front and back were equally tantalizing, he decided.

He felt himself stir. What the hell? No. This wasn't attraction at all. No way he'd feel attracted to his unwanted wife. The only reason his dick quickly thickened was because he'd just woken up. Men his age still suffered from annoying morning erections. To keep his mind off his wife's tantalizing figure, he looked at the gurgling coffeepot "I smell coffee."

"I just made a pot. Sit down. Breakfast is almost ready."

"Thanks. Need help? Looks like you're busy cooking."

"No thank you. This kitchen is too small for two people. Not enough room to maneuver here."

"I hear Walmart is missing a tablecloth."

"What? How do you know?"

"'Cause you're wearing it."

"Oh my God! You're horribly mean."

Julian tried not to chuckle at the way Joanie scrunched up her nose. "Why are you wearing that? It's not Halloween yet."

"Funny. I'm going to work. Can't you tell? I am wearing my ugly uniform, and I am running late."

"Ahh. When I spotted you this morning, I thought you'd wrapped yourself with a tablecloth."

"Dr Ravenwood, you better not make fun of my uniform if you want breakfast."

"Okay. But your uniform is—"

"I know. Ugly." Joanie looked down at herself and smoothed her hands on the side of her skirt.

"You look pretty in it, though."

"Uh-huh. Breakfast consists of eggs, bacon, coffee and toast. Want all of them?"

"Sure. Where is Sam?"

"Outside."

"Alone?"

"Of course not. She's with Mark."

"Mark?" Who the hell was Mark? He walked to the fogged-up window and peered outside. Sure enough, Sam was out there skipping over a small puddle of water. The man smiled as he scooped Sam up when she slipped and tossed her up in the air. Sam giggled, telling him to do it again and again. "Who's Mark?" An ass. The kind that preyed on single moms with young children, he told himself.

"Sam's godfather. He comes here on weekends when I work late — like today."

"How long have you known him? Can he be trusted around children? Around women? Did you run a background check on this prick?"

"I've known him since we moved here. He was the one who drove Dad and me to the hospital when I was in labor with Sam. I broke my damn water in his brand new car. But he didn't mind at all. He's been a part of my family since then. Sam likes him, and Mark is not a prick. He's a pilot."

A pilot my ass. He looked outside. Mark had Sam on his shoulders and they were jumping over puddles. Couldn't this guy see the ground was slippery? What if he slipped and dropped Sam? Damn idiot.

Seeing his daughter laughing with another man made him gnash his teeth, but when Sam leaned forward to kiss Mark's cheek, pain like no other slashed at his heart. Obviously, Mark was playing dad with Sam. Damn it, he should be the one playing with Sam, not this dick. He pushed away from the window. "We made a deal. I'll stay here until Sam's birthday. While I am here, I want Sam with me. I'll watch her while you go to work. Starting today."

"Sam's been looking forward to staying with Mark today. He promised to take — "

"I want to know my daughter, Joanie. And I want her to get to know me. We made a fucking deal."

"I know and I will not renege on my words. Things happened so quickly. You just dropped in on me like a meteor. So unexpected. I forgot to look at my calendar to check on Sam's play date schedule. Today's trip to the Woodland Park Zoo with Mark slipped my mind."

"I'll take her."

"If you want to win Sam's or any kid's affection, I suggest you don't interfere with their social life—including trips to the zoo. She's a child, Julian. She'd think of you as a man who said no to her going to the zoo with her friend."

"I'll take her and her friend to the zoo, Disneyland, San Diego Zoo, Paris, London. Wherever. I don't give a fu—"

The back door opened and in came Sam with her cheeks bright red, curls flying everywhere and a big smile on her face. Mark followed behind her. As soon as his eyes met Mark's, he knew right away that Mark didn't like him. Well, the fucking feeling was mutual.

"Hi, Dr Julian. I skipped over the puddle many times and didn't get wet." Sam beamed.

Julian looked at his daughter, from her curls down to her shoes. She hadn't got wet, but her shoes were muddy. "Good girl. You had a great time skipping?"

"Uh-huh. Uncle Mark helped me, and I want to do it again. Uncle Mark, will you do it again?"

"Sure, bug. After breakfast."

"I'm going to see animals and butterflies today."

Sure, bug? So Joanie gave this prick right to call Sam bug. "You're going to the zoo, I heard."

"Yup, I looove the zoo. I like the penguins and the tent with lots of butterflies."

"Hey, beautiful," said Mark to Joanie. "Breakfast ready?"

Julian wanted to punch Mark in the nose. How dare he call his wife beautiful? Endearments were saved only for couples. He scowled at Joanie, who scowled at him in return.

"Mark, this is Dr Julian Ravenwood. He's the one I've been telling you about."

"The vet from New York."

"Yes. He'll be staying with us until Sam's birthday. Doctor, this is Mark."

Mark extended his hand to Julian. "Dr Ravenwood."

"Mark," Julian shook the man's hand. Normally, he'd encourage someone he met outside his office to call him Julian. With this man, he didn't feel like it.

"I didn't know Joanie has a pet that needs attention. Aren't you too far away from your clinic? You have one, I'm sure."

"Yes, I have a clinic. I'm a good vet." One of the top leading veterinary clinics in Manhattan and recently mentioned in the New York Post as the best, he wanted to add. But Julian wasn't a braggart. He kept the information to himself.

"I'm sure." Mark said. His tone was heavy with sarcasm.

"You want me to check your ears for ticks? Do you always scoot your rear end on the ground? Most likely you have an anal sac problem. I could help you with that."

"I bet you're good at sticking your fingers in —"

"Guys, please. Sit down and have breakfast. Good God."

Julian looked at Joanie, then at Mark. He wondered if they'd known each other intimately. Shoving the thought aside, he gave his attention to his daughter. *What the fuck do I care if Joanie's sleeping with another man?* He shouldn't care, but his ego told him otherwise. *Fuck.*

"Come here, Sam. I'll help you wash your hands."

"And my feet, too?"

"And your feet too." After washing Sam's hands and feet, he dried them off with the towel Joanie handed him. He tickled Sam's feet and felt delighted for making her laugh.

Joanie served everyone breakfast. Just like the hotdogs, she'd burned the eggs and toast. The bacon was crunchy and crumpled like brittle nuts. Good God, Joanie was a horrible cook. Considering how chubby Sam looked and her healthy color, he bet it was old Saint Claire who'd done the cooking when he'd been around.

"Mark, you want coffee?"

"No thanks, Joanie. I'm okay with my orange juice."

"Julian?"

"Sure." What kind of a man preferred orange juice over coffee in the morning? A weakling. He watched Joanie pour coffee in a white mug. Jesus. It looked like tar. He looked at Mark. The bastard was grinning from ear to ear.

Mark lifted his glass of orange juice and drank it with gusto.

Breakfast was horrible. His coffee was so strong even three heaping teaspoons of sugar couldn't make it sweet enough. His teeth felt loose from biting his bacon, and he didn't like Mark at all. The whole time, he listened to Joanie and Mark talk about things he couldn't take part in, people he didn't know, and places they'd been together. Joanie tried to include him in the conversation, but he had a feeling Mark didn't care if his saliva turned sour in his mouth while not saying anything. Fuck him. And why had Joanie kept calling him Dr Ravenwood? What the hell was that about?

He focused his attention on Sam to avoid looking across the table where Joanie sat in her seductive uniform. What the hell kind of job did she have? From where he was sitting, he could see half the top of her breasts and the beginning of her cleavage. Mark, who was sitting closer to her, could probably see her nipples. His wife's nipples.

The thought irritated him. He wanted to hit Mark in between the eyes with the damn hard toast. Oh, yeah, that would be satisfying. He almost smiled at the thought.

"Okay, you guys. I'm really going to get in trouble at work if I don't leave now. Dr Ravenwood, Sam is going to the zoo today."

"Joanie, call me Julian," he snapped.

Joanie scowled at him before smiling at her daughter. "Sam, listen to your Uncle Mark and Aunt Dana. They might not invite you again if you don't. And be nice to Marcus. No punching, okay?"

"I always behave, Mama." Sam finished her glass of juice, then ran up to her mama and gave her a wet kiss.

Julian wanted that kiss. No matter how wet it was. As if Joanie had read his mind, she whispered in Sam's ear. Sam ran to his side and stood with her puckered lips like a goldfish.

"I get a wet kiss, too?"

"Uh-huh. And a hug."

Joanie gave him a quick smile and stood up. "Okay, you guys. I'll leave you now."

"We're leaving too." As soon as Mark said the word, Sam latched onto him and grabbed his hand.

"Okay." Joanie grabbed her purse from the counter. "You have Sam's Hello Kitty bag, Mark?"

"Yes, darling. You already asked me that five times." Mark shook his head at Joanie. To Julian he said, "She acts like a parrot sometimes. But I still love her."

Joanie punched his arm. "Don't be mean. I just want to make sure." She gave Mark a hug.

The goodbye hug was too long in Julian's estimation, and the fucking asshole called his wife darling. Goddamn, he wanted to kill the man.

Joanie finally gave him her attentions. "I am sorry, but I have to leave you here. Feel free to use the television. We have local channels, no cable. Uhm, we have lots of home videos on VHS tapes that you can watch. Most of them about Sam. I think the player is still working. Oh, if you leave the house, make sure you lock the front door. The spare key is on top of the porch light. Mark, call me anytime."

"I will, darling." Mark winked.

Joanie burst out laughing. The two looked at Julian as if they knew something he didn't.

"Bye, Sam. Mama will miss you." Joanie kissed the top of Sam's head then disappeared in a hurry.

Julian cringed at the sound of Joanie's car starting. He walked toward the window and watched Joanie leave. The Subaru rumbled its way out of the driveway.

"She'll make it to work." Mark picked up Sam and headed for the door, too, but Julian stopped him.

"Wait."

"Yeah?" Mark turned around, his stare unfriendly.

"Where does Joanie work?"

"At the Pink Mermaid. You must have seen it when you drove here. It's the restaurant on the side of the road with a huge mermaid on top."

"I've seen it. But I didn't know it's a restaurant."

"Now you know." Mark turned and walked out the door.

Julian wanted to flip Mark off for his sarcastic remark, but controlled himself. If he was right, Joanie had already told the man who he was, which explained his instant dislike for him. He wouldn't give Mark a reason to think he wasn't fit to be around children. He stood on the porch as he watched Mark open his beamer's back passenger door.

"Hey, Mark," he called.

Mark looked at him with an annoyed look written all over his face. "Yeah?"

"Who's Dana?"

"My wife." Mark shut the door and walked to the driver's side.

Wife? Mark was married. So Mark had been baiting him when he'd called Joanie darling. The prick wasn't trying to inch his way in on his wife and daughter's life after all. Julian waved at Sam and watched the car disappear around the corner.

When the quietness of the morning finally settled around him, he could hear the birds chirping and a creek running. He liked it. Sam was lucky to have the wooded property to play in, something that city kids were missing.

Leaning against the doorjamb, he pulled out his cell and called his lawyer. Rick's voicemail picked up. He left a message about Sam and Joanie then hung up. He looked around the kitchen and snorted in amusement. It looked like Hurricane Katrina had gone by and destroyed Joanie's kitchen. "Wow, what a mess." He picked up the plates on the table and piled them all in the sink. "Hell, why not? I know how to wash dishes."

What he had thought would be an easy task turned out to be hours of labor. The cupboards were unorganized, the utensils were all mixed up and the dishwasher full of dirty dishes crusty from who knew how many days of sitting there.

Joanie wasn't only a bad cook, but a horrible housekeeper also. Julian decided to extend his dishwashing help to cleaning the house, well, the downstairs at least. He bet Joanie would be grateful for his help. The woman needed all the help she could get. He'd be living here for two weeks. Might as well be the one to lend a hand.

He found a basket full of dirty clothes. He dumped them in the washer, sprinkled powdered soap on top, closed the lid then pushed the start button. While waiting, he searched for the vacuum cleaner. He found it on the back porch beside the grill Joanie had used to burn the hotdogs. He pushed the vacuum around the house like it was a hungry manatee grazing at the bottom of the sea. It seemed like in every room of the house, there were things that needed to be fixed.

Done with the vacuum, he searched for a screwdriver to fix the cupboards' loose hinges and the coffee table's wobbly legs. Underneath the sink, he found a wooden box full of carpenter tools. He grabbed a hammer and a screwdriver, then walked around the house. He had just tightened the screws on the cabinet doors when his cell phone rang.

"Hey, Rick. You got my message?"

"Yes. What a shock. Is she really yours?"

"I'd bet my life on it."

"So what are Joanie's demands?"

"What?"

"Julian, you're rich. She's been denying you freedom for how long now? Why? Simple. Money. I'm sure she is using the child to milk you."

Divorce lawyers, he thought, were too smart when it comes to money. "Yeah. She wants money." After explaining everything, Rick insisted he could come up with a case against Joanie. One would be blackmail. Julian discarded the idea in a heartbeat.

"By the way, when did you say you're coming back?"

"Two weeks."

"All right. Be smart, Julian. Make her sign the papers now. You can always push the issue about the kid later."

"I'll think about it."

"By the way, sorry to hear Georgina moved out."

"Yeah I know. Thanks for the advice, Rick. I'll call if I need you." Why didn't he think about that? Rick had a point. He could give Joanie the money now in exchange for her signature instead of waiting until Sam's birthday. The sooner he ended his marriage with Joanie the better. The woman was a temptation he didn't need. If there was one person he had to avoid at all cost, it was Joanie. She spelled trouble.

The clock struck five. Julian grabbed his jacket and left the house. He'd driven by a grocery store yesterday. He'd make a quick trip there. The only items in Joanie's refrigerator were orange juice and milk. The freezer looked sad with just the frozen hotdogs and Sara Lee in there, and the cupboards were bare.

On his way to the grocery store, he drove by the Pink Mermaid restaurant. The words 'Bend's Best Burger' in big bright pink letters were painted on the grimiest glass window he'd ever seen. Whoever called the damn place a restaurant was nuts. It was more like an old barn or a gigantic tinderbox. The building tilted to the left, practically leaning against a tree. Battered and weather worn, the restaurant's sign stood directly above the door. He stared at it.

Fry my ass if that's a mermaid.

The tip of its tail was missing, hair was the color of the restaurant's roof—brown—PVC pipes were used for the arms and to keep it upright and the torso was wrapped with soot covered duct tape. The thing didn't look like a mermaid at all. No wonder he hadn't recognized it. Julian wondered how long the poor mermaid had been sitting there.

His stomach grumbled. Except for breakfast, he hadn't eaten anything today. He looked at the sign again. "Best burger, huh? We'll see." He drove around the parking lot and was lucky enough to find a spot. Pink Mermaid must have a great chef to draw this many customers.

Inside the restaurant was as bad as it looked outside. The place was dank, smoky, and smelled of stale beer and body odor. Julian had to stand by the door to give his lungs a chance to adjust to the offensive smell.

A young waitress wearing the same uniform Joanie had worn approached him. "Come in or stand outside. We need to shut the door."

Shut the door? Fuck, they needed to keep all the windows and doors in this place open. Better yet, remove the roof. Julian shut the door behind him. Jesus. He'd need a good shower to get rid of the smoke he could feel clinging to his skin, hair and clothes.

The waitress leaned in closer and yelled in his ear. "You need a table?"

Julian nodded, although he wasn't sure if she'd find one for him. For a run-down restaurant, this place was packed. "Sweetmelon. Is that your real name?" he asked, pointing at the waitress's name tag.

She chewed her gum as if it was a chewy fat steak before she answered, "Do you think my mother is so stupid to name me Sweetmelon? That man there." She pointed at the middle-aged man with a mustache so thick his mouth disappeared beneath it. "His name is Bogart. He owns this place so he gets to name all the waitresses. Anything to drink?"

"Tap beer, please. Anything dark." He wondered what name Mustachio had given Joanie.

The room was full of men, all of them drinking and smoking. It looked like there was a celebration of some kind happening at the moment. The music was in full blast and all the tables, as far as he could see, were full. He stood in the corner closest to the door, the best place in the room since there weren't any emergency exits in sight. If a brawl or fire started, he could run outside quickly. He hoped Joanie knew the fire exit if she needed to escape. It was hard to believe Joanie worked in this sleazy joint. Julian scanned the room, but didn't see Joanie. The waitress came back and gave him his beer—in a bottle.

"Sorry, this is what we got left. Widmer Brothers, locally brewed. It's good. You must be from out of town."

"What made you say that?"

"Because men in this town always come here early every Tuesday, Thursday, Saturday and Sunday." Sweetmelon blew her bubblegum to a size of a saucer and sucked the air back in until it resembled a bull's old wrinkled testicle.

"Why, what's the occasion?"

Instead of answering, Sweetmelon pointed at the stage the same time all the lights went out, except for the spotlights.

Men started chanting the name Cherrybomb. When soft music floated in the air, everyone quieted.

Ah-hah! A show. These people weren't here to eat, but to watch a freaking show. A minute after, a masked woman in a red silk gown and red stilettos came out to stand in the middle of the stage. She made a low bow, giving those who were in front a tantalizing view of her nicely rounded breasts.

Julian found himself staring. The dancer looked like God's creation. A goddess. She was close to being perfect if it weren't for her height.

From where he stood, he could see just a hint of her smile. An expert, he thought. The woman knew how seductive her smile looked, and she was using it to her advantage—a smart move for a dancer.

Slowly, the woman's hips swayed in tune to the music.

Mixtures of grunts, gasps and groans collided in the air when the woman's gown slid down her shoulders until it pooled around her feet. A red skimpy thong with what looked like chicken feathers barely covered her pubic mound. And her top—if one could call it a top—covered practically nothing. Now he knew why the men were here early. To secure a front seat. Hell, he wished he were there in the front.

Without a doubt, this woman possessed the greatest body he had ever seen. Georgina, he bet, would kill to have a waistline and flat abs like this goddess. It must have taken her years of practice to move like that— slow, sensual, provocative. And to have such a small waist—damn. He could wrap his fingers around her waist while she was on all fours and he standing behind her.

Someone whistled. The dancer smiled.

Julian took a sip of his beer, cursing the primal beast inside him for thinking lustful thoughts.

The dancer flipped her long cascading dark brown hair. Lights made it shine so beautifully. Julian thought the woman's hair was her other weapon, on top of her spectacular figure. When the music picked up a faster beat, the woman's seductive movements quickened as well. The crowd came back to life and started throwing money on stage, calling the dancer's name. He noticed the dancer mixed jazz, modern, and ballet in her movements. She arched and swayed her body as if there were invisible hands caressing her and she was responding to the touch. Her mouth was slightly open, and a thin sheen of perspiration shined above her lips. Julian stood mesmerized. He'd never seen anyone dance so erotically as the way she did. She looked like she was making love and on the verge of having her orgasm.

He couldn't take his eyes off her.

It was amazing how she held the men enthralled, including him. Surely, if his body were on fire, he'd bet his Porsche the rest of the men were too.

Julian continued to watch, ignoring the warm bottle of beer in his hand. The woman looked his way. Through her mask, he could see her eyes. She was staring at him. He must have distracted her because she stumbled a bit. What, did he make her nervous? She started biting her lower lip and her tongued darted in and out the way Joanie would when... Goddamn son of a bitch. He narrowed his eyes. No fucking way. Could she be Joanie? He turned around to find Sweetmelon.

Sweetmelon was standing by the bar watching the dancer too. He wound his way to her. "Sweetmelon," he called.

"Hey. Want another beer?"

"No. Please tell me, what is Cherrybomb's real name?"

"Get in line. See those men, they've been asking for Cherrybomb's real name since she started working here. Bogart told us not to tell anyone our real names. It's private."

Julian took out his wallet and offered her a hundred dollar bill. It was too much, but he didn't like bargaining. "Tell me."

"Customers are not allowed to know —"

"I'm sure I can find someone here who will give me the dancer's name in exchange for a hundred dollars."

"I knew I should be dancing on that stage. Men would not only pay to see me dance, but pay just to know my real identity, but damn Bogart said the cedar trees could swing better than me."

"Do you want the money or not?"

"One C note isn't gonna help you. I've been offered more than that."

"Here. Two hundred. Tell me her name."

"Fine." Sweetmelon snatched the money out of his hand, then looked toward Bogart. "I hope he won't see me taking money from you. He'll suspect something."

Julian smirked. Bogart was so busy watching the dancer he wouldn't know if his restaurant was on fire.

"Well, I can tell you but promise not to tell anyone."

Julian nodded. He had a feeling he already knew who Cherrybomb was, but he wanted to hear Sweetmelon confirm his suspicion. "I promise."

"That's our star dancer, Joanie Saint Claire."

"Goddamn it."

"Hey, you promised not to tell anyone. My ass will get fired for telling you."

"How long has she been doing this?"

"Almost two weeks, I think. She started a few days after her father died. She used to live in Seattle, you know. She had that city like air around her before. Not anymore. I heard she moved here because some loser knocked her up and left her like an old broken down car on the side of the road. Her kid's gonna be four years old soon, I think. Sexy for a mother, huh?"

Sexy. She was a goddess dancing in hell. "Damn it, Joanie," he mumbled.

"Don't tell Joanie I squealed on her."

"Tell me, how do I get backstage?"

"Now that's another—"

"Tell me or I'll have this joint shut down for failing to follow proper safety codes. You'll find yourself looking for another job. Take me to the backstage."

"Oh, God, you're really gonna get my ass kicked all the way to China."

"Sweetmelon, I swear I'll do what I can to get you another job. Just take me backstage. Or I'll find it myself."

"Why? Got the hots for her? All the men here have boners—"

"Criminy sakes, Sweetmelon."

"You're one eager... Wait a minute. Do you know Joanie?"

"Yeah, I know her. Intimately." Julian stressed the last word.

"Intimately? Oh, crap." Sweetmelon spat her gum on her hand. "You're the one who knocked her up and—"

"Yes. The loser who left her on the road like a broken down car."

Sweetmelon's eyes grew big. She popped the gum back in her mouth and chewed it faster than a hungry goat. "Now this is better than a *Lifetime* television show. Follow me."

* * * *

Joanie had spotted Julian right away. She had wanted to run back to her dressing room, but Bogart had already threatened he'd fire her heinie if she didn't dance tonight. What the hell was Julian doing here, anyway? She continued dancing, but her body felt stiff. She might as well do the strut or do a jig. She tried concentrating again. Beaches, famous rock, white-capped waves... Ah, drat. She couldn't. Blocking the sound, the stale smells of beer and sweat was impossible now that her concentration was broken. Thanks to Julian.

Now where the hell is he going? Why is he talking to Sweetmelon? She did a pirouette. When she glanced back to the spot where she had spotted Julian, he was gone. Damn the man. Did he recognize her? Maybe not. And maybe he didn't like her performance so he'd decided to leave. Joanie wished the music would play faster. Seeing Julian among the crowd had made her uncomfortable. What if he had indeed recognized her? Oh my God. Would he use her dancing against her so he could take Sam away? Her steps faltered. Luckily, the men were more interested in staring at her body than her dance movements.

Bill tried reaching for her calf. She stepped back and smiled at him. The fool was so drunk he probably didn't realize he'd just thrown her a fifty-dollar bill. Joanie made a mental note to give the money back to his wife. She'd tell Marie that Bill had dropped the money under the table because he'd been so drunk. God, his family needed the money more than she did.

Finally, the music ended. She forced a smile on her face and made super low bows—to the left, right and middle. The bowing was Bogart's idea. To give the audience a chance to see every side of her, he'd said.

She blew the audience a kiss before turning around. She sashayed her hips until she reached the curtains. Once the curtain had closed behind her, she took off running. But she didn't make it far enough to reach her dressing room. She hit something solid. A chest. Julian's chest.

"Yikes!"

She looked up and met Julian's angry glare. He blocked her path, practically smothering her with his coat.

"Have you lost your mind?"

"What are you doing here?"

"I should ask you that question. What the hell are you doing? No. What are you thinking?"

"What do you mean? I'm working. Didn't I tell you that this morning?"

"You said you're a waitress." He wrapped his arm around her and dragged her with him. "One who serves beer and chips to fucking drunks?"

"I am a waitress in the morning and a dancer late in the afternoon."

"Good God. Can't you just be a waitress morning, afternoon, and night?"

Joanie dug her heels on the floor, forcing Julian to stop. "I can't work at night. Sam needs me at home."

"But it's already late. You should be home preparing dinner and yet you're working. Get your fucking story straight."

"I work when Mark and Dana can watch her. And for your information, I make more money being a dancer, and dancing is decent."

"Not if you show your ass and boobs for everyone to ogle."

"So what? That's the plan. Those men come here to see me on stage. They look but I never let anyone touch me while I dance." She removed the coat from her shoulders and shoved it against Julian's chest.

"The way those men looked at you, it didn't matter whether you let them touch you or not. To them—in their heads—they were fu—feeling you."

"Is that what you were thinking when you watched me dance?" she blurted.

Julian pierced her with his angry blue eyes. His nostrils flared and jaw locked tight. She noticed his chest was heaving. Lord, he looked like a mad rhino. But why? What the hell had ticked him off? Definitely not because he saw her dance. He wouldn't care, would he?

"Let's go home," he said in a nasty, demanding tone. "I think I inhaled enough second-hand smoke here to turn my lungs black."

Joanie wanted to hear his answer, but she had a feeling she wouldn't have liked his answer anyway. "I can't go home. I still have an hour left."

"Joanie, don't be a fool. A woman like you should be at home. Let's go." Once again, he wrapped his coat around her.

"I can't. I'll lose my—"

"Joanie, what's going on?" It was Bogart standing by the door, twirling his baseball bat like a baton.

"Nothing, Bogart. This is a friend of mine and he's going to drive me home."

"You know you're not done for tonight."

"I know. That's what I kept telling him."

"She is done here. Forever," Julian said, putting heavy stress on each word.

"I am? What are you—?"

"Let's go, Joanie." Julian tugged her hand.

"Stop! Are you for real? You can't order me around like—"

"I am for real. And yes, I am ordering you."

Joanie couldn't believe it. How could he boss her like this after showing up only yesterday?

"She can't be done here." Bogart moved, intending to block them.

"Yes, she can. Why? Because I said she is. Now, move out of our way." Julian snarled.

"Better watch your tone. We don't bow to anyone wearing fancy shirts and shoes here. Take your arrogance back where you came from. Don't forget where you are."

"Believe me, I know where I am. Hell on earth. Now, move."

"She works for me, jackass. I decide whether she can leave early or not."

"Fuck you and your barn. I'm taking Joanie with me."

"You're a stupid man in a fancy outfit. Didn't you hear what I said? She can't leave this soon and definitely not forever."

"Why?"

"She owes me money." Bogart pointed the tip of his bat at Joanie, then he began smacking the bat on the palm of his hand.

"Do you owe him money, Joanie?"

"No."

"My ass. You owe me. For the damage in the kitchen, stove, and wasted food. You can't leave this place without paying me back."

"You didn't tell me I have to pay for those."

"Why do you think I kept you?"

"Because you need me. I brought in more customers since I started dancing here. I don't owe you money. And it wasn't my fault your stove was faulty."

"Faulty? You lying whore."

Smack! Julian punched Bogart in the face. Blood spurted out of his nose.

Bogart touched his nose and looked at his bloody hand. "You're fucking dead." He attacked with his bat.

Joanie moved in front of Julian. "Bogart, don't—"

Julian shoved her away seconds before Bogart swung his bat.

What happened next was a blur. First Julian was throwing punches then within a span of a heartbeat, Joanie saw him on the floor fending off Bogart's blows to his head. The sound of flesh hitting flesh made her cringe. Joanie recognized Julian's grunt. The sound pulled her out of her shock.

"Stop! You ugly beast." she pulled Bogart's hair, forcing his head to lean backward.

"Yeoowww!"

Bogart's hand flew and hit her on the cheek.

Joanie saw a million tiny stars swirling around in the midst of darkness. She released her hold on Bogart's long greasy hair to cover her cheekbone and left eye. She heard unbridled anger in Julian's voice as he called her name, followed by a hair-raising growl.

Through one eye, Joanie could see Julian's fist connect with Bogart's face and stomach. She watched him elbow Bogart in the ribs and follow it up with a knee to Bogart's groin.

Bogart crumpled on the floor.

Good God, Julian looked menacing and not like a veterinarian at all.

"Call my wife a whore again and I'll have the authorities tear this whole place down and you—I'll see to it that you rot in jail."

Bogart panted. His nose was oozing dark red blood that dripped down his lips and chin. He looked at her with pure hate on his face. "Wife? I hired your wife to work for me because she needed a job. She's penniless, you asshole. She said she could cook. Cook my ass. She destroyed my kitchen and nearly set this place on fire. But I—stupid me—gave her a chance and hired her to bus tables. But she broke plates faster than I could replace them." Bogart spat bloody saliva on the floor. "This fancy man here your husband, Joanie? What a joke. You, asshole," he pointed his middle finger at Julian. "Get your wife out of here. Make sure she doesn't come back. The only thing she's good at is grinding her hips. She's fired."

"I want my paycheck. It's the end of the month, Bogart."

"Shit. You owe me more than what you earned for two weeks." He winced as he wiped the blood with his sleeve. "And your damn husband broke my nose. I'm going to sue you for this."

Julian took money out of his wallet and threw it on Bogart. "Have your damn nose X-rayed. Sue me and we'll see who goes to jail first. Let's go, Joanie."

"Julian, you're bleeding."

"Forget it. Let's go." Julian gripped her arm tight, pulling her with him as he walked toward the back door.

"Wait, the money. I have to get it, otherwise Bogart will take it."

"He should get the money and give it to you."

"That's not the way we do it here. When I'm done dancing, I'm supposed to pick it up while the audience is watching. Bogart said that way men would toss more money on stage."

"Why didn't you pick the money up?"

"Because I saw you. You distracted me. Let me go back."

"He can have it." He tightened his hold on her shoulder, preventing her from turning.

"But Bill tossed me a fifty. I want to give it back to his wife. His family needs it."

"I'll give her the damn fifty. Move your feet, Joanie."

"But—"

"No buts. Don't make me carry you out of here."

"You're a rotten bully, you know that?"

"I know and I am your husband."

"Until Sam's birthday."

"Right. Until then I will exercise my right."

"What? What right?"

"The right to haul your ass out of here and spank you when necessary."

Joanie let out a deep breath. For a moment, she thought he was talking about his other right. And she wasn't thinking about mowing the lawn or the right to possess the television's remote control.

"Dr Ravenwood, you can't just show up here and start a fight like that."

"I am saving you from this hell of a place."

"Excuse me. I can take care of myself."

"Looks like you're doing a fine job of it too."

"Don't talk to me like I'm a child. I am not a seventeen-year-old anymore."

"Joanie, anyone who looks at you would know you're a full grown woman."

"Good. Now you know—you can't scare me. Oh, no. I'm not scared of you, Dr Ravenwood."

"I'm not trying to scare you. Just trying to knock some sense in that beautiful head of yours. We need to come home. Right now."

"Dr Ravenwood—"

"Joanie, if you call me Dr Ravenwood one more time, I won't be responsible for what I'll do to you."

"Bully. This place you call hell is where I work. Or used to be. Damn it. You cost me a job."

"Find another one. Wear this. You'll catch a cold dressed like that." Julian wrapped the jacket around her and zipped it all the way up so that only Joanie's head was showing.

"So easy for you to say. You have a degree. I don't." Since the jacket was too big, she was able to shove her arms inside its sleeves.

Julian took her hand and led her out of the Pink Mermaid. Joanie looked at their laced fingers. *Lord, did he just tell Bogart that I'm his wife?*

Dragging Joanie with him, they made it to the parking lot in a short time. Julian pushed a button on his remote to unlock his car. "Come on. Get in the car." He wanted Joanie away from the building in case Bogart called for backup. Most likely, the bastard wouldn't follow them, but he couldn't be so sure about that. Damn, his side hurt like a son of a bitch.

As soon as both of them were inside the car, he locked the doors, turned on the ignition and revved his engine. He waited until Joanie had buckled her seatbelt, then he drove off. The tires crunched the gravel, kicking it back as he sped up. The bar was out of sight when he finally pulled over on the shoulder of the road. Shutting the engine off, he released the breath he hadn't realized he'd been holding.

Damn, his whole body shook from anger, annoyance, and fear. Not for his safety but Joanie's. The bastard had hurt Joanie. When he'd seen Bogart's fist had made contact with her cheek, rage had surged out of his chest. He'd wanted to kill him for hurting the wife he barely knew. He couldn't believe how worried he had been.

Turning in his seat, pain shot from his side where Bogart's bat had made contact. He ignored the pain and unbuckled his and Joanie's seatbelts. "Are you okay? Did you get hit anywhere else?"

"No. I'm fine."

"Next time, do not try to block anyone or me during a fight. Running is the best thing you could do in a situation like that."

"Bogart was going to hit you with a bat." She looked at him with a scowl. "I'm not just going to run and leave you."

"I know." And he had felt the bat too. Shoving Joanie aside had lost him a second to dodge Bogart's blow. Although, if she hadn't alerted him, he would have broken ribs now. "Thanks for trying to save me. But like I said, next time—"

"Julian, you have a cut on your upper lip."

"I like it better when you call me Julian."

"It's too personal," Joanie mumbled.

"No, it's normal."

"If you say so. Here." She took out the handkerchief she kept inside her bra and dabbed his lip. "Does it hurt?"

The handkerchief was warm and held her scent. Soap and that unique scent of a woman. Like a switch to a light bulb it turned him on. Julian closed his eyes. Cool it, boy. You don't want her.

"It hurts, doesn't it?"

Julian opened his eyes. "A bit." Even with the pale light coming from the moon, he could see the mark on her cheek. "You didn't have to help me. You got hit. You'll have a bruise here." He touched the part that was beginning to show signs of swelling.

"It'll go away."

"Did you really burn all the food in there when you were their cook?"

"Not all. Bogart exaggerated his story. But—"

"It wasn't your fault." He doubted it. She probably burned the food the way she did the hotdogs.

"Exactly. When I dropped the meat on the hot pan it just caught on fire."

Most likely the oil was too hot. Joanie shouldn't be left alone in the kitchen. She was a horrible cook. He bet Bogart had hired her without checking her qualifications. He'd just seen her pretty face and accepted her right away. "You put meat on the hot pan and a fire started? Just like that?"

"Just like that."

God, it was a good thing she hadn't burnt the whole place down and herself. Sam wouldn't have a mother right now. "Why didn't you just apply to bus tables to begin with?"

"Bogart's girlfriend was still working there and he didn't need any more staff at the time."

"Did he fire her so he could give you the job?"

"No. She left. She and Bogart had a misunderstanding."

Most likely triggered by my wife. He knew the way Bogart had looked at him and Joanie. The man was jealous. He liked Joanie so he let her work for him. Who wouldn't? Joanie was a knockout mama. "Why not work at a different restaurant?"

"Pink Mermaid is the closest and the hours worked great for me. I can work and still have time to pick up Sam from daycare. Well, now I won't have to leave her there."

"No, you won't."

"Julian, you didn't have to fight him for calling me names. Good thing you got only a little cut here. What if something horrible happened? If you got killed? You won't have a chance to get to know Sam if you're dead."

"You're right." Bizarre, but he knew he'd fight another Bogart to defend her.

The moon cast a glow on her face, giving her an ethereal look. He'd bet his life savings Bogart fought him because of jealousy. Now, what about him? Machismo, he supposed. No man would like another man to call his wife a whore. Damn, he hoped he wouldn't have to fight another one because his wife had transformed into a hottie.

"Thanks, anyway," Joanie whispered.

"You're welcome."

"What were you doing in the bar?"

Why was he at the bar? He'd thought about trying the Mermaid's burger, perhaps talking to Joanie about giving her the money ahead of time like his lawyer had suggested. "I wanted to see you. You were gone a long time." A lie. But he blamed Bogart's blow to the side of his head for his lying. People with scattered brains couldn't think right, so they lied. Right?

"You couldn't wait until I got home?"

"Glad I didn't."

She folded the handkerchief and used the clean part to wipe his forehead.

"You'll have a fat lip."

"And you'll have a shiner."

Joanie surprised him with her laugh. The sound was melodious, unpretentious, sexy.

"Tomorrow we'll be quite a pair."

"How did you learn to dance like that?"

"Like what?"

"Like you were alone in the bedroom with someone, making love."

"I was."

"What?"

Joanie brought her hand up to stifle her giggles. The sound was infectious. "Let me explain. Mind you, before this job, the extent of my dancing experience was ballet dancing and that was eons ago. So to stand in front of drunken, nasty, stinky customers, I had to do something. And that's when I thought about the beach close to where Dad and I used to live."

"Innis Arden."

"Right. While dancing, I often imagined myself standing on the beach making love with the wind, nature, the sound of waves, while the sun watched."

What she said was so erotic that he thought about kissing her. And he did just that.

Cupping both sides of her head, he covered her mouth with his, the way he had imagined doing it last night and while she was dancing. Joanie tasted like gum. She must have chewed some like — what was her name? — something melon. Damn, he couldn't think right. He shifted his position, leaning closer so he could kiss her better.

Joanie sighed and ran her hand through his hair. She wasn't kissing him back actually, just waiting for him to do the kissing.

"Joanie, you taste —"

Bright lights shined on them followed by a loud horn. Joanie suddenly opened her eyes then ducked. Her head connected with his chin.

"Ow. Damn, woman."

"Oh, I'm sorry, sorry."

Julian rubbed his chin. "What are you doing?"

"I didn't want the driver to see you kissing me."

"Ah."

"And you shouldn't have kissed me."

"I know."

"Then why?"

"The fuck I know. It was a mistake," he snapped. Finding out she tasted so good and felt soft beneath his palms was definitely a mistake. It wouldn't happen again. Better not or he'd be screwed. *What the fuck am I doing?* "Buckle up. Let's go home."

He blamed his action on four things—her provocative dancing, her sexy and erotic description of making love with the wind, the punch on the side of his head, and the need to know that she was all right.

Chapter Nine

The moon was still bright, but the spell was gone. The moment and the kiss were brief, but Joanie was sure they would stay in her mind forever. She hadn't known what to do when their lips had made contact. She had even forgotten how to breathe. But one thing she was sure of — it was their first kiss as husband and wife, and it had been a mistake just like their first night. She was his mistake. Somehow, Julian's admission stung.

She shouldn't have let him. What was wrong with her? Shivers had run up her spine when their lips had touched and she'd moaned like a...a slut. Good God, if the car's headlights hadn't disturbed them, she would've opened up to him willingly... Like last time.

The realization hit her. After the pain, humiliation, and endless nights of crying, she was still in love with Julian. Why? How could she love the man who had openly showed his anger during the wedding and had snarled his 'I do'?

Watching the road ahead, she said, "Julian, I think it would be best if you stay somewhere else."

"Why? Afraid I'll try to kiss you again?"

"No. You wouldn't do it again because like you said, it was a mistake. It's just, I don't want Sam to get used to having you around. That's all." *I don't want to get used to having you around.*

"Tough luck. That's what I want to happen. When is she coming home?"

"She's not. She's staying overnight at Mark and Dana's." Crap. She was so rattled by his sudden visit she'd forgotten to tell him that information too. She'd better check her calendar.

"And you just remembered to tell me this?" Julian practically snarled the words.

Oh dear. She was saved from answering when they reached her driveway. As soon as the car had stopped beside where her Subaru should have been, she unbuckled her seatbelt and hopped out. She'd have to get a ride back out to pick it up. Julian was hard on her heels. Fumbling with her house key, she managed to open the door after jiggling the doorknob.

The moment she stepped inside, she knew something changed. "Oh my God. My house. What happened to my house?" She went directly to the kitchen where she was used to finding morning dishes still sitting on the table. "And what happened to my dirty dishes, the floor…?" Joanie looked at Julian leaning casually against the doorjamb with his hands on his pockets and one ankle over the other. God, he looked so handsome. Like a cowboy without his hat and guns. The urge to run and hug him reminded her of the way she felt when she saw Hugh Jackman at Benaroya Hall in downtown Seattle. The feeling made her whimper. "You did the cleaning while I was gone?"

He grinned like a little boy who had caught a toad and hidden it in his pocket. "Thought I'd help since I'll be eating your food and sleeping on your couch. The paintings aren't missing, by the way. I put them in the vacant room upstairs. I was careful. I know good quality when I see it."

"I don't know what to say."

"A 'thank you' would be nice."

"Thank you."

"You're welcome." Julian walked toward the refrigerator, opened the freezer and grabbed a handful of ice. "Can I borrow your handkerchief? Your cheek must hurt when you grin like that."

"Can't stop. It's like I hired the Maid Brigade to clean my house. Here." She handed Julian the handkerchief and watched him wrap the ice with it.

"Press this on your cheek."

"Thanks. What about you? You need ice for your cut."

"I'm good. You kissed my owwie away."

"Very funny."

"No. It's very arousing and cured all my pains."

Joanie closed her eyes and took a deep breath. Arousing. She didn't think she was capable of eliciting a sexual response from him, especially after he'd treated her with contempt at their wedding. What had changed? "The kiss was a mistake but a very arousing one?"

"Mistake or not, a kiss is still a kiss. By the way, thanks for the toothbrush."

"Dora's the only one I could find. This," she swept her hand around the room, "is incredible. I forgot how good it felt to come home to a clean house. I've been so busy lately, cleaning's the last thing on my list."

"Did you eat?"

"I had an apple and a handful of grapes. I don't eat at the restaurant. Food's as greasy as Bogart's hair. How about you? Did you eat?"

"It was part of my plan when I went to the restaurant."

"Oh, no. I forgot to tell you there are frozen TV dinners in the freezer. You must be hungry. We can microwave Sara Lee's pot pie or I can make tuna fish sandwiches."

"Tuna fish is fine. Can we add coffee to our dinner?"

"Sure." She reached to open her cupboard and felt the jacket hike up. Turning around, she looked at Julian to see if he was looking. He was. She pulled the jacket down. Showing her ass while dancing was fine, but flashing it off stage was an entirely different matter.

"Could you reach the can?"

"Sure. Tuna's here, right?

"Right. I'll make coffee."

"No."

"Sheez. You don't have to yell. I thought you wanted coffee?"

"I do. But I can make it. Why don't you go upstairs and change — if you want."

"Are you sure you want to make coffee? I can make it in a hurry then I'll change."

"I've been using a Starbucks espresso machine. I think I can handle your Krups."

"All right. Thanks. Be right back." Joanie quickly left the kitchen. She needed to change and pull her brain out of the clouds. Good Lord, all the way home she'd kept thinking about the kiss. It was just a short, simple kiss but enough to make her imagine the wicked things they could do in his cramped car. Her imagination even went as far as making love in there, the way the porn stars did on *Papa Long Porn,* the VHS tape her friend Dana had forced her to watch. When his hand had brushed against her thigh as he shifted gears, she'd had to bite her lips to stop from whimpering.

Dana was right. She should have accepted one of her date proposals. If she had, she wouldn't be acting like a deprived horny bitch who'd bottled her sexual desire for a long time. But dating wasn't on her to-do list. Even when her father had been around, she'd spent her time and energy raising Sam. There just wasn't enough room in her life for a man. And even if she'd made an effort to find a date, she would only have ruined it by being hypercritical. After her experience with Julian, she'd judged every man who'd shown interest in her critically. Except for her dad, men, she'd told herself, were all the same. They just wanted room in between her legs and not in her life.

* * * *

It took her only five minutes to change and wash off her make-up. She hated waiting so she made it a point of not letting anyone wait on her. Wearing her gray sweats and old Huskies T-shirt, she went back downstairs and headed straight to the kitchen. Julian was already preparing their sandwiches.

"You must have spent hours in here to know where to find everything. You even found the can opener. I've been looking for that for days."

"If you washed your dishes you would have found the can opener. Because that's where I found it."

"But I looked in the sink."

Julian pulled a lock of her hair. "Just kidding."

"Very funny. Really, where did you find it?"

"In your pot drawer."

"God, don't know how it got there."

"Well, now it's found. Coffee's ready. Sit down."

"I should be serving you, not the other way around." She pulled a chair out, sat down, and let out a loud sigh. It felt too good to sit down after hours of standing and walking in heels. Her feet ached from wearing the shoes Bogart insisted she wear on stage. She wanted to massage her arches. *Later. Right now, I just want to enjoy visiting with Julian.* They were talking like old friends seeing each other again for the first time. She didn't want to end the moment.

Amazing how life experiences and maturity could change a person.

"Long day, huh?" Julian placed a plate in front of her before pulling the chair close to hers.

"Yeah. Try walking on heels for hours and you'll know exactly how I am feeling right now."

"Here. Prop your feet." Julian leaned down. Before she'd realized what he was about to do, he'd grabbed her ankles and raised her feet to place them on his lap.

"Oh no, it's okay. I don't—"

"Relax. Come on, eat your food. You need your energy back. After your performance on stage, it's no wonder you're tired."

"I served customers too. Have you any idea how heavy a tray full of drinks is? Yikes! Stop. What are you doing?"

"Massaging your foot."

"While eating?"

"Why not? I can use one hand to rub your foot and use the other to eat."

"Julian. I appreciate what you're doing, but oohhh... So good."

Julian chuckled and pressed harder on her heel. "Just relax."

She took a sip of her coffee. "Lord, how did you make this coffee? This is soooo good."

"I am not a lord, but thanks."

"This is so wrong."

"Why?" He rubbed her heel, but in her mind, he was rubbing something else.

"Because I'm going to miss this coffee and the foot rubs."

"I'll show you how to make good coffee."

Her shoulders slumped. She wanted to hear a different answer. What exactly, she didn't know. "That would be nice."

"So, Sam's not coming home tonight."

"Sorry about that. I forgot about her play date with the Marsdens." She took a bite of her sandwich. "Yum." Tuna sandwich on an empty stomach and a foot rub—great combination. Julian pressed on her heel. Joanie felt her eyelids lower. When was the last time she'd had a massage... Come to think of it, never.

"You falling asleep on me?" Julian chuckled.

"No. I'm just savoring your pampering my feet."

"Anything else I need to know about Sam that you forgot to mention?"

"Hmm? Oh, yeah. Sam's last day of preschool was yesterday so she'll be able to spend two full weeks with you. What else...?" She tapped her fingers on the table to keep her mind off Julian's hands now moving up her calves. "She's allergic to insect bites, cashew nuts, hates any kinds of jam, and eats butter the way I eat Oreos. So don't leave her alone with butter within her reach. And... Well, you'll be spending time with Sam. I think it's best if you learn who your daughter is. Discover who she is, what she likes, and her favorites. You'll get to know her better that way."

"I look forward to spending time with her. Was hers a difficult pregnancy?"

Joanie met Julian's stare. She had been sick the whole nine months, but finding out she was pregnant by a husband who had abandoned her had made the pregnancy even worse. But he need not know that fact. He was here to get to know Sam, not her. "I think in every pregnancy, there's always a part where a mother experiences a bit of difficulty. Like tying her shoes, going to the bathroom all the time, or getting off the couch without groaning. But Dad was here to help me through, and Mark and Dana."

Julian nodded. His brow was wrinkled as if he was deep in thought. "I was a jerk. You didn't deserve to be treated the way I treated you."

"Yeah, I agree. You acted like a jerk."

Julian's brows shot up. "A big fat jerk?"

"Yup. A meanie, as Sam would say. Well, it's history."

"I'm sorry for putting you through the hardships of carrying a child. You should have told me. I'm not a monster, Joanie. I would have come to help if I knew. You didn't have to shoulder the burden. The mistake wasn't yours alone."

"Don't say that. Sam is not a mistake—for me. If I were given a chance to change my past, getting pregnant so young is the part I would never change. My mistake—as you called it—gave me a beautiful daughter. I love Sam too much to think she was a result of bad action. She's my heart, my life, my everything. I can't imagine living without my little bug. I know what happened between us caused you to lose your high school sweetheart, and you hated everything about me, the wedding…but I wouldn't change the past. I have Sam because of it. I am not sorry, Julian."

From the very start, Julian had been repelled by their union. He'd never once looked at her after the wedding. He hadn't even said goodbye before he'd left. Like he'd said, he'd acted like a jerk toward her, but hearing him say to her face how sorry he was for touching her, for getting her pregnant, made her ache all over. Her nose began to sting.

Damn it, I'm not going to cry. I am done crying over you.

"Thanks for the yummy dinner." She placed the half-eaten sandwich on the plate. Removing her feet from their heavenly perch, she stood up and picked up her mug and plate to take to the sink, but Julian rose from his chair to stop her.

"Leave them. I'll clean up."

"No. You've done enough. Just leave them. I'll wash the dishes tomorrow. Thanks. Do you need more blankets for tonight? I have an extra." She kept her gaze downcast and tried to step around him. Julian blocked her by placing a hand around her waist.

"Joanie, look at me."

"I'm tired. I'll see you tomorrow."

"Look at me." He cupped her face gently, forcing her to look at him. "I'm sorry. You're right. Sam isn't a mistake. She's a miracle. Listen. What I did to you was cowardly, even cruel. But believe me, Joanie. I didn't mean to hurt you. When I left that night, I was mad at your dad, my grandma, and myself. And to be honest, I was mad at you also. At the time, the only right thing to do, I thought, was to leave. Everyone was blaming me for what had happened to you. To me, you were guilty too. But because of your age, the blame fell hard on my shoulders."

"I'm sorry."

"Joanie, you let me make love with you that night. Why?"

He didn't know? How could he not? Why would a girl make love with a man if not for love?

"What happened doesn't matter now. It's all in the past, and I can't undo it. I'm sorry, too, for putting you in the position you never imagined to be in."

Julian nodded.

The sincere look on his face undid her. Like water from a broken dam, tears quickly found their way down her cheeks.

Julian's thumb wiped them away. "I'm not going to ask you to forgive me. You can hit me with your pots and pans if that's how you truly feel toward me right now. I wouldn't mind. All I am asking is you give me a chance to show you and Sam that I am not the monster you probably thought me to be."

"Not once did I think of you as a monster. An a-hole maybe, but not a monster."

"Boy, I'm not sure which one is better." He laughed and kissed her forehead before hugging her tight. "Grandma is right about you. You're a good person, Joanie. A cry-baby, but good."

It was unexpected. Nevertheless, she welcomed his embrace. "You wouldn't think that I'm a good person if you were around before and after I had Sam. Dad seriously thought of calling a psychiatrist. He said being around me was like being in the middle of a monsoon."

"I wish I had seen you when you were heavy with Sam."

"Just go look at a cow. I was hideously big. Couldn't even see my feet."

"Hmmm… I once helped a pregnant cow named Lucy. I didn't think she was hideous. In fact, she was lovely. Unlike you, though, she remained fat after she had her calf. But I didn't tell her that."

If she weren't feeling sad, she would have laughed out loud. She rubbed her nose on his white polo shirt. He smelled of Pink Mermaid but she could still smell a hint of his cologne. "Carrying Sam around helped me shed my fat. She was a big baby."

"And dancing. I bet it helped you gain back your figure?"

"No. I only started dancing recently."

"Really?" he drawled. "I wouldn't have taken you for a newbie, Cherrybomb."

"Hey, don't call me that." Joanie scrunched her nose and pushed on his chest. It was like pushing her car whenever it stalled on her. His hard chest felt good beneath her palms. Whatever she was feeling at the moment made her splay her fingers against his hard muscles.

Julian answered by pulling her closer to him sandwiching her hands between their chests. "The name was apt. You're a fantastic dancer and you rocked the bar tonight."

"You didn't think so when you smothered me with your jacket."

"I didn't say you're a bad dancer. What I didn't like was the job itself and your costume."

"Bogart picked the costume. Nobody would watch me dance if I wore pants and T-shirts, he said." Joanie was having a hard time focusing on their discussion. Her mind kept switching to the feel of Julian's hands resting above the rise of her hips. She took a deep breath and let it out in a whoosh. Standing so close to him like this, no one would think Julian had abandoned her four years ago because he hadn't liked being married to her. She thought of her father. What would he say if he saw her enjoying Julian's touch? He'd probably say, "Where is your pride?" With regret, she stepped out of his embrace. Julian loosened his hold but didn't let go of her. Instead, he slid his hands up to stop below the undersides of her breasts.

"Nobody could wear your costume and look great. But you know what? You could wear anything and the customers would watch you. Bogart was wrong."

"The customers were always drunk. They'd yell and clap for any woman who danced on the stage wearing my costume."

"I wasn't drunk."

Julian knew he shouldn't be flirting with Joanie, but he couldn't seem to stop. His wife, he'd found out, was easy to like. There was something about her that made him want to keep the conversation going and be with her, like being at a party. You see a woman you like and you stick with her all night long to see where you'll end up when the night was over. It must be her round green eyes or the softness of her mouth, so pleasant to look at. Lowering his gaze to focus on her mouth, the desire to kiss her again rose to a higher degree. If the headlights hadn't shined on them, who knew what he could have done while sitting in the car.

Shit. Didn't he make a promise not to touch her again? Yet, here he was feeling her soft curves. On their way back to her house, he'd wondered how her body would feel pressed against him. Now he knew — wonderful — and his whole body responded to her wonderfulness. He felt his dick thicken.

The top of Joanie's head barely reached his lips. She wasn't tall like Georgina, did not possess a Hollywood type beauty, wore old and unattractive sweatpants Georgina wouldn't be caught wearing, and she smelled of soap, not perfume, but he found her so appealing. What the hell was up with that?

Her face was scrubbed clean, free of makeup, her plump lips the color of a red rose. Up close he could see tiny freckles smattered on her cheeks and the bridge of her nose. Man, she was a beautiful creature in her own natural way, imperfect, but beautiful. Vanity, he thought, failed to possess Joanie. He liked that about her.

"Grandma will be very happy to hear she's a great-grandma now."

"I've missed her. How is she doing?"

"She's living with me. I hired a nurse to care for her. She's blind now."

"Oh, I'm so sorry. That's awful." Joanie's eyes quickly brightened with tears.

"You're a cry-baby." He took both her hands and placed them behind him. Without her arms in between them, he could feel her soft breasts and hard nipples against him, which meant... She wasn't wearing a bra.

"What are you doing?" Joanie asked in a soft breathy voice.

"Doing what the drunks—I am sure—were thinking of doing to you." He dipped his head and captured her mouth. Joanie sighed as she leaned against him. Using his tongue, he traced the shape of her lips.

"Julian, you're kissing me again."

"I know."

"But you said it was—" He silenced her, his tongue snaking deep inside her mouth. He chuckled at Joanie's reaction. If he were to make a guess, he'd think she didn't know how to kiss. She didn't know what to do with his tongue. But that was impossible. No twenty-one-year-old remained ignorant about the art of kissing. Was he wrong? "I think whoever showed you how to kiss was a bad tutor."

Joanie moved her head back an inch. A red hue quickly painted her cheeks. "I think he was. But we didn't get a chance to practice."

"You've got to be kidding me." He didn't know what to think of her revelation, but one thing for sure—it made him smile. Why? He searched for an answer but failed to find one. "There must be something wrong with the men here in Bend. If I were them I wouldn't stop until I…"

Joanie smiled. "Some of them tried, but I didn't let them."

During their wedding, he hadn't kissed her properly when the bushy-eyebrowed priest had said he could kiss the bride. Suddenly he didn't feel like smiling anymore. He realized the humiliation he had caused Joanie. Damn, he'd been a cruel son of a bitch. "I didn't kiss you properly after the wedding, either."

"No. I think your mind was somewhere else that day. Maybe you were thinking about finding a way to get out of our marriage. Or wishing for a miracle to happen. I-I understand, though. Who would want to kiss a bride who looked more like a twig—?"

He stopped her with a kiss. It could be the burgeoning urge to kiss her or guilt that drove him to tighten his arm around her waist and cup the back of her head, but whichever it was, he didn't care. Joanie's soft body held flush against him felt so great. And her mouth—damn. She tasted like honey. "I should have kissed you after we got married." He dipped his tongue inside her mouth again. "Every bride deserves to be kissed on her wedding day," he added in between kisses. "Especially by her groom."

Joanie moaned. Her tongue touched the tip of his and began sparring with him. She was a quick learner.

"And I should have kissed you when I took your virginity. I would have known then how good you tasted."

"And I would have known how good it was to be kissed," she said when he left her mouth to suck on her neck.

"Yes, it is good." Bending his knees a bit to align his body with hers, he ground his hips against her pubic mound. "God, you feel wonderful."

"Julian... Oh..."

Wedging his knee in between her legs, he gripped Joanie's ass and pulled her up. She felt hot against his thigh. When Joanie let out a sexy whimper, he began rocking her hips.

Joanie whimpered again, moving her body against his.

"Yes, rub it like that. Hit the right spot." Unable to stand it, he pulled her shirt over her head and exposed her breasts. Just as he'd thought—they were beautiful with rosy areolas and big nipples. He cupped her breasts and massaged them while devouring her mouth.

The tightness of his jeans was so uncomfortable he wanted to unbutton his fly and whip out his hard dick. But not yet. He wanted Joanie to take control, enjoy the foreplay, which he was sure hadn't happened during the first time he'd had her. Tearing his mouth from Joanie's unbelievably sweet one, he followed the length of her neck, bit lightly on her soft skin and enjoyed her quiet moan.

"Julian, this is so good."

"Yes, I know. And there's more." He supported her as he leaned her back a bit. His mouth didn't leave her skin but continued to taste her, leaving a wet trail of kisses all the way down until he reached her hard nipple. "Beautiful." He licked it over and over until it shined with his saliva. The sight only heightened his need. Opening his mouth, he sucked it hard.

"My God, Julian."

Joanie's hips were moving in a thrusting motion, rubbing her pussy hard on his thigh. She'd be sore if he didn't help her. He snaked his hand inside her sweatpants and didn't stop until he reached the top of her mound. Only then did he press his thigh in between her legs again. "Julian, oh my God."

"Hmm, you're close, babe. You're going to have your orgasm."

Joanie moaned. Pure undulated pleasure registered on her face. Not only was she a natural beauty, but also an unpretentious woman. Her uninhibited side aroused him. He was close to ejaculating inside his pants, but he had to control himself. He'd give Joanie what her body screamed for. Pressing the tip of his middle finger on her clit, he rotated her nub—that he knew, would drive her wild.

Joanie panted. She was nearing her peak. A thin sheen of perspiration appeared on her upper lip. He leaned forward to lick her mouth, at the same time he plunged two fingers inside her tight pussy. She was so damn tight and hot. And he was having a great time.

"Oh God, oh God. Julian…"

"Yes, babe." He continued to finger fuck her until he felt her contract. With his fingers inside her vagina, he pressed his thumb against her clitoris.

"Julian… Julian…" She convulsed in his arms.

He covered her mouth to swallow her screams. Vaguely, he heard his cell phone ring. He ignored it. With his heart beating against his ribs, he held Joanie tight. Her heart, too, was pumping so fast. "Are you all right?"

"Yes. For a moment, I thought I'd died and gone to heaven."

"Well, you did go to heaven. Now you're back." He wanted to stay the way they were until her heartbeat slowed down, but his cell phone kept intruding. He reached in his pocket and checked the LCD display. It was Georgina.

"You need to get that," Joanie said as a statement rather than a question.

"No, I can call back later." He kissed her before handing her the shirt. "Let me help you."

"No, it's okay. Answer your phone." Joanie stepped out of his embrace. She gave him a smile, turned around, then walked out of the kitchen.

He waited until she was out of sight before he flipped the cell phone open. "Hey, what's up?"

"What's up? What happened to hey, sweetheart?"

"I, I'm sorry. It's just I didn't expect your call."

"Aww. And here I thought you'd be happy to hear from me."

"I am. But it's been a month, Georgina. Last time we talked you weren't my sweetheart anymore."

"I know. But you know what? I miss you so much. Sweetheart, I'm still yours. Body and soul."

"Really?" Julian didn't know what to make of Georgina's statement. He should have felt happy, excited that she'd called and declared her love for him, but he felt nothing.

"Really. Guess what?"

"What?"

"I came by your apartment today and read to Grandma this afternoon."

"Thanks. Bet she loved that."

"She did. Sweetheart, I have something to tell you."

"What is it?"

"I realized moving out was a big mistake. Will you forgive me for giving you a hard time about your wife and for leaving?"

"There is nothing to forgive, Georgina."

"Oh, you are so wonderful. I love you and I miss you so much. You know what?"

"No. What?"

"I'll be in your bed when you get back. I can't wait to see you."

"I'm still married, you know."

"I'm aware. Rick told me, but I don't care. I realized that you deserve another chance. Besides, you promised that you would make your wife sign the papers. I'm bending my rules just for you, you know."

"Thanks."

"Rick told me about your daughter."

Damn it. Why would Rick tell Georgina about Sam? He'd have a talk with him. Julian combed his hair back. Before Georgina had left him, he'd kept promising that he'd be back as a free man. Now, she wanted him back, which should have made him feel happy. But it didn't. Right now, all he wanted to do was follow his little wife who had fallen apart in his arms a minute ago. How could this happen so fast? What was wrong with him? "Yeah, Sam. She's turning four in two weeks. She's a beauty."

"I'm sure. How's your day?"

"Busy. Yours?"

"Lonely. But Rick came over this afternoon and kept me company. So your wife hasn't signed the papers, huh?"

"No. Not yet."

"Awww...poo. I was hoping to celebrate our engagement next week."

"Engagement?"

"Yes. Once your stubborn wife signs the papers, I know you'll ask me to marry you, so I went ahead and told my friends to expect an engagement party. You said you would make her sign."

Julian pinched the bridge of his nose. In such a short time, Joanie had managed to make him forget about Georgina. What had happened to his bravado, eagerness, the in-and-out theory? Caput. They had gone *pfft* like a balloon because he had looked at Joanie's ass. *Damn, what a fucker I am.*

This afternoon, he had already decided to cut Joanie a check in exchange for her signature, to end their marriage sooner, just as Rick had suggested. His mind had changed when he'd seen her dancing on stage wearing a skimpy outfit, looking so delectable and moving so sensually she could raise any man's dick. Seeing drunken assholes throw money at her feet, hooting obscene words as if she was an indecent woman, had cemented the idea that he would not let Joanie work in that bar again, or in any bar for that matter. Estranged or not, she was still his wife and he'd protect her.

Protection. That was something he could provide. Julian thought for a moment. Protection? He'd just seduced Joanie in her kitchen. *I'm such a hypocrite. Shit.* If truth be told, he didn't want other men ogling Joanie because he wanted her for himself. He'd touched her like a husband exercising his right, and holy hell, he wanted to do it again.

There was something about Joanie that set her apart from the rest. She was innocent, unpretentious, uninhibited, inexperienced—these were all qualities that oozed naturally from her being.

"...come back soon," Georgina was saying.

Julian pulled his thoughts together. "Georgina, I'm gonna be staying here longer than I thought. Didn't Rick tell you that?"

"What?" Georgina whined the word.

"Yes, I want to get to know my daughter."

Georgina tsked. "Julian, don't believe anything your wife said. You didn't see her for years. Who knows, maybe the brat belongs to someone else?"

"Don't call Sam a brat, Georgina," he snapped. "She's a smart and wonderful child. Not a brat."

"Oh, I'm sorry. I thought brat meant child. I didn't know brat is a bad word. Anyway, if she insists that Sam is yours, have a DNA test done."

Joanie wouldn't have let Sam wear his wedding ring, which he'd kept in his pocket since he'd taken it, if Sam wasn't his. If Georgina could see Sam, she'd be able to tell, just by looking at her dark blue eyes, that she was a Ravenwood. "I believe she's mine, Georgina."

"Make sure you really are the father, Julian. Your wife could be using the child to get money from you. Rick should go there to help you slap her with, with...cases and lawsuits and whatever."

"I already talked to Rick about that. Thanks for the concern, Georgina."

There was a long silence before Georgina spoke again. "Well, I trust you, sweetheart. Maybe you're right. Is she a beautiful child?"

"She is beautiful. We have the same blue eyes."

"Oh, Julian. That is great. Good thing she didn't inherit her mother's eyes. You said Joanie had bug eyes, right?"

He imagined Joanie's passion filled green eyes. No, they were far from a bug's eyes. They were beautiful. Round and clear with thick eyelashes that could be mistaken for the fake kind Georgina sometimes wore. "Joanie's eyes are dark green, the color of a forest."

"Hmm. Sam. Beautiful name, especially for a boy. Tell me more about her."

Georgina's comment annoyed the hell out of him. He shouldn't say more about Sam, but knowing Georgina, she wouldn't relent until she got what she wanted. "You really want to hear more about her?"

"Of course. If she's going to be my stepdaughter, I should know her. Don't you think?"

"Georgina, I don't—"

"Aww, come on."

What the heck? Where was the spark, the excitement, whenever he was on the phone with Georgina? Gone. It was as if they'd never shared those many nights together. He really must have his brain checked. "Sam is turning four in two weeks. She loves hotdogs and butterflies. She's always wearing pink clothes, is allergic to insect bites and cashew nuts, loves butter, and I love her. She's the reason why I am staying here for two weeks, Georgina. She invited me to her birthday."

"Aww... You're going to celebrate her birthday. That's sweet. Should I go there to celebrate with her?"

"I don't think that would be a good idea."

"Right. Wives are bitchy about their husbands' girlfriends. Do you think you could bring her here for a week or a month?"

"I doubt Joanie will allow that."

"Hmm... Sounds like she's a greedy bitch. Play all your cards, Julian. Don't let your unwanted wife take full custody of our Sam. Don't let her fool you."

"I think I was wrong about her, Georgina."

"What do you mean?"

The snappy tone told him it would be best to keep his thoughts about Joanie to himself. "Never mind. I'll talk to you later."

"I'll be here waiting. When you're done with your business over there, come home right away. I miss you. Do you miss me?"

Julian cleared his throat. Replying that he missed her as well would be a lie.

The moment he'd laid his eyes on Joanie, he'd thought about nothing else. Not once had he missed Georgina. *Crap.* What would a smart man do in a situation like this? He took the safest route. "Yeah. Thanks, Georgina." He listened to Georgina blow kisses through the phone then hung up.

Damn. It was incredible how fate played with humans. Two days ago, he had cringed at the thought of seeing Joanie again. Only yesterday, he'd been so adamant about seeing Joanie's signature on the dotted line. Now it felt like he had bad indigestion whenever he thought about divorcing his wife.

Fuckin' A. This is unbelievable. I'm lusting over Joanie. That's all.

He clenched his hand, feeling his fingers still sticky from Joanie's juice. God, within a span of two days he'd become physically attracted to his wife, the woman he had tried to forget, the woman who'd borne him the beautiful Sam.

Two weeks. He would spend two weeks to be with her and Sam. He'd focus his time with her. Perhaps that way, whatever spell Joanie had cast over him would disappear. When that happened, he'd go back to Manhattan, meet up with Georgina, spend a whole day with her in bed and rekindle their relationship. Then perhaps, he would forget about his green-eyed wife.

He was just suffering from great desire over an ugly duckling turned into a beautiful swan. That was all. Maybe if he avoided touching her, he'd be okay.

The floorboard creaked above him. Julian looked up at the ceiling. Seconds later, he heard the sound of water running. Joanie was taking a shower. Blood pumped into his dick. "Maybe."

Chapter Ten

"Bitch!" Georgina threw her cell phone against the wall. Parts of her brand new iPhone flew everywhere. She didn't care. Julian would buy her a new one. Oh, yeah, if the bitch he called Joanie signed the damn papers, he'd beg her to come back to him and she'd get more than expensive trinkets from Julian. Listening to Julian, she could tell he'd gone cold on her.

Chest heaving, she stood in the middle of Julian's living room. She knew Julian's grandma was out with her nurse. The old woman always went for a stroll in the park. Freaking God knew why. The old bat couldn't even see a damn thing. Whatever. She must find Joanie's address in Oregon before blind Grandma caught up with her and begged her to read again.

It was Rick's fucking fault. He'd told her to play hard to get, to pretend she was leaving Julian so he'd be pushed to face his wife in person and ask for her signature. She'd endured a month of being away from Julian, thinking he would realize how much she meant to him. Now, the threat of losing him loomed like dark clouds above her. When Julian had told her about the brat, she'd wanted to curse him for being such an idiot. But she had to play her cards well. Her future, her dream, was at stake here.

Julian would be gone for two weeks. Two fucking weeks to spend with his child. Not good. Anything could happen in two weeks. Joanie had the advantage—she would dangle the brat in front of Julian's nose.

I hate fucking kids. Dirty, loud pests, and they're smelly. Julian had said he loved his daughter. Shit, how could he have known that in two days? By the tone of Julian's voice, she could tell that Julian liked his wife with the fucking forest green eyes.

Julian's marital status was no secret to her. She'd known all about it. She might have been blonde, but stupid she wasn't. When she had spotted him at a dinner party, she had made inquiries. Julian was a catch with money coming out of his ears. His parents were long dead—no in-laws to deal with—and he had only one relative close to him, his grandma. Julian was her stop, the big fish she needed to reel in, in a hurry.

She had to do something before his bitch of a wife won.

She was done sucking up the pruny testicles of politicians who only used her in bed. She would never go back to dating old pricks in exchange for a signature handbag, and she was done dating empty-headed models who, like her, were only waiting for their big breaks. She'd found Julian, an established doctor—not a heart doctor, but who the fuck cared?—with money and the first lover who'd actually had any interest in marrying her. Dr Julian Ravenwood would be her ticket to achieving her long-time goal, to live the high life. She could almost feel it now, her success, and she would do anything to remove the obstacles that would prevent her from claiming that success, be it a woman or a small child.

With Julian's child around, he would never be hers alone. The child would need support, would whine about school and tuition for college. The ugly mother would use the child the way she was doing now — detaining Julian, refusing to sign the divorce papers in exchange for who knows what. No. One thing she hated most was sharing her possessions. She would never, ever share Julian with anyone.

Damn it, this was all Rick's fault. That damn useless asshole of a lawyer. She'd let him fuck her from behind because he had promised to help her snag Julian.

"Trust me, Georgina," he'd said. "If you let me fuck your magnificent cunt doggie-style, I'll help you get Julian to the altar. Come on. I've been dreaming about having a taste of your pussy. Julian wouldn't know."

Those were the words of a horny jerk, and she had believed him. His idea of sending Julian to Oregon had failed. What an asshole.

Julian had said something about the brat's birthday in two weeks. If Joanie planned to use the kid to keep Julian on her side, she'd use the child, too, to bring Julian back to her bed. What better way to do it than show her genuine adoration for his child? She would go to Oregon next week. First, she must make a plan.

Georgina went to Julian's home office, a place that she always found dull and boring. Books about animals filled his shelves. The magazines on the console table were also about animals. She opened his desk drawers and riffled through the papers and whatnot. While pushing pens and paperclips around, she noticed something that didn't quite belong there, a hair ornament.

It was old and made out of some kind of shell, kind of like the shells pearls came from. *It must have belonged to Julian's grandmother.* But the engraved letters on the back told her otherwise.

To my beloved Julie. A token of my affection, love, heart and soul.
Yours,
James Saint Claire.

So this old thing belonged to Joanie's mom. So how did it end up in Julian's drawer? Joanie must have given it to him. Well, too bad because she wouldn't see this in one piece again. With all her might, Georgina snapped the clip in half and laughed her heart out.

Grinning, Georgina turned on Julian's MacBook, logged onto the Internet and searched for a flight. It didn't take long for her to book a business class flight to Oregon. Now if she could just find the address in Bend, she'd be set.

Chapter Eleven

Julian smelled pancakes. His lovely wife must be up and cooking—no, more like burning food again. He tried opening his eyes, but the flimsy, faded curtains failed to block the sun from shining on his face. God, it was five o'clock when he'd finally fallen asleep. The clock on the wall showed he'd slept for only three hours but it seemed like it was only ten minutes. Maybe if he slept another hour, he'd feel better. He covered his eyes with his arm and did just that when something soft and heavy landed on his stomach.

"Yeooww!"

"Wake up, Doctor. Wake up."

"Hello, hon."

Sam whacked him with her stuffed monkey. "I have something for you."

"I'm up, I'm up. Morning, Sam." He picked up Sam, whose eyes were shining like sapphires in the sun and gave her a hug. His daughter smelled of toast and milk. For a moment, he just inhaled her scent. God, he wished he'd seen her when she was just a little baby.

How many hugs and kisses had he missed? So many. His throat constricted. God, he wanted to cry.

Sam wriggled from his hold. Reluctantly, he released her. "Did you bathe in milk? Because you smell so good."

"Noooo. I drank milk. Look. It's for you."

He cleared his throat and pretended to look shocked. "Wow, for me? I've never had a stuffed butterfly before."

"His name is Midnight Blue. See, this is the color of your eyes like mine. See? See?" Sam nearly poked her eyes to make a point.

"Yeah, I see."

"His wings are your hair. Black. What's you gonna call him?"

"I thought his name is Midnight Blue?"

"Yessss, but what's you gonna call him?"

"Let me see... How about Midnight? So I won't forget what kind of butterfly he is."

"Okay. See my butterfly balloon?"

"I see. Really nice."

"I got icky feet again. See."

"Hmm. And looks like your hands are icky too. What have you been doing?"

"Picking flowers."

"All right. I think I know how to fix your icky hands and feet." He knew what Sam wanted — to get tickled. Julian picked Sam up and tossed her up in the air. "Here we go."

Sam squalled, her eyes closed tight. Julian had never been so happy. He carried his daughter to the kitchen and sat her beside the sink.

Sam's eyes were big with anticipation as she waited for the water to turn warm. The moment Julian said okay, Sam kicked and stomped her feet inside the sink. Soapy water splashed everywhere. He tried cleaning her soles where the sticky sap from the rhododendrons was stuck, but she kicked her feet, squealing. His little girl giggled so much drool dripped down her chin. He was counting Sam's toes making her squirm and laugh when Joanie walked in on them. She was carrying the pink bag she'd given Mark the day he took Sam to the zoo, a butterfly balloon, and a bouquet of wilted flowers. Her cheeks were flushed and there was dirt on her forehead where she must have wiped her hand.

"Oh, no. Mark's been spoiling her with gifts. Now you're spoiling her by washing her feet."

"Jealous?"

Joanie rolled her eyes. "Yeah. In your dreams. You guys, next time you play this game, do it in the tub. Look at this mess."

"Uh-oh. We're busted and Mama's huffing and puffing like an angry wolf."

"And she's gonna blow us down." Sam tittered.

"Excuse me. I need to get my vase from under the sink."

Julian moved a bit to make room for Joanie. "Need water for that. Here." He changed the water temperature to cold.

"Here, Mama," Sam mimicked, then giggled when Julian rubbed soap in between her toes. "Stop. It tickles."

"You want me to stop?"

"No."

"I thought so."

"That's enough. Your feet are clean now, bug."

"Mama's turn?"

Julian grinned. "Wanna have a turn, Mama? I'll gladly wash more than your feet."

"Ha ha. Very funny. Come on, you guys. I made breakfast."

"Mama's too big for the sink, Sam. I think we'll have to use the tub for her," he said without taking his eyes off Joanie. She looked so pretty, especially when bright red spots painted her cheeks.

"And purple bubbles to make her smell yummy."

"Sam, that's our secret. Don't tell."

"Okay. Can I tell Dr Julian you always cry when you look at my ring?" Sam looked inside her shirt. "Mama, it's gone." Sam's lips quivered and her eyes welled with tears before Julian could search his pocket for the ring.

"Sam, baby. The ring is not missing. I have it." Quickly, he took the ring out and showed it to her.

"You do?" Sam blinked her tears away.

"See? You can wear it now, but not while you sleep. It's not safe. I think Mama cries when she sees your ring because you're growing up too fast. You're going to be four soon."

"Uh-huh." Sam wiped her cheeks with the back of her chubby hands. "I will have big pink balloons, chocolate cake with butter, ice cream with butter, and more butter. Yum."

"Sam, Julian will be staying with us until your birthday."

"Yeesss. Can I go play now?"

"Sure. In the living room, not outside."

"Okay, Mama."

Julian dried Sam's feet and helped Sam put her sandals on. He gave her a tight squeeze before letting her run around the house with her butterfly balloon. Then he faced Joanie. "Good morning, Joanie."

"Good morning."

"You still cry about us?"

"I stopped crying about you a long time ago. If I cry now it's not all about you. How about breakfast?"

Julian didn't force the subject. Before his two weeks was up, he'd sit down with her. They needed to talk. Yeah, they'd talked last night, but it wasn't enough. There were so many things bottled up inside Joanie. She must let it out, clear her chest, then maybe she'd forgive him for being an ass and accept him as friend. A lot of divorced couples ended up being good friends. Maybe they could be too.

"Breakfast sounds good. What are we having?"

"Pancakes. I made them this morning while you slept. I could have burned the whole house down and you would have just kept on sleeping. Did you stay up late?"

Yeah. I was up all night contemplating whether to go upstairs and sleep with you or not. "Someone's face kept me awake all night."

Joanie frowned then nodded her head. "I see. I'll make coffee."

"No, I mean, thanks but I'll make it."

"You don't like my coffee, do you?"

"I do. It's just..."

Joanie leaned against the counter top, clasped her slender hands together and sighed. "It's okay, you know. I think Mark doesn't like my coffee, either."

"Don't look sad." He stood in front of her and leveled his eyes with hers by bracing his hands on each side of her. "Making coffee is quite tricky."

"And grilling hotdogs. They said that the best way to a man's heart is through his stomach. Well, I'll never make it into anyone's heart if I can't make coffee."

"Is there a special heart you want to reach?"

"I'm just saying..."

He thought about showing her how to measure the grounds and water to make a good pot of coffee. Now, with her statement he just might not. If her tar-looking coffee kept men away, he shouldn't meddle. Julian took a deep breath and let it out in a whoosh. Why should he care about her coffee? All he knew right now was he wanted to kiss her, find out how she tasted in the morning, and feel her sun-kissed cheeks against his unshaven ones.

"Is my coffee really that bad?"

"Babe, you make horrible coffee." The pain in Joanie's eyes made him discard the kissing idea. Instead, he touched her forehead to wipe off the smudged dirt. "I didn't mean to hurt your feelings."

"Oh, no. You didn't. I just remembered what Dad told me about coffee."

"Care to share?"

"He said, if a man is in love with his woman, her coffee would always taste good to him."

What a crock of bullshit, Julian thought. But then old Saint Claire had loved his wife. And he didn't love Joanie. Attracted to her, yes. But love her? Definitely not. "Bet he's right. Your coffee is not really that bad. Just a bit of sugar and honey and it'll be good."

"You don't have to say that to make me feel better. Honestly, you didn't hurt my feelings. Maybe there's a bit of truth about Dad's theory, but then it's debatable. Mark doesn't like my coffee, but I know he loves me. As a friend, of course."

And he knew why. Joanie was pleasant to be around, likeable and for sure easy to love. For the first time since he'd left her, he wondered if he had made a mistake by not giving their marriage a chance. He stared at Joanie's big, clear eyes, eyes that had cried for him and had probably looked outside many times, hoping he'd come back. Julian's chest felt heavy. The impact of what he'd done crashed on top of him. He didn't deserve to be treated like a guest in her home after what he'd done to her. But Joanie, like his grandma had said, was a good soul.

"You deserve someone who would love you the way your dad loved your mom." He smiled at Joanie.

"I already found that someone."

"You have?" Hearing that Joanie loved someone was a blow in his gut. It hurt like a son of a bitch, but Julian kept a smile on his face. Any husband would feel the same way, he thought. Even the estranged ones.

"Yeah. But the thing is, he has yet to find me."

"Whoever he is, he must be blind." And stupid. He brushed a gentle kiss on each corner of her mouth.

"How many times do you have to make the mistake of kissing me?"

"I suppose for the whole duration of my stay. It's hard not to kiss you, Joanie. You have beautiful, shapely lips that are begging to be kissed."

"You're just saying that."

Raising his mouth from hers, he gazed into her eyes.

"No. I am telling you the truth."

Sam's pattering sandals on the floor reined in the temptation to kiss Joanie full on the mouth.

"I want to go to the woods. Midnight should see her family."

"Later, bug. I have things to do."

"How about we all go and have a picnic in the woods?"

"I'm staying. You two can go after breakfast." Joanie tried to move his hand out of her way, but he didn't budge.

"Party-pooper. Are you a party-pooper, Joanie?" he whispered in her ear.

"Mama's a party-pooper," Sam repeated in a singsong voice.

"I'm not. Go find your hat, bug."

Once Sam was out of earshot, Joanie continued, "You're here to spend time with Sam, Julian, not with me. I think you'd better spend your two weeks getting to know her."

She was right. He was still here because of Sam. But God help him, he wanted to get to know Joanie as well. "Please join us."

"Why? The only reason you're still here is because of our condition — your two weeks with Sam in exchange for the one hundred thousand. You and me, we're divorced in every sense. We're not supposed to be having a picnic or…or kissing."

He cupped her head, forcing Joanie to look at him. "Ah, yes. I forgot about the money. Well, I am adding kissing and going on picnics to my condition."

"You, Dr Julian Henry Ravenwood, are nuts."

"Please join us. I'll wash the dishes and fold the laundry. Just come."

"How about ironing?"

"Yes. I'll even cook and rub your feet."

"Dear, how can I say no to that? Fine, make your coffee. Pancakes are cold already. You can microwave them. Let me make a phone call and I'll join you two. Sam, come in the kitchen please."

* * * *

The afternoon sun was high in the sky when the three of them trekked into the woods. Julian watched Sam run ahead of them with her net waving in the air.

Her feet left small prints on ground still soggy from last night's rain.

He'd grown up in Seattle where trees were abundant. On many occasions, he had hiked up Mount Rainier and Wallace Falls. There was something about the green environment that helped soothed a weary spirit. A walk in the woods was far better than a stroll in Manhattan Park, and the best part was walking with Sam and Joanie. Yeah, especially with Joanie.

He glanced at his wife. The strong urge to wrap his arms around her and wrestle with her on the soft grass—to once again feel her soft curves and sun-kissed skin—struck him. Every minute he spent with Joanie increased his unexpected infatuation with her. Man, he couldn't imagine what would happen during the remainder of his stay. Fall in love with her? Nah. That would be crazy. "You sounded happy when you were talking on the phone."

"Yeah. I was talking to Carmen Smith. She's a Windermere agent."

"You're selling something?"

She shifted the old quilt tucked underneath her arm. "How much do you want to bet Sam will ask you to wash her feet again?"

Joanie, he thought, would change topics to avoid answering questions she didn't like answering. "I like washing her feet, but if she wears boots instead of sandals we could keep her clean—maybe."

"Her last pair finally quit on her. I haven't had the chance to buy her a new pair."

Julian made a mental note to take Sam to the mall tomorrow. "What does she want for her birthday— aside from butterfly wings? Do they sell those?"

"Amazon, Sears, Costume Store. But you don't have to buy the wings. She wants everything that has wings and pink. Anything about butterflies is fine."

"How about you, Joanie. Do you need anything?"

"No. I have Sam."

He gently touched her elbow.

Joanie stopped walking and faced him with her brows arched high.

"You can also have me—as a friend. We didn't get a chance to be husband and wife. How about we try to be friends?"

"You're not trying to trick me into signing your papers for free, are you?"

Joanie gave him a smile that took his breath away. Damn, if he weren't careful he might find himself in love with Joanie. "No. We made a deal."

"Good. Sam, bug. We can stop here now." Joanie stepped away from him. She spread the old quilt on the pine needle covered grass and placed the pink bag in the corner. "Are you guys hungry?"

"Me." Sam answered. She kneeled on the blanket and watched Joanie open the basket.

"I forgot how nice it is to be in the woods."

"You live in the city now." Joanie handed Sam a sandwich, then gave him one.

"Yeah. In the middle of Manhattan. My office is only a few blocks away from my apartment. I walk every day, but the walk isn't as nice as our walk here in the woods."

"My woods," Sam said while chewing.

"Sam, remember. No talking while you're chewing."

Sam smiled, showing her little teeth. "Oohh, butterfly." Sam dropped her sandwich on the quilt and took off running.

"Who's running your business while you're here?" Joanie wrapped Sam's sandwich again.

"My business partner. Warren is probably digging himself out of the fur balls now because I left without waiting for my sub."

"Business is good?"

"Business is good. I noticed your paintings. They're wonderful. Bet each one could fetch a good amount."

"Not with the economy down."

"Yeah, true. The way you have them around your house looks like you just moved in or something."

"I don't have room for them. That's all."

"Would you sell some of them to me?"

"Why? You think shelters in Manhattan need paintings to decorate their walls?"

"No. But my apartment is dreary. I need something to remind me of this place."

"Of course. I'd be glad to get rid of some of them. Are you sure?"

"Yeah. I'm sure. Also I'm thinking maybe I should buy a house here, and I could —"

"Wait. When we made the deal, you didn't say anything about buying a house here. You said you'll send Sam occasional cards or see her online."

"I know."

"Julian…"

"Yes?"

"If you feel guilty about us, don't. Just, just give me the money and I'll sign the papers and we'll go our separate ways. Someday, like you said, Sam can decide if she wants you in her life or not. For now, we'll stick to our conditions."

Julian should thank her for her condition. Most men seeking a divorce would jump at the opportunity she was offering him. Give her money, she'd sign the papers and that would be the end of them. He'd go home a single man. Simple. Painless. But damn it, he felt the opposite. He didn't want to leave, didn't want to talk about the damn divorce papers again. And Joanie pushing him away hurt like hell. Why?

He leaned forward to touch her cheek. Her skin was soft like Sam's and smelled like Sam's too. "What will you do when I leave?"

Joanie closed her eyes and leaned on his hand. When she looked at him again, her eyes were devoid of shine and laughter. "Go back to living without you in our lives again. Find another job, raise Sam. Maybe ask Dana to hook me up again with another one of Mark's pilot friends. What will you do when you leave here? Aside from working. "

First, kill any pilot you hook up with before I leave, then make love with you so you won't forget me. "I don't know." It was the truth. Freedom. Yes, that was what he had wanted. To be free of her, but now the idea certainly didn't make him happy. "I shouldn't have left you. I should have stayed and tried to make our marriage work."

"We had a horrible start. You couldn't stand being in the same room with me. Hate, regret, guilt. Those were our marriage's foundation. A marriage like ours would have never worked."

"But you would have given us a try, right, Joanie?"

"Yes." Joanie picked up the pine needles off the blanket and tossed them in the air.

"Why?"

He'd be here for only two weeks so he might as well talk to her now. There were so many questions begging to be answered, such as why she'd let him take her that night. "Joanie, answer me."

"Why not try us, Julian? Every marriage deserves a chance to grow, including ours."

"I was nothing but mean to you. I hated the wedding, the idea of getting married, of marrying you. I don't remember anything about our wedding but curiosity from the attendees."

"I do. I remember everything about it. It was a beautiful wedding. The sun shined through the colored glass windows giving the chapel an incandescent glow, and the chapel smelled like incense, flowers, and candles. Everybody had a smile on their faces. And you, you stood by the altar with your best man, Nolan. You both looked wonderful. Nolan, I remember, gave me a shy grin when I saw him check his watch."

"To see his girlfriend, Gypsy. Nolan fell hard for her."

"How are they doing?"

"Gypsy's dad caught Nolan in her bed. The old man exchanged words with Nolan. It was a bad scene from what I understand."

"Oh, no."

"Yeah. Nolan walked away that day. He's engaged to someone else."

"Sad. Things happen for a reason. Maybe Nolan and Gypsy weren't meant to be or fate is not done playing with their lives. You never know. Did you know that your friends cornered me after the wedding?"

"No."

"They all have foul vocabularies, but I like them. They made me laugh. At least for a brief moment."

"What did they say?"

"Nolan gave me a tight hug and said, 'Don't let Julian bully you. He's a wuss with a poundcake for a heart. He'll miss the fun in Florida, but he's luckier than the three of us.' Trey told me to be patient and wait. I didn't know what he meant by it so I just said okay. Henry kissed my hand and said to me, 'Julian is one lucky son of a...you know.' I like your friends. Aside from the fact that they're all breathtaking, they gave me reason to believe that they're all gentlemen, regardless of their reputations as skirt-chasers."

"You think they're breathtaking?"

"Oh, God, yes. Blue eyes, dark hair, tall. I mean, the four of you looked like gods from Olympus who came down to earth to torment females. Are you still called the Blue-Eyed Four?"

Julian laughed. "Sadly. So you remember everything that happened during our wedding, huh?"

"Yes. I thought at the time I was only dreaming because I was marrying the man I loved since I— It was a beautiful wedding." She said the last words in a hurry, but Julian had heard her. He'd heard what she'd said clearly.

"You loved me?"

"I would have picked a different song, though." Joanie avoided looking at him. "The music was so old-fashioned. Jason Mraz's *I'm Yours* would have been nice or *In Your Eyes* by Peter Gabriel."

"Joanie, you loved me since when?"

"The flowers were orchids—all white. I was so nervous walking I couldn't even hold my bouquet."

"Joanie..."

"Father Keeley did a great job. I loved everything about that wedding except... I wished that day never happened."

"What? Why?"

"Because it wasn't what you wanted. I told Dad to stop the wedding, but he wouldn't hear me out. He said you must make a decent woman out of me and you did. You showed up at the church looking so handsome. That was all Dad wanted. For you to be there."

"He was most likely happy when I disappeared."

"I can't say that he was happy. But he wasn't surprised."

"How come he didn't come after me? Especially when you found out you were pregnant with Sam?"

"In the beginning, he felt victorious. He said with you running away from me, you missed something so wonderful. But months before he passed away, he started talking about you, why we should let you in on Sam. I swear to you, I said no. Not because I didn't want to share Sam with you. Believe me, all I dreamed about during her first years were for you to see her, hear her say strings of words and watch her play."

"Then why didn't you inform me?"

"Because I didn't think you'd like to know. I didn't think you would be happy. Marrying me was hard enough for you to take. To know you had gotten me pregnant, I thought, would be too much. I didn't want to give you more grief, more responsibilities."

"So you decided to keep Sam from me."

"Yes."

"You could have done that if you filed for a divorce, Joanie. I wouldn't have come back here to see you. Why didn't you?"

Joanie looked at him, frowning deeply. "I did."

"What?"

"Yes. When you came here, I thought you brought the papers I sent to you. But then you started spouting about your papers that I returned and didn't say anything about mine. So I figured you didn't get the papers?"

"No, I didn't."

176

Joanie shook her head. "Dad. He must have kept the papers instead of taking them to the post office."

"Did you wonder why I didn't reply?"

"I did. Dad said your silence was your way of getting even with me. To delay whatever plans I had."

"And what was your plan for filing for a divorce?"

"Aside from I got tired of waiting?" Joanie chuckled but it lacked mirth. She picked a crumb off the blanket and threw it on the grass. "A day after our supposedly first wedding anniversary, I thought it was time that I should do something about our situation, give you your freedom back. Unfortunately Dad, for some reason, decided to go against my will. He was always old school. Anyway, you'll soon be free."

He cupped her face and looked at her flushed cheeks, her sad eyes brimming with unshed tears. He remembered seeing her sad — during their wedding day. God, he wished he knew how to take her sadness away.

Her tears began to fall. Wiping her face with his thumbs, he kissed her forehead. "I'm sorry, baby. I really am. I think we were both victims of circumstance. But you, you faced the brunt alone." He pulled her against him and hugged her tight.

"No. Not alone. Dad was with me. He moved me out of Seattle to spare me from the talk, the gossip. Well, we survived and everything turned out okay."

Unable to stop himself, he kissed her cheeks, nose, and mouth. She tasted sweet and salty from her tears. Joanie sighed into his mouth and wrapped her arms around his neck. Julian lowered her onto the quilt. His body followed and partly covered her small and supple length. Now he knew why she'd reacted the way she had whenever he'd seen her reading to his grandma. "You loved me. But you love the blind guy now."

"The blind guy?"

"The one who is yet to find you."

"Ah, yeah. I love the blind guy."

"Lucky for him. If he wasn't blind, I might have killed him for ignoring you. Where is he?"

"Around," she replied with a shrug. "He's a knuckle-butt."

"A knuckle-butt?"

Joanie grinned.

The man, he thought, wasn't only blind but also stupid. Definitely blind and it was a good thing. With his free hand, he kneaded her hip, waist, and the flesh underneath her breast. Joanie returned his kisses with an equal eagerness. Her fingers raked his scalp as she arched her body to press against him. God, he wanted her so badly. He cupped her breast.

"Whatcha doing?"

Joanie stilled beneath him. He moved his head a bit to look at her. Her lips were red and puffy from his kisses.

"What're you doing?" Sam asked again.

"Kissing Mama, Sam," he answered without moving from his position.

"Why are you kissing my mama?"

"Because she's beautiful and she's my wife." He could feel Joanie's heart beating hard against his chest. She didn't say anything. Her tears flowed like rain on a glass window. He kissed her again before he rolled off Joanie and lay on his back.

"Why is Mama your wife?"

"Because we're married."

"Marcus said he's gonna marry me."

"Really. What did you say?"

"No."

"Why?"

"Cause Mark and Dana always kiss. And they're Marcus' mom and dad. I don't have a dad. I have a papa."

"Do you want me to be your daddy?"

"Uh-huh. Do you want me to be your Sam?" A simple, innocent question, but enough to crumble every bit of his being.

Julian felt a prick in his heart painful enough to bring tears to his eyes. He wondered if it was because she didn't have a daddy. Of course, she was too young to understand why she didn't have one. Besides, she'd had a papa until two weeks ago. "I want you to be my Sam forever. I love you, baby Sam." He pulled Sam gently against him and embraced her tight. "You're my little honey. Don't you forget that."

"I won't. I'm good in remembering, but I am not a elephant."

Joanie half cried and half laughed. She buried her face on Julian's arm. "No, you're not."

"I'll tell Marcus I have a Dr Daddy Julian."

"Daddy is fine, Sam."

"Okay. I want a ladybug."

* * * *

After a languorous day and what seemed to be endless kissing while lying on the blanket, they'd decided to wrap things up and go home. Joanie hadn't wanted the day to end, but it was late and Sam was tired and whining about not catching any butterflies. The sun was already hiding behind the clouds when they finally emerged from the woods.

Julian carried Sam all the way to the house, promising his daughter that he'd give her a good foot washing again. Sam's eyes lit up and she stopped whining about not catching anything today.

It didn't take long before Joanie had Sam tucked in her bed. "Tired, bug?"

"Yeah. Hug?"

"Of course. I love you, Sam. You're my sunshine, my moon, my stars and…pancake. Let me have a taste of my pancake." She blew on Sam's neck, making a gurgling sound that made her daughter giggle.

"Mama! Stop, you're tickling me."

"Okay, I'll stop. Goodnight."

"I love you, Mama."

"Love you too."

"Is it my turn?"

Joanie stood up to leave, but Julian intercepted her. He wrapped his arms around her and kissed her hard. He smelled of Sam's shampoo and bubblegum toothpaste. *I could easily get used to all of this.*

"Kiss, kiss, again."

Julian released his hold on her. "It's my turn to taste the pancake."

Sam squealed and tried to hide under her blanket. Joanie left the two with a smile on her face and went into her room. She was tired, but didn't want to sleep. Not yet. She stood by the window and looked at the starry night. They'd had a great time today. It was too bad it had to end so soon.

Within the span of two days, her upside-down life had turned right side up again. What about when he said his goodbyes? Would she be able to handle the reality that Julian was no longer hers? Yes, she'd offered to end their marriage three years ago, but that was before they'd had this—the picnic, kissing, and walking with Sam while they held her hands.

It was hard to explain how signing the divorce papers had turned into a wonderful picnic in the woods, but whatever it was that had changed things between her and Julian would end soon. What came easy would disappear in a hurry. This was momentary. She and Julian were fused together by years of regret, guilt and perhaps pity. And Sam. She should put an end to all of this. Nothing good would come by letting Julian get too close to her.

The floorboard squeaked behind her. She didn't turn around. She knew it was Julian. As in the past, she always knew when he was around, even when he thought she didn't.

"The pancake is out." He wrapped his arms around her waist and flattened his hands on her belly. Joanie was aware of Julian's erection pressed intimately into her, just above the rise of her butt. Desire quickly consumed her as he pressed hard against her. Dear God, why? After all these years, the pain and tears, she still wanted him. All of him.

"She had a great time."

"Did you have a great time?"

It was the best time of her life. One that she wouldn't forget. "Yes. Thank you for suggesting a picnic."

"We could do it again tomorrow and the next day. We'll do it every day while I am here."

While you're here.

Julian's hand tightened around her waist as he began to nuzzle her neck. "I love your smell."

"Julian, why are you doing this?"

"I don't know. All I know is I want you."

God, she had wanted to hear him say those words for years. This—with Julian—was a dream coming true. She should be happy. But what she felt right now was the opposite. "I think we need to stop this."

"I think we should continue."

"I'm not sure if this is wise."

"I don't see anything wrong with us like this. You're my wife and I want you, Joanie, badly."

As God was her witness, she wanted him too. Julian's mouth found the sensitive spot behind her ear and licked it. "Julian... Please..."

"Let me love you, Joanie. Let me show you what we could have had if circumstances were totally different."

Joanie didn't get a chance to answer. Julian pulled the sash tying her robe and slid his hand inside to cup her breasts. The heat of his palm quickly spread around her body. Gently he massaged her breast until her nipple hardened and pushed against his palm. His mouth was hot against her skin.

Julian was breathing hard. She could feel the quick rise and fall of his chest against her back. With her good sense screaming no, she tilted her neck to the side, giving him more access to the column of her throat.

Julian removed his robe and let it drop on the floor. From behind, he slowly moved his hands around her to cover both of her heavy breasts. Then he started kneading them with pressure, sending delicious feelings cascading down to her warm pussy and all the way to the very tips of her toes.

"I want to touch you." She tried to turn around, but Julian stopped her.

"In time. Close your eyes, Joanie."

"This is wicked."

"Yes. I know."

With her eyes closed, her sense of feeling heightened. The anticipation doubled her heart rate and intensified her sexual desire. "Julian..." One strong hand moved down her belly and stopped at the top of her mound. She arched to press her breast against his hand, her butt against his hard cock.

When his finger dipped low to touch her clitoris, she opened her legs. "Julian..."

"Oh, yeah, open for me. Joanie, tell me you want this. Tell me you want me."

"I want you, Julian." Finally, he let her turn around.

"Show me how much you want me. You're in charge, Joanie. Unlike our first time, you can set your pace. Show me what you want, how you want it, and I'll give it to you."

Feeling bold and wanton, she smiled. "I'll take you up on that." She pushed him. He didn't budge, but acquiesced when she prodded him again. He kept walking backward until they reached the bed. "Sit."

"My, my. I didn't know you were capable of being a wicked wench." With his gaze focused on her, he sat on the edge of the bed.

"Even an abandoned wife can use her imagination, Julian. I didn't stay innocent. You'll be surprised." She would thank Dana later for forcing her to watch those porn tapes. Both hands on his shoulders, she brazenly lifted one knee, then the other, on each side of him, leaving her wide open. She didn't dare lower herself though. Not yet.

She pressed her lips against his. Julian's tongue was inside her mouth in a heartbeat, dueling with hers. His taste was so good she couldn't get enough of him. She sucked his tongue gently, savoring him.

Between them, Julian caressed her breasts with one hand while the other snaked down to touch her hot pussy. She moaned against his mouth.

"You feel so good, hon. So good." He lowered his head and sucked on her nipple. At the same time he plunged his fingers inside her.

"Ohh…"

Julian gave each breast equal attention before he lowered himself on the bed. "Take me."

Closing her hand on his hard cock, she guided him to her open pussy and sank herself down slowly until he was buried deep inside her. Julian groaned and grabbed her hips. Beneath her, he moved rhythmically.

Joanie tried to move, but Julian's hold on her prevented her from doing so. He was staring at her with an intense expression. Suddenly, he pulled her down then rolled. Joanie found herself on her back with Julian on top.

"What happened to I'm in control?"

"Later. Honey, you're so tight."

"Lack of use, I guess."

"Not since…"

"No."

"You're kidding."

"I'm not."

"Oh, God. Wrap your legs around me. Yes. That's it." Slowly, he thrust inside. His strokes were measured and careful.

"I'm not going to break, Julian. I didn't the first time."

Julian smiled and kissed her nose. His hand drifted between their bodies to touch her clitoris. "Wet for me, huh?"

"Oh, God."

While he slowly fucked her, he rotated her clit. "Come for me, hon. Oh, yeah, fuck. So good."

Her pussy throbbed. She was nearing her peak. "Don't stop."

Julian did. He pulled out and started slithering down. Kissing her neck, belly, and...

"Julian, what are you doing?"

"Shh..." He lifted her leg and anchored it on his shoulder. Without any warning, he spread her pussy and gave her one long lick.

"Oh, Julian."

"I want to taste you, hon. Stay like that. Yes."

Embarrassment flooded her, but it vanished the moment Julian's tongue moved up and down her folds. "This must be illegal."

"It's not. This is perfectly natural."

Julian dipped his tongue in her entrance repeatedly before he sucked her clitoris. She felt the sign of her oncoming orgasm. "Julian... I think... Don't stop."

"Hmm... Sweet." Julian didn't stop sucking her clit until she cried his name the second time. It was only then that he lowered her foot down. "This is your first time to be kissed here?" he asked while gently running his fingers along her wet folds

"Yes."

"Do you like it?"

"Yes."

"Good. Me too." He poised his glistening cock at her entrance, then fucked her hard and good. "I like your taste and I want to do it again." Two more hard thrusts and Julian pulled out his engorged dick. He growled on her neck. It was low, guttural, then he came, spilling his semen on her belly.

In the dimness of the room, Joanie smiled.

Chapter Twelve

Julian's breath was hot on her neck and his thigh heavy on hers. She couldn't sleep. The minutes, seconds, were too precious to spend sleeping. It had been a week since Julian had come back to her life. One more week and he would be gone again — for good.

Lying on her side, Joanie stared at her fingers entwined with Julian's. The difference between their hands was so obvious. Hers were much shorter than his, rough from busing tables at the bar and years of exposure to paint. Rough from scrubbing to get rid of paints and stains and from mundane tasks around the house. Julian's was obviously pampered — no calluses, smooth, and the nails were neatly trimmed. She'd never had a professional manicurist work on her nails. She was, as she recalled, different compared to Julian's ex-girlfriend, the beauty queen.

She wondered if the reason for Julian's strong desire for divorce was another woman. What else would drive him to leave his work and come here if not for a woman? She wondered if his current girlfriend was beautiful.

She had stopped thinking about Julian being with another woman a long time ago because the thought only brought her endless pain, akin to what she was feeling right now. She mustn't start again.

"But who could she be?" She closed her eyes. Minutes passed before Julian squeezed her fingers.

"Who?" Julian asked.

His breath fanned the fine hairs on the back of her neck, sending goose bumps all over her. He shifted a bit, pressing his nude body more intimately—if that was even possible—against hers. Spooning with a man, more so with her husband, was a position she never thought she'd be able to experience.

"Joanie? You awake?"

Joanie sighed. She really must stop thinking out loud. It was too late to take it back. "I asked who she is. Your reason for coming here in person, for demanding that I sign the papers."

Julian squeezed her hand tighter this time. "Georgina Myers."

"I bet she is as beautiful as her name. Like your high school sweetheart Emily." Thinking about Julian in the arms of another was painful, but to hear the woman's name come from his own lips—a deep stab in her heart.

"She is. Georgina's a model, prim and proper. Always immaculately dressed and she hates reading. Although she always tells me that she loves it."

Of course, if Julian found another woman she would be altogether different from Joanie, both in nature and in quality—the exact opposite of her. Joanie fisted her hand, suddenly embarrassed. "Do you plan to marry her?"

"Joanie, do you really want to discuss Georgina?"

"I do."

Julian sighed. "We've been living together for months. Now I—"

"You love her. That's good. At least this time when you marry, it's because you love your bride. You wouldn't want a repeat of the past, would you?"

"No. Joanie, listen."

"I wished this for you, you know. To find happiness, to find a woman you truly want to be with. And you should be faithful to her, Julian."

"Georgina and I... I'm not even sure what we are anymore. When she found out about my marital status, she left. Just like the others."

"What do you mean like the others?"

"Georgina wasn't the first to run out the door. They, the women I've dated in the past, all thought I wasn't a good catch because I'm married."

"Sorry. That's my fault."

"Stop it. They also thought that you were trouble, that you'd cut their hair, and throw rotten tomatoes at them. They didn't want that."

"I would never do that."

"They didn't know that about you. I am glad Georgina and the others left, because they made me come home to you. I met my daughter and my wife who burns hotdogs and who'd throw herself into the middle of a fight to protect me."

"For the record, I pulled Bogart's hair to stop you from fighting so I wouldn't lose my job."

"Liar. You didn't want me to get hurt."

"Of course I didn't want you to get hurt. I need your money."

"Ha ha."

"What changed, Julian? Last time you barely looked at me. Now…you're in my bed."

"Is wanting you not enough of an answer?"

Joanie sighed. *Wanting me is definitely enough.* "It's enough."

Julian pressed gently on her shoulder, urging her to face him. "You are a remarkable woman." He kissed her forehead. "A precious gem."

"But unpolished."

"You shine enough to brighten up any gloomy day, hon. You don't need any more polishing."

"You know you can flatter me all you want, but you're still giving me the money I asked for."

"Joanie, let's not talk about the money or the damn divorce, okay?"

"What do you want to talk about?"

"I don't want to talk. I want to make love with you."

"Again?"

"Again. It would be my greatest pleasure."

Julian made love with Joanie as if it was the end of the world, or as though he were sitting on death row and this was the only time they could be together.

It was stupid. What he was doing was even beyond that. Both of them knew they were together because of a deal they had agreed on. But he couldn't explain why letting go of Joanie was harder than putting a wounded or sick pet to sleep. Why couldn't he just leave her alone?

Joanie responded to his touch without inhibitions. She opened up to him like a blooming flower. So beautiful and innocent.

"I will not forget this, love. You will always be my first wife. My Joanie." He moved against her slowly, savoring each stroke, each grip of her throbbing walls.

This time, he wanted to make love with her the way a groom should to his bride on their first night. This time, he wanted their union to be unforgettable.

Julian kissed her, his tongue deep in her mouth, tasting, probing. He sucked her tongue, bit her lower lip, caressed her breasts, and every part of her that he could reach as if she were a divine goddess.

Sheer pleasure registered on her face. "Joanie, look at me." Heavy lidded and passion filled green eyes stared back at him. Julian's heart thudded and he knew what he felt for her was beyond need.

"Yes, Julian."

"This, what we are doing, is making love. I am making love with you."

"And I with you. Now, please do something."

He snaked his hand in between them to touch her clitoris. "Like this?"

"Yes."

"Ahh... You're tight and wet." He pressed deeper until his whole middle finger was buried, then he pumped it slowly while looking at her beautiful face. Without taking his eyes off her, he pulled his finger out of her pussy and licked it dry. "You taste like honey."

Joanie's eyes widened for a brief second. Then she surprised him. She took his finger and sucked it. "You're right, and this honey is all yours."

Julian's cock pulsed at her words. "Spread your legs wide, hon. Yes. Look at me. I want to see your beautiful eyes when you come." He settled himself between her legs and watched her eyes flutter shut as he slowly penetrated her.

"Julian..."

He pulled out then plunged his cock deep inside her again. The pleasure was unbelievable, but the knowledge that he was giving it to Joanie made his heart swell.

Joanie met him thrust for thrust until she was racked with spasms. Then he released his own on the soap-scented sheet.

All night he made love with her, showed her everything he knew about pleasing a woman. When the sign of the new day showed visibly through her window, he let her sleep. Another day had gone by. Soon, it would be Sam's birthday. Soon it would be time for him to leave. Damn, why did that thought hurt so much?

* * * *

Julian woke up when Joanie shifted her position. Early morning sun filtered through the crack in the curtains. *Morning already.* This was the first time he'd woken up beside Joanie, and it felt wonderful. He planted a kiss on Joanie's shoulder, adjusted the sheet around them both and hugged her close to him. He thought about going back to sleep when he heard Sam's footsteps. He had just lifted his head to see her when Sam came in running and tugged at the blanket with all her might. Julian, luckily, was quick enough to hang onto the edge of the sheet. It was fine and dandy for her to see Mom and Dad kissing, but to see them sleeping together without their clothes would be a shock to her innocent, big blue eyes.

"I want pancakes."

"Sam!" Joanie grabbed the blanket and covered herself. "Sam, it's too early. Uhm, hang on, bug, okay?" she said in a muffled voice.

Julian ensured the other part of the blanket was safely covering his lower half.

"I want Cheerios."

"I'll get it for you, Sam. We'll give Mama another hour to sleep. She worked hard last night riding a stud so she's tired." Joanie pinched his side. "Oww."

"I wanna ride a stud." Sam pouted, obviously miffed she didn't get to ride her own.

Julian laughed.

"Not funny."

"No, not funny. Someday, Sam. When you're thirty-five."

"After my birthday?"

"Close. Can you turn around and count to twenty, hon?"

"Uh-huh. Mama's playing hide-and-seek?"

"Kind of."

"Okay." Sam turned around and started counting. Julian joined Joanie under the blanket.

"Good morning, beautiful. Care to give me a morning kiss?"

Sam heard him. "I want a kiss from Mama."

"Of course you'll get a kiss. Keep counting Sam." He kissed Joanie. It was a long languorous one. Joanie returned a kiss so sensuous that he felt himself stir. "I had a great time."

"Me too. Julian, Sam can't count up to twenty yet," she whispered.

"Damn." Kissing her one more time, he got out from under the sheet. "Sam, baby, I got a kiss from Mama. Come to Daddy, and I'll give it to you."

Sam, who was already done counting and was facing them, ran to his side. She presented her pudgy cheek and giggled when he made a loud kissing sound. "I want cheese sticks."

"Sure. You can have whatever we can find in the kitchen."

"Yeee. I'll go get Dolly." Sam disappeared from the room.

"Thanks. I don't think I'll be able to face her again if she sees us like this." Joanie sat up. The blanket slid off her shoulders and exposed one luscious breast.

"Hmm... How long do you think before Sam finds her doll?" He inched closer, forcing Joanie to fall back on the bed.

"Seconds. And, Julian, don't look at me like that. I'm still sore — hmm."

"Just want more of your honey taste." He kissed each corner of her mouth before capturing her full lips. "Sweet. Joanie — "

"Daddy, Daddy! Dolly and me want Cheerios." Sam's voice drifted in from the other room.

"Demanding little bug. I better leave you here. Otherwise, our child will starve to death. I plan to take her to the mall. You can come if you want, but if you'd rather stay and sleep that's fine too."

"You need time alone with Sam. I'll stay."

"Need anything?"

"Häagen-Dazs's double chocolate chip coffee ice cream."

"Got it." Julian put his pants on. He didn't want to leave Joanie's bed, but he had a hungry child waiting. Besides, it was time for him to think straight. He was here on a mission — to divorce Joanie, not to love...

He gripped his shirt tight and looked straight at the woman he'd tried to forget, the woman he hadn't wished to see again, the woman who was looking at him with a smile he would never forget. Could it be that in such a short period of time — a week in fact — he'd fallen in love with her? Impossible. It would take more than a week for a person to truly fall in love with someone. Not merely a day or two. Or three.

"Are you okay?"

"I'm not sure." He strode toward the door and scooped up his daughter who was coming out of her room.

Chapter Thirteen

Joanie stretched on the bed, which still held Julian's scent of sex. Losing her virginity to Julian four years ago had been her own doing. She'd wanted it to happen, and it had, with the help of alcohol. But last night... Julian had been sober. They'd had sex—lots and lots of it—because he'd wanted it to happen too.

Feeling smug, she hugged the pillow Julian used and inhaled his lingering scent.

Sam's and Julian's voices floated upstairs and into her room. She couldn't make out what Sam was saying but whatever it was must have been funny because Julian chuckled loudly. She wanted to join the two people she loved most, but decided to stay in bed and be lazy. Julian had asked for Sam's time. He could have it. Later, when the night was quiet and the moon was high in the sky, she would have her time with Julian. She hoped.

Joanie closed her eyes and listened to the murmurs from downstairs until she couldn't hear anything anymore.

It was past noon when she woke up. Lord, she hadn't stayed this late in bed since she'd had Sam. She felt rested, invigorated, charged and wonderful.

Joanie yawned. The house was quiet. Julian and Sam must still be gone. She decided she had lounged long enough in bed. It was time to clean up. Quickly, she took a shower and put on her old jeans and green tank top.

Downstairs, she found the kitchen tidy and on the table was her vase full of crudely cut flowers she recognized from her garden. The stems were broken and leaves were torn. There were petals on the table. It was the most beautiful, saddest looking bunch of flowers she had ever seen.

Tears rolled down her cheeks and she smiled. For the first time since her father had died, she felt happy.

The coffee pot was full and already cold, but she could always microwave some. She had just finished her second cup when the phone rang. It was Carmen, the Windermere agent, telling her the buyer had arrived in town yesterday and was really interested in buying her property. After a lengthy apology and explanation about why she had decided not to sell the property anymore, she ended the conversation on a positive note, saying that if ever she changed her mind, she'd contact Carmen right away.

She couldn't believe she'd actually held off a buyer when a few days ago she had been advertising the property online. The house, Sam's insurance, her lack of dependable job, all of these had been a thorn in her side. Then Julian had shown up. His presence had made the financial part of her life much better.

The clock struck two. Time to prepare dinner. This time, she'd try harder not to burn the food.

* * * *

Julian must have spent fifty bucks on the coin-operated rides in Bend River Mall. It was incredible how the rides could keep a child occupied for hours. Finally, when Sam had got tired of riding each one of them, she'd asked for an ice cream cone. Shopping with Sam was fun and easy. There was no perusing labels, trying on clothes, and preening in front of the mirror involved.

He kept her on his shoulders while they walked around different toy stores. By the time they left the mall, they had accumulated three bags full of everything pink and a bag from Victoria's Secret. He smiled at the image he conjured in his mind—Joanie in her new dark pink negligee. He could hardly wait for night-time to come, when he could be alone with her, while his little honey slept in her own new pink pajamas. He thought green would look good on Joanie, but Sam had insisted he buy the pink one.

By the time he had buckled Sam in his car, she was half asleep.

Through the rear-view mirror, Julian looked at his daughter hugging her doll, her pudgy cheek leaning against the cushion. Her puckered lips reminded him of Joanie's. He could buy Sam all the toys in the world, but none could ever replace Dolly.

Sam yawned, opened her eyes and met his gaze through the rear-view mirror.

"Hi, baby, are you tired?"

"I want Mama."

"Me too." It was the truth. He had wanted Joanie the first time he'd seen her in the woods. All morning, he'd wished Joanie had gone with them. He'd missed her smile, her laughter, her eyes, her scent. He'd missed her.

The mall wasn't too far from Joanie's house, only about fifteen minutes. He passed the Pink Mermaid and wondered if Bogart had found a replacement for Joanie. Taking the street to Joanie's, a surge of excitement at the prospect of seeing his wife overwhelmed him.

Julian shook his head in disbelief. He was acting like a teenager excited to see his girlfriend. He took the bend that led to Joanie's house. A few minutes later, the old house loomed up ahead. Something was wrong, though. Smoke was coming out of the kitchen windows. *Fuck.* Was the house on fire?

As if he was on fire himself, he floored the car and nearly parked it on the porch. "Sam, baby. Stay here. Daddy will be back."

"Okay."

Without wasting any time, he yanked the front door open and ran into the kitchen calling Joanie's name. The living room was engulfed in smoke and the burnt scent heavy in the air. "Joanie! Joanie! Where are you?"

"I'm here. Stop shouting."

"You okay? What the hell is going on? Is the house on fire?"

"Yes, I'm okay and no the house isn't on fire. Only my pork roast. Damn it."

Julian opened the windows and the back door wide. With the amount of smoke, a fire alarm should be blaring now. "You don't have a fire alarm?"

"Yeah, I do. It needs new batteries. Where is Sam?"

"In the car. I left her there because I thought the house is on fire. What happened?"

Joanie pointed to the baking pan. "That's what happened."

The meat was burned beyond recognition. It might have been pork when she put it in the pan, but it wasn't anymore. It resembled a black lava rock he'd once seen in Hawaii. The little round black things around it were probably potatoes. He wanted to laugh, but thought better of it. His wife couldn't cook shit. "We might be able to salvage it." And end up having broken teeth.

"I doubt it. I don't understand. It says on the directions to set the temperature to three hundred fifty degrees, which I did, so I don't know why it got too hot and burned my roast."

Joanie looked so crestfallen, he had to hug her. Her hair smelled of smoke and shampoo. He didn't care. And he didn't care about the roast, he was just glad Joanie wasn't the one that had ended up charred.

When he'd seen Bogart's fist hit her on the cheek, fear had gripped his heart.

Now, the thought that the house had been on fire while she'd been inside had made his heart stop beating. Well, at least it had felt that way. Sheez, if this continued, he'd have a heart attack before he reached the age of thirty-five. He gave Joanie a squeeze before he released her. "There must be something wrong with the elements. I'll take a look. Don't worry about the roast."

"Well, that's supposed to be dinner."

"We could always order pizza. Go get Sam." The oven must have been older than his grandma. It had seen better days and who knew how many Thanksgiving turkeys. Peering inside, he found a portable temperature-sensor timer. The kind that a cook would hang on the grill if the oven temperature gauge were broken. Joanie must have missed it since the color was the same as the oven's black walls. If Joanie had used this oven before, she would have known about the timer. Heck, he bet Joanie had never used this oven before. Her dad had done all the cooking for Joanie and Sam.

Mentally, he added an oven to his list of things to buy. Later, he'd take the oven to the junkyard if only to keep his wife from using it again.

* * * *

Dinner had been great. He'd ordered three different pizzas—cheese for Sam, pepperoni and pineapple for him and chicken with spinach for Joanie. Before he'd had his third slice, Sam had already zonked out on his lap.

Joanie didn't fight him when he said he'd take Sam up to her room. He could tell she was still feeling bad about the pot roast and taking her frustration out on her slice of pizza. Julian stared at Sam sleeping so innocently on her tiny pink bed. He hoped someday when she was grown she would find someone who would love and take good care of her. He adjusted Sam's blanket and kissed her again, then he reached under the bed to get the bag he'd stashed there. He walked over to Joanie's room and placed the bag in the middle of the bed before he went downstairs.

Joanie was still on the couch, nibbling her slice of pizza and muttering something about a stupid cooking instruction, her feet propped on the coffee table. "She must be really tired to fall asleep without asking for her papa."

"Yeah. The owner of the coin-operated rides at the mall is fifty dollars richer today because of her. And Sam is a very satisfied customer."

"Fifty bucks? Julian, I always ignore the rides. You shouldn't—"

"It was worth it, Joanie." He would tell her later about the gift he had ordered for Sam's birthday. "At least I got to sit down and watch her while she was yippee-ing."

"Thank you for taking her to the mall. You shouldn't have bought all those toys. Her room looks like a toy store now."

He sat beside Joanie on the couch and propped his feet on the table too. "She twisted my arm."

"Oh, I bet. She can be persuasive. Especially when her lips pout and the tears... Oh, God."

"So what do you do when Sam goes to bed early?" Julian asked.

"If I am too lazy to clean the house, sometimes I watch a movie I borrowed from the library or read my torrid novels. Sometimes, I simply lie in bed and wait until sleep visits me."

"Torrid novels? I didn't know Browning wrote those kinds of novels."

Joanie tittered. "I read her books so many times I know *How Do I Love Thee?* by heart. I'm older now. I thought it was time to move on to more mature reading materials."

"Thus, the torrid novels. Grandma didn't graduate from Browning's works. And she's like you. An avid fan of reading—when she could still see."

"Because she had found a reason to continue reading love poems. I believed in its power when I was young."

"Not anymore?"

"I can't say I do. But like Mister Darcy of *Pride and Prejudice* said, love sonnets are the food of love. If there isn't love to feed—it doesn't have any use. Your grandma experienced love. The poems have been keeping the feeling alive for her."

He covered her hand with his and rubbed her knuckles. She said her wedding ring was somewhere. In her dresser maybe? "You believed in Browning's poems. Loved reading each line, phrases, stanzas. You read the words as if they were coming from your heart."

"How did you know?"

"I listened to you read to Grandma. Joanie, you gave yourself to me that night because you believed in love."

"Yes, I gave myself to you without reservations."

"My grandmother suspected that you had feelings for me. But I didn't believe her."

"Now you heard the truth from me."

"You have no idea how happy I am to hear that. Now, about this blind guy you found but who has yet to find you."

"What about him?"

"He's a big jerk, is he?"

"Yeah. But he's been nice lately."

"Really?" He looked at Joanie. Her eyes were humorous and tender. Reality hit him. *He* was the blind guy. "Does he happen to live in Manhattan?"

"That's what he told me."

"Do you really love him?"

"With my heart and soul."

"And you will put your life before him."

"Without second thought," she answered.

"You still love me."

"I didn't say it was you."

"Joanie…"

The amused look suddenly left her eyes. "I thought I was done loving you. But I was wrong."

"I don't deserve your love."

"No, you don't."

"Still…"

"Still…" she repeated.

He cupped her face and took her mouth with his. Last night, he'd felt her love through her uninhibited acts in bed. She'd made love with him, not sex. She'd given him her body and soul. Good God. Joanie loved him.

"Joanie." He devoured her mouth. This time it was a hot tongue-twining kiss. Joanie loved him and God knew he was beginning to love her too. He removed her shirt and unhooked her bra.

Now standing in the middle of the room, he stared at her naked breasts before he slowly lowered his head and sucked a nipple. Joanie gripped his hair, pressing him closer against her. He thought about the negligee he'd bought for her. "Let's go upstairs," he said, between sucking her breasts and unbuttoning her pants.

As soon as her zipper had been lowered, he snaked his hand inside and cupped her warm pussy. She was already wet. Joanie slid her pants lower. She twisted and bent a little, then she was totally naked.

Her flushed skin glowed. "Julian, I love you."

He felt a tug. Joanie was unbuckling his belt. Not a moment too soon, he felt her fingers wrapped around his cock, her thumb rubbing his tip. His mouth left her breasts. "Joanie, Joanie, my wife… Oh, yeah… That's it." Watching her hand go up and down the length of his cock was so erotic. He moved his hips in a thrusting motion. His little wife was learning, exploring. He'd let her.

"You feel so velvety," she said.

Then to his delight Joanie kneeled.

"Joanie, hon. Ahhh…"

Joanie licked his cockhead repeatedly. The feeling of her tongue rasping on his sensitive slit was too good, but when she sucked him, he thought he'd come in her mouth. With all the strength that he could muster, he held his orgasm.

He moved his hips as he watched his cock go in and out of her mouth until he couldn't take it anymore. Grabbing her arms, he pulled her up. It was too late to go upstairs. "Place one foot on the table and the other on the couch." He held her ass as she did what he'd told her.

"Julian."

"From now on, you are mine." He guided his hard cock into her waiting pussy. Joanie was so wide open he could penetrate her deeply.

"Oh, my God, this is so wonderful."

"Yes, love. It is." Using his middle finger, he helped her reach her orgasm by rubbing her sensitive spot.

Joanie moaned and met his thrusts.

"You like that, love?"

"Yes. Oh, Julian, I can't wait. Please…"

"Just let it go, love. Let it go."

Joanie's inner walls gripped his dick then her ass contracted.

"Good. Now, hang onto me." He placed his hands just below her ass and thrust so hard Joanie screamed. "Almost there, yeah… Fudge." His orgasm was so explosive he bit her shoulder to stop himself from shouting. "Hmm…" His cock was already half aroused when he realized something—he hadn't pulled out. The thought that she might get pregnant actually made him smile.

He helped Joanie find her footing back on the floor before burying his nose in her neck. "Was it like your torrid novels?"

"Much better."

Chapter Fourteen

Joanie emptied the dishwasher, thinking about the pink negligee that she'd found spread on top of the pillow and the short note beside it. "Gone into the woods. See you later, Mama. Love J and S."

Pink negligee. Sam most likely had picked the color. She was never a fan of anything pink, but it would do. Tonight, she'd wear it.

She was making a list of things to do and buy for Sam's birthday when she heard a car. One thing she liked about a graveled driveway, the crunching sound always alerted her if a car was coming. Kind of like a barking dog.

Wondering who it was, she went outside. A black, dust-covered Mercedes was parked in front of her house. It could be another buyer. Dang, she should go to the library and remove her advertisement. Soon she'd have the money to fix her house. There was no need to keep the ads up.

A woman with straight blonde hair wearing a red mini skirt, white halter top, and huge dark glasses—

Joanie had seen Hollywood stars wear — got out of the car.

Joanie simply looked at her. She was a woman from the big city, no doubt. What was she doing here? From her porch, Joanie watched the woman plant her hands on her hips.

Her blonde hair shined in the afternoon sun like corn silk. Her high-heeled shoes were so pointy Joanie was sure they'd get stuck in the soft ground like nails in wood.

The woman waved and gave her a Colgate smile as if she was posing for a camera.

I doubt this is my classmate from Seattle. Joanie racked her brain, trying to remember if they'd met before while she waved back.

The woman quickly walked behind the car to open the trunk, and disappeared from view. When she emerged, she was carrying the biggest stuffed butterfly Joanie had ever seen in her life. How she had managed to stuff it in her trunk, she had no idea. The woman wasn't finished. She opened her passenger door and pulled out six big shopping bags.

Who in the world is this?

Joanie ran her clammy hands on the front of her jeans and met the woman halfway. "Hello," she greeted.

"Oh, hi there. Is this the Saint Claire residence?"

"Yes." Joanie watched the woman walk gingerly onto her front steps. She was so careful one would think Joanie's porch was covered with dog poo.

"Thank God. I'm Georgina Myers, Dr Julian Ravenwood's fiancée."

Stunned, Joanie just looked at the woman's unblemished face. Did she say fiancée? Julian had told her last night they were not together anymore. Had he lied to her? If he had, what was his fiancée doing here?

"Whew. I thought if I kept on driving, I'd end up in Japan or China. I'm not even sure if I'm still in the US of A," Georgina said lightly. It sounded rehearsed.

"Last time I checked, Bend, Oregon was still part of America." Joanie quickly imagined a world map. It had been years since she had last stepped inside a classroom, but she would bet Japan or China were still Asian countries. Asia was the biggest continent separated by large bodies of water from the other continents. Therefore, one couldn't just drive there.

"Well, you have a neat area here. Different from what Julian had told me over the phone. So, are you the hired help for the Saint Claires?"

"Hired help?"

"A maid or housekeeper." Georgina smiled.

Self-consciously, Joanie smoothed her hair. "No, I'm not the maid. I'm Joanie Saint Claire."

"Oh, Joanie. So wonderful to meet you." Joanie staggered backward when Georgina gave her a fierce hug.

"Julian isn't here right now."

"That's all right. It's you I want to talk to anyway." Georgina struggled with her load.

Did she say she wanted to talk to me? Whatever for?

"Can I help you?"

"With these? Yes. I didn't know toy stores were so massive."

Joanie grabbed the shopping bags overflowing with stuffed toys. Emblazoned on the bags were the big fancy letters, FAO Schwartz.

"Glad Julian mentioned his precious Sam likes butterflies, so I didn't have to walk around the mall looking for a perfect gift."

"Did you say this stuff is for Sam?"

"Yes. I have more in the trunk, but I'll ask Julian to get them for me. Is Sam home?"

"No. Julian took her into the woods for a walk. They'll be back soon."

"Pooh. I was hoping I'd meet Sam right away."

"Why?" The question came out so quickly.

"Well, since Julian and I are engaged—unofficial, of course, since you're still married to him—I thought I should get to know Sam so when she comes over to see Julian—"

"Sam is not going anywhere." The sound of her own teeth grinding were loud in Joanie's ears. What the hell was this woman talking about? Julian didn't say anything about taking Sam to Manhattan. Besides, that wasn't part of their agreement. Joanie felt her flesh start to quiver.

Georgina turned her diamond ring around and around so it caught the light. The stone sparkled. "Oh, I am sure Julian said he'd take Sam to our apartment to visit her great-grandma. May I come in?"

"Sure." Joanie walked ahead of Georgina and dumped the bags on the couch.

"Oh, wow. What a lovely home. Julian told me your house was a shack. I don't think so. I love it. Simple and homey."

A shack? Had Julian really called her house that? Yes, she'd made him sleep on the man-eating couch, and he'd seen the sorry state of her house, but she doubted he would call her home a shack. Whom should she believe, this woman or Julian? Her woman's intuition kicked in. Why was she really here?

"Can I offer you anything?"

"Orange juice or milk or whatever you have available."

"I'll be right back." Julian had told her Georgina was a model, but he had neglected to mention she was Venus walking on earth. So Julian had told her about Sam and her upcoming birthday. When did he tell Georgina all of this? When she was asleep?

She poured orange juice into her clearest, nicest drinking glass. After all, the woman had brought Sam presents and thought her house was lovely.

"It must have been hard on you to know your husband is planning on marrying another."

Joanie turned. She didn't expect Georgina to follow her into the kitchen. Hard was an understatement, but she didn't have to know that. "Not really. Julian and I are married only on paper. We hardly knew each other when we got married, and he left while I was still in my gown." Planning on marrying another? But Julian told me he and Georgina weren't an item anymore.

"That's horrible. So no honeymoon for you, eh?" Georgina lowered her painted lips the way one would when feeling disappointed. Joanie doubted she felt anything like that.

Joanie didn't answer the question. "Have a seat." She placed the glass on the table. "Here you go."

"Thank you. Hmm... Real good. Is that Sam in the picture on the refrigerator?"

"Yes. She was only a year old in that picture."

"Joanie, she is beautiful. I wanted to have my own pretty girl, but Julian didn't want a brat—yeah, he said a brat—running around his apartment. He hates kids."

"Excuse me?"

"Oh, I shouldn't have said that. I know brat is a bad word. And I'm assuming Sam isn't one."

"She's not. Sam and Julian are getting along fine. He loves our daughter and is really enjoying his time with her."

"Really. That is so good to know. You just gave me hope, Joanie. I should ask, no, beg him again to have a baby with me."

Why was she telling her all of this? Something wasn't right here. And this woman rubbed her like sandpaper on skin. Abrasive. "What exactly is your reason for being here? I doubt just to tell me how much you wanted a baby with Julian. That's personal. And we've just met."

Georgina's pale blue eyes betrayed her ardor. Her smile wavered. "You're right. I shouldn't have told you about my eagerness to have a baby. I'm sorry. I got carried away. Well, I'm here to talk about us and Sam."

Joanie's hackles rose. Why would this stranger talk to her about her daughter? No, she hadn't travelled from New York to Oregon to talk. *That's bullshit. What is your game, bitch?*

"You came here to talk about my daughter?"

"Yes. You probably didn't know this since you didn't actually live with Julian. He's a meticulous one, you know. Always washing and cleaning, and babies are messy, he said. I suppose that's understandable. All doctors are clean. Julian hates dirt, snot, and dirty feet. Kids are always dirty. He said dealing with animals in his clinic is bad enough. Coming home with a brat in the house is the last thing that he wanted in his well-organized life. If Sam is a messy eater or a puddle-stomping kind of kid, then Julian won't like that. Maybe our Sam is different. Maybe Julian wouldn't get mad if she gets dirty."

Our Sam? "Sam could swim in mud and Julian would just laugh about it. I don't know where you got the idea that he hates kids. And I highly doubt that Julian would compare the pets he treated to kids. I may not know him that well, but I know enough that he's not that mean."

Joanie remembered the first day she'd left Julian in her house. He'd cleaned and washed everything. She thought he liked to wash Sam's feet because he enjoyed doing it. Were his niceties all for show? If yes, for what? So she would change her mind and sign the papers without asking for the money and he would still get his wish about spending time with Sam?

Georgina waved her hand as if dismissing her comment. "Oh, I knew you'd say that. See, that's what Julian wanted you to think. He planned this act." She sat on the chair with her back straight.

Or you're the one acting. "I'm sorry, but did you come here to talk bad about Julian?"

"Oh no. Goodness, of course not. I'm just letting you in on Julian's plan. Kind of warning you. Like I said, I wanted to talk about Sam. Julian said Sam's turning four and she's having a birthday party. So I came right away to meet my future stepdaughter. I have all kinds of toys for her, mostly things with butterflies. You don't mind, do you?"

Stepdaughter? Joanie's head began to throb. "Thank you for all the trouble. But Sam doesn't need the toys."

"Joanie, I knew you'd say that. It's just… I thought if I joined the birthday celebration, she might like me. Believe it or not, I want us to be friends, too, for Sam, but only if it's okay."

Julian had said the same thing. He'd wanted us to become friends.

Engaged. His fiancée wanted to be her friend. Sam, a stepdaughter. Joanie shook her head no. This woman was lying. Julian didn't plan to stay here. He didn't know anything about Sam before he came. His idea of staying only came up because she made a demand and he countermanded. "You said Julian planned his act. What about you? What is your plan?"

"Plan? No, Joanie. I came here as a friend. You see, Julian was open about his past. He told me he was forced to marry you and that your father pointed a gun at him. I told him he deserved it and I laughed. He didn't think it was funny. What happened the night that cost him his bachelorship was unthinkable, he said. He said he'd rather die a bachelor than marry someone like you. I think he just said that because he had a girlfriend at the time." Georgina tapped her painted finger on the rim of the glass. "Joanie, Julian was just mad at what happened. When he said he was married to his unwanted, untidy wife — which, by the way, I don't believe because you look great in your green top — I stayed away from him. You know, married men are trouble. With my line of work, I know. I even explained to Julian that I didn't want another scorned wife chasing me with her sharp scissors."

"Not all wives are the same."

Georgina waved her hand in the air dismissing what Joanie had just said. "But Julian pursued me. When he wants something, Julian gets it. Even if he has to use seduction, which, by the way, he's really good at. The rest is history. So, I came to ask for your friendship. Do you think we could be friends?"

Not in a million years. Joanie thought about the first night Julian had wrapped his arm around her. Seduction. That was what it was, to get to Sam. "I regard my friends with affection and trust. The friends I have, I can rely on. I'm sorry, but you don't fall into that category." Snakes belonged in a cold pit, not in the warm embrace of friends.

"I understand. But in time, I'll gain your trust. My being here is the first step. I wanted to explain, to let you know I didn't steal Julian from you. We just fell in love. Julian is here to make you sign the divorce papers. I should be happy. Well yes, I am happy. But knowing another woman's heart is breaking because of me kept me awake all night. Please don't hate me."

Awake all night fucking Julian. Julian had told her everything but missed the part about his unofficial engagement. He had made it clear he would go back to New York, maybe to go back to this woman throwing bile at her with her words. "The only hold I have on Julian is the wedding certificate. He can marry anyone he wishes when our divorce is final. Let me tell you this — insist on seeing my Sam, and I won't just hate you. I'll cut your hair and choke you with it. We have nothing in common. Friends are bound by things they both love. We don't have that."

Georgina's eyes turned icy, but only for a brief second. Her smile, however, remained pasted on her face. "Oh, Joanie. Soon I will be Julian's wife. Sam will be our connection. Julian would want to see Sam again. Maybe buy her stuff or ask her for a visit. Wait, he did mention over the phone that he'd bring Sam to New York to see her great-grandma. Grandma's staying with us, you see. So, when that happens I hope we can meet without hostility."

What visit? Joanie seethed with anger. She wanted to scream, send the woman out of her house, but she would not lose her composure, not in front of this woman trying to kill her with her offer of false friendship and sincerity.

Julian, that rat. She'd eat dirt before she'd let him take Sam away so he and this viper could be with her. She rubbed her temples. She could feel a migraine starting.

"No. Julian and I agree that after his time with Sam is over, he won't be back here again."

"Oh, I see. Well, I guess that is for the best."

"I beg your pardon, but I'm going to ask you to leave. Please take all the things you brought for Sam. Don't worry, if you and Julian marry, I won't chase you with my scissors. Just don't pretend that you like my daughter. I can see that you don't."

"Oh, if that's what you want, and if no contact would make our lives wonderful, consider it done." Georgina opened her purse and took out a purple lace handkerchief. "By the way, when I was getting ready to leave, I found this on his desk. I think it belonged to your mother."

Joanie couldn't imagine what it was. She took the bundle from Georgina's hand and opened it. "Oh, my God. Oh, my God." A lump formed in her throat. She swallowed, but it was hard. Her head began to buzz. She'd been looking for this clip. She remembered wearing it on her wedding day, but it had kept slipping off her hair. She stared at her mother's heirloom. The precious clip her dad had given her on their wedding day was broken in half. Tears blurred her vision until she couldn't see the clip anymore. "How did this happen?"

"I don't know. I am guessing Julian broke it, because when I found that in his drawer, there were angry notes about you. I could be wrong. Joanie, I am so sorry. If I knew this would bring you grief, I would have kept this in my safe or had it fixed before giving it back to you, but you see, this is not mine to keep. It's yours, although I am not sure how it ended up in Julian's desk."

"I wore this to our wedding. It was falling off my hair so I asked Julian to hold it for me. God, why didn't he just give this to me? Why break it?"

"Because he hates you. For what you've done. But he's willing to forgive you, for Sam's sake."

Joanie looked at the woman Julian had most likely bedded countless times. The insincerity in her voice and triumph in her eyes were obvious. No, she wasn't sorry at all. She had only brought the clip back to hurt Joanie further. "Thank you for bringing this to me."

"You're welcome. I am staying at the Riverhouse Premier Hotel tonight. Please tell Julian where to find me. If you need anything, just call me."

I'll call you from my grave. "As soon as Julian and Sam come back, I will tell him where you're staying. I'm sorry, but I'm going to ask you to leave. My head hurts."

"I don't mind at all. Should I help you with anything? Put the toys away? There are goodies in the bag too."

"I don't need help. Please take your toys back."

"Here is my card. Call me if you need anything or if you just want to talk."

Joanie didn't see Georgina leave. She stayed sitting on her father's chair, mourning the loss of a special memento.

* * * *

Now that she'd planted the bad seed, all Georgina had to do was wait for the roots to grow. Before the brat's birthday, Joanie would sign Julian's divorce papers. Yeah, then *she* would be Julian's wife.

Georgina drove on the rough road, cursing every time she hit a rut. She couldn't imagine why people would live in a miserable place like this. There was nothing here but gnarly trees, old houses and restaurants she wouldn't dare step foot inside.

She thought about Joanie Saint Claire. The moment she'd spotted her on the porch, she'd known who she was, and she'd hated her. She was the opposite of the woman Julian had described to her. Joanie's face and body — even she could admit — were more than beautiful. Not as tall as she, but what was height when you had a package any man fantasized having. Freaking Joanie was a doll, the kind of woman the modeling business hated — young and beautiful and with an innocent look on her face. God, she wanted to claw her eyes out.

Well, she might do just that if her first plan failed.

Chapter Fifteen

Sam wrapped her arms around Julian's neck as he carried her home. Joanie's house loomed in the distance. It looked like a house taken from nature itself. The neutral color of the sidings, moss on the roof, even the weathered porch added character to the home. Rustic. How come he'd never noticed how beautiful it was?

He looked for any sign that Joanie was burning something in the kitchen again. No smoke coming out of the house this time. Good. His wife hadn't burned the house or herself yet, but what if she'd used the knife and cut her wrist and now lay bleeding on the floor? The other night, he'd watched her cut Sam's pizza and he thought she'd take out her thumb before she could remove the crust. Damn. He hurried his steps, eager to see his wife's smile.

The front door opened and Joanie came out. It was only then that he was able to breathe. He smiled, but Joanie didn't. The moment he met her eyes, he knew something wasn't right. Her eyes were red-rimmed and it looked like she had been crying. He didn't like what he was seeing. She was looking at him the same way she had when they'd met in the woods. Not good. Still, he kept his smile. When he reached her, he leaned in for a kiss, but Joanie turned her face. He kissed her temple instead.

"We had a great time."

"Hey, bug. I missed you."

"Mama, I caught a frog and a butterfly and a ladybug. But we let them go. They need to go home to their mama."

"Good girl."

"Something wrong, Joanie?"

She took Sam from him. "Sam, go in the kitchen. Your lemonade is on the table."

"Yum, lemonade."

Something was definitely not right here. When he'd left her this morning, everything had been fine. Damn it, what had happened?

The whole time they were gone, his mind had been focused on Joanie. How he'd wished they were watching Sam together. And by the time Sam released the frog she'd named Art, he had arrived at a conclusion—he wouldn't go back to Manhattan a single man. He would give their marriage a chance to bloom, to flourish.

For years he had tried erasing Joanie's face from his mind. He'd dated blondes or brunettes and tall women left and right. But for some odd reason, he'd always spotted women with hair just like Joanie's. Each time he would look, to find out if it was Joanie. He tucked his hand in his pocket and followed Joanie inside.

She stopped in the middle of the room. When she faced him, her features were as hard as granite. "Thanks for spending time with Sam."

"We had fun. We wished you were with us."

"I bet." Her words were heavy with sarcasm.

"What's going on? Got a bee in your brain?"

"Brain? What brain? Because the way I've been acting for the past few days one would think I didn't have a brain at all."

Okay, PMSing. She's just suffering from cramps. That's all. "Acting like what? Trying to become a great cook? Is it the oven? Don't worry about it."

"You know what I'm talking about. Don't try to be funny, Julian. You're a vet, not a comedian."

"Okay. I give up. What's wrong? And what's up with the brown bags? Recycling?"

"No. You're taking them with you when you leave today."

What the fuck? "Joanie…"

"I bet Sam had a great time. We appreciate everything. But it's time for you to leave."

"What's wrong, love?"

Joanie shook her head. Tears welled in her eyes. "Here, take it." He recognized the envelope right away.

"What's this, Joanie?"

"This is the reason why you came here. I am giving it to you now—signed. You don't have to give me the money. I don't need it anymore. Your condition still stands. You can spend time with Sam until her birthday, but you are not staying with us anymore."

Count to three… Count to three… "Joanie, I need an explanation. I thought we had an understanding. Last night—"

"Was just that—last night. Already in the past and will never happen again."

Sam came back, licking her hands, which were covered with butter. "Sam, honey, come say goodbye to Dr Ravenwood. He's leaving now."

"The hell I am." So she's back to formality again. Joanie was seriously pissing him off.

"Daddy said hell."

"Sam, say your goodbyes."

"I don't want to say goodbye."

"Then come in the kitchen with me."

"I'm not leaving, Joanie," he yelled, but Joanie was already gone.

"Are you going to wash my feet?"

"Of course, Sam, baby. I'm not going anywhere." He picked up Sam then sat her on Saint Claire's chair. "Stay here. I need to talk to Mama, okay?"

"Okay."

He went to the kitchen and found Joanie pacing back and forth. He grabbed her hand. "Sit down. You need a drink? We have a bottle of white wine."

"No. What I need is for you to leave us now. Come back tomorrow if you still want to see Sam."

"Of course I want to see Sam. We thought we could all go to the fair together. What's going on, Joanie? What did I do?"

"Stop pretending. You know what you did."

"Please spare me from racking my brain. Just tell me."

"You lied, that's what you did."

"Joanie, I know this may sound crazy but — "

"She's staying at the Riverhouse Premier Hotel. And that's where you should be also."

"Who?"

"Your unofficial fiancée, Georgina Myers."

"Oh, fuck."

"When you leave, take the bags with you. They're full of toys from Georgina. Sam doesn't need them. I told her to take them back, but she didn't. We live in a shack, but I can still put food on the table and send her to preschool. We don't need charity from either of you."

"Joanie, I don't know why she's here and what she told you. But—"

"Please leave. Go see your fiancée. The forms are signed. You two can get married now."

Julian stared at Joanie. She'd signed the forms. He was free of her, free of his unwanted, innocent wife. Georgina was here waiting for him. He didn't have to beg her to come back to him. He could go see her now and spend hours in bed with her. Hadn't he thought Georgina's was the hottest ass he'd ever seen? He tried to imagine himself in bed with her, but couldn't. All he could see was his wife and her unrestrained passion.

"But I don't want to marry her. And that's the truth. Do you want to know what else?"

"More lies?"

"Goddamn it, listen to me."

"Why? What for? I don't want you here anymore. Leave, Julian. She's waiting."

"Don't push me away. I am not leaving you or Sam. Never again, Joanie. Within the span of…of what? Seven days, you—maybe unknowingly—cast a spell on me. You bewitched me. It's hard to believe. Even I'm having a hard time believing how fast you made me change. But it's true."

"Guilt, Julian. That's what's talking here. You feel guilty. That's why you want to stay. And lust, lust could easily be mistaken for something else."

"I am not stupid. I can distinguish the difference between the two. I want to stay here and be with you and Sam."

"Is that why you broke this?" Joanie put the two pieces of the hairclip on the table.

"What the hell? Joanie — "

Cough! Cough!

"Sam, are you okay?"

More coughing came from the other room. Julian followed as Joanie ran into the living room. "Sam, baby."

Sam was on the floor holding her throat, her little legs kicking hard. Joanie pushed him out of the way and kneeled beside their daughter. "Samantha. Oh my God! What's wrong, bug? Look at me, Samantha Rose. Bug, what did you eat? Julian, she can't breathe. EpiPen, she needs the EpiPen."

"Give her to me. Call 911, Joanie. Open your mouth, Sam." He forced her mouth open to look for anything lodged inside. He didn't see anything, but her breath smelled like nuts. "Joanie, where's the EpiPen? Bring it here. Now!"

Joanie disappeared and came back with the pink bag she carried all the time. "EpiPen, EpiPen," she chanted shakily. "Here." She practically threw the clear, yellow-tipped tube at him. She dialed the numbers all the while screaming Sam's name.

He'd used an EpiPen on a dummy, but never on human flesh, and especially not a child. He looked at his daughter. Sam's eyes were rolling back and her face was beet red. Good God, he was losing her. "Sam, baby, this is going to hurt." He removed the yellow tip of the EpiPen. "Joanie, hold her leg. Keep it steady."

"Use it now, Julian. Now!"

With one more look at Sam's face, he stabbed her leg with the EpiPen. Sam jerked and made a gurgling sound. He held the pen for a few seconds before pulling it out. He hadn't seen the needle, but it had gone into Sam's thigh. He'd known when it had struck Sam. He'd felt the needle penetrate her soft flesh. Still, he checked the needle. If it was out, Sam had received the dose. It was.

Joanie was screaming Sam's name. The agony in her voice was that of a child, piercing his heart. "Sam, baby. Open your eyes... Samantha. Sam!"

Sam stopped kicking. Her arms went limp at her sides then her lips turned blue.

"Sam, honey? Samantha!" Julian screamed her name over and over. He placed the side of his face directly over her mouth to see if she was breathing. She wasn't. Heart hammering against his chest, he felt for Sam's pulse. It was there but faint.

Julian began the rescue breathing. He blew steadily into her mouth, watching her chest rise. Removing his mouth from Sam's, he watched her chest fall. Again, he felt for Sam's breath on his cheek. Nothing. He blew air into her mouth again, counting three seconds for each breath. Shaking, he remained focused on what he was doing.

"Oh, God. Samantha, honey, be strong. Mama needs you. Mama needs you."

Julian's vision blurred as he breathed air through Sam's tiny mouth. The little bug, the sweet pancake who loved animals and anything pink now lay unmoving on the floor.

The sound of a siren came closer and closer. Help was coming. His throat constricted at the sight of his daughter's face.

Only minutes ago, she had been laughing, happy. Now, she was inches from death. He opened Sam's mouth to feel her breath. A cry of relief broke from his lips when he felt Sam breathing again.

"Julian, is she okay? Is my baby okay?"

"She's breathing now. But she still needs to go to the hospital. The ambulance is here."

"Thank you, thank you. Oh, God, I've already lost Dad. I can't lose Sam."

Julian picked up Sam, hating the fact that her chubby, soft arms didn't wind around his neck. "Daddy loves you, Sam."

The drive to the hospital seemed like an eternity. Sam was given another dose of epinephrine because she hadn't got enough from the EpiPen. She was breathing but still unconscious. Her heartbeat was faster than normal, but the medic assured them that it was the effect of the medicine.

Julian was beside her, holding Sam's tiny hand, kissing her little fingers over and over again, whispering "I'm sorry" as if what had happened had been his fault. "Sam, honey. It's going to be your birthday soon. You need to wake up so you could see what Daddy got you, okay? I love you, little pancake," Julian sobbed.

Joanie didn't say a thing. She just watched, feeling the love, grief, remorse mixed with anger pour out of Julian for his little Sam.

Two hospital staff shoved Julian away from the gurney because he wouldn't let go of Sam's hand. The doctor snarled at him, telling him that he was only delaying his daughter's treatment. Julian, who seemed to realize what he was doing, raised his arms up then nodded his head and stepped back.

The doctors whisked Sam away, leaving Joanie and Julian standing together, watching the silver double doors leading to the emergency room close.

Then Joanie let it out. She wailed and screamed like she had wanted to do when she'd seen Sam on the floor. Julian pulled her roughly against him and whispered, "She'll be okay. She's tough like you. She's tough."

* * * *

It was incredible how even a nonbeliever, secular, or whatever he was could remember God in times like this. When was the last time he'd been to church to pray? Shit, if this was His way of nudging him, to let him know that He existed, well, this was one fucking harsh way to do it. Who in the world with a right mind would use a child to teach an adult a lesson? No, God had nothing to do with this, but he had a pretty good idea who had put his daughter's life in danger.

After what had seemed to be an eternity of waiting, the doctor had come out and called him and Joanie. Sam was out of danger and sleeping.

In the small room where Sam had been transferred, Julian had kept his eyes on his daughter and wife. Sam had woken up only to fall asleep again, this time because of the Children's Tylenol the nurse had given her to ease Sam's discomfort. Sam would sleep even better if her Dolly were beside her. She'd be staying here overnight for observation. Sam would want Dolly.

"Joanie."

Joanie looked up. She had already stopped crying but her eyes looked utterly sad and tired. "Yes?"

"I'll go back to the house to get Sam's doll. You have my cell. Call me if she wakes up or anything."

"Okay. But you don't have to do that. Sam will ask for you when she wakes up."

"Tell her I'll be back. I have to check on something."

"We'll be here."

Julian nodded then turned to walk away. He was almost at the door when Joanie called him. "Yeah?"

"Thank you."

"No need to thank me, Joanie. I will give my life for Sam, for you." He walked away in a state of emotional upheaval. One thing was clear—he loved his family, and those who dared hurt them would fucking pay.

Chapter Sixteen

"What the hell did you say?"

Georgina winced. Rick screaming on the phone didn't help her frayed nerves. She marched back to the bed where she had dumped the contents of her purse. Damn it. Where had she put her pill bottle?

When she'd realized putting a can of cashew nuts in one of the gifts bags had been a bad idea, it had been too late. She had already left Joanie's house. Well, maybe the brat wouldn't find it. After all, she had brought her nice toys. Unless of course she was a pig and would rather eat nuts than play with stuffed animals. *But what if...? Fuck.*

Calm down.

She took a deep breath and tried to slow down her breathing the way her doctor had told her to do when having an anxiety attack.

Where the hell are my pills?

"Georgina!" Rick's angry tone jarred her thoughts back to him.

"Stop screaming at me, Rick. You're not helping."

"What the fuck did you do? Try to kill Julian's daughter?"

"I thought of it, but I changed my mind. But it's too late because I already left the stupid can of cashew nuts in—"

"Oh, my God. Do you have any idea what could happen if the little girl finds the nuts?"

"I do! That's why I left it for her to find. But like I said I changed my mind. Joanie probably found it by now anyway. Besides, why would they think that it was me who left the can?" She rolled her eyes when Rick sighed heavily over the phone. She hated it when he did that. It was as though she had just said something stupid.

"Georgina, I told you to play your cards well. Not like this."

She sat on the bed then kicked off her shoes. "Well, your plan didn't work, so I had to do something."

"Like premeditated murder?"

"I changed my mind."

"In the court of law, that doesn't change the fact, Georgina, that you planned to kill Sam Ravenwood."

"This is your fault, you know. If only you had answered your phone then you would have told me what to do."

"Shit."

She heard multiple beeps. "What was that? You're recording our conversation? You're an asshole."

"Me? Who tried to kill an innocent child? "

Why had she even called Rick? Oh, yeah. He'd been Julian's lawyer for years. Fucking ass. "No one would know unless you tell, Rick. And if you do, I'll tell whoever is willing to listen that you're involved." With that, she hung up the phone.

Looking around the room, she decided it was time to pack up. If Julian asked for an explanation, she'd do it in their apartment, in his bedroom. Naked.

Laughing, she began picking up her scattered clothes.

* * * *

Joanie's house was awfully quiet. No singing, giggling, pitter-pattering of little feet. No Joanie in the kitchen burning food. Julian stood in the middle of the room. Sam's sandal was on the floor. She must have lost it when she was kicking hard, trying to breathe. His vision blurred at the memory of little Sam fighting for precious air, clawing her neck. Julian picked up the sandal and stared at it. Imprints of Sam's little toes were there. He tucked the sandal in his back pocket and looked around the floor. It was a mess, but he spotted Sam's necklace. The chain was broken but the ring was still there.

Because of the stupid necklace, he'd learned about Sam. The necklace was the reason he had insisted he'd stay and get to know her. What had Joanie said about his decision? Ah, playing with people's lives. His selfishness had brought all of this to Sam and Joanie. If he had just taken her offer, given her the money, he would have been back in Manhattan looking after his animal patients and Georgina wouldn't have come here.

Georgina. The woman he had thought was perfect for him had hurt his family. Without a doubt in his mind, she'd brought nuts into the house. What a dumb fuck. He'd smelled nuts on Sam's breath. He kept scanning the room. Sam had eaten nuts that had made her sick. Wherever it was, he'd find it. Joanie would never buy anything with a hint of nuts in it, and he would never do that, either. So where had Sam got the freaking nuts? Georgina. He kicked the brand new toys that were on the floor until he spotted a ratty looking ragdoll peeking out from under the couch. Dolly. Beside it was a can of cashew nuts.

"Fuck." He picked up the can and thought about throwing it against the wall, but changed his mind. He'd go after who'd brought it. "Georgina, I'm going to kill you for this." He put the can and all the toys back in the brown bags including the shopping bags. When he was sure he had got them all, he strode toward the back of the house where he dumped the bags in the garbage bin.

He was leaving the kitchen when he spotted Joanie's broken hairclip on the table. He pocketed the two pieces. With certainty that Joanie would never want him in their lives, especially after what had happened, he moved around the house, cleaning. At least Joanie wouldn't have to worry about cleaning when they got home. When he'd finished, he started packing his things, including the small Dora toothbrush Joanie had given him the first night he'd insisted that he stay there. With a big lump forming in his throat, he straightened up the living room, making sure no more nuts or candies were lying around the house. He was making one more sweep when a scrapbook caught his eyes. It was Sam's baby scrapbook. Joanie had recorded and collected everything, including Sam's dried umbilical cord.

Sam was a big baby and according to Joanie's records, was colicky. She'd started walking at the age of one and was potty trained when she was eighteen months. The first time Sam had been diagnosed with severe allergies had been during her first birthday. Someone had given her a peanut butter cracker.

Julian continued to look through the book until he reached the page about Sam's parents. Joanie's picture holding Sam was glued on the corner and beside it was a short note. *Daddy's in your heart, bug.* Shaking his head, he closed the scrapbook and put it back where he'd found it. He hitched his overnight bag over his shoulder and walked toward the door. But the sound of the phone ringing made him stop. His heart leaped. Had something happened in the hospital while he'd been gone? If it was Joanie, why hadn't she called his cell? Without waiting for the second ring, he picked up the receiver.

"Saint Claire's residence."

"Oh, hi. Is Joanie available? This is Carmen, Windermere real estate agent."

"Hi, this is Julian. I'm sorry, but Joanie is not available right now. Can I take a message?"

"Joanie called me again earlier today and said the property is up for sale again. Oh, I'm so happy. Please tell her that my client is happy that Joanie finally changed her mind—again—about her property. I will be there early tomorrow to close the deal."

"Sure. Joanie talked to me about the property but she didn't mention that the deal is already made. When did she put it on the market?"

"Oh, she put Sam's Woods on the market a few weeks ago. The name caught my attention and I contacted her right away. She said her house needs immediate repairs because of her child. She's super nice. I'm glad I called her. That property is a prime lot. Anyway, my client is eager to put up the fence so he could bring in his horses. So, please tell Joanie that the papers are ready. She has my number. Tell her to call me right away, please. It's Julian, right?"

Julian gripped the phone hard until his fingers ached from the pressure. "Right."

"Well, thank you. And please pass the message to Joanie." Carmen repeated, obviously eager to close out a deal.

"I will, Carmen, but listen..."

"Yes?"

Julian knew what he was about to tell Carmen would really upset Joanie, but he had to do this. It didn't take him long to say what he wanted to say. He pulled out a horrendous idea that made Carmen scream, "What?"

Poor Carmen. She sputtered and sighed, but she acquiesced and promised to come meet him pronto.

Joanie needed the money—desperately. He should have figured it out. Why else would she dance at the Mermaid if she hadn't needed money? His little wife had offered him a deal so she wouldn't have to sell Sam's Woods. But why sell the property? Didn't Saint Claire leave her anything? Well, he'd find out soon. Julian closed the door and left the home he'd learned to love.

* * * *

There was only one Mercedes parked outside the hotel. If he was right, Georgina was still in her room. Julian approached the desk.

The tired-looking receptionist was on the phone. She asked Julian to hold on and covered the receiver. "Can I help you?"

"I lost my key and forgot my room number. The room is under my girlfriend's name—Georgina Myers."

"Is Miss Myers in the room?"

"Yes."

"I'll have to call—" The other phone line started ringing.

"You can call Georgina. She's in our room."

"It's okay." She quickly checked her computer then opened a drawer in front of her. She took a key card, swiped it on a machine then tucked it into a small envelope. She wrote the room number on the outside. "Here you go," she said then resumed talking on the phone.

That was easy. Jesus, the hotel was practically empty. Everyone was hurting because of the collapse of the economy. Even he and his partner had felt it.

It didn't take long before he reached Georgina's suite. He rapped on the door.

"Who is it?"

"Open the door, Georgina."

The door opened. Georgina practically flew out and landed on his chest. She started crying, mumbling something about shock and a horrible mother. It took extra effort to extract Georgina from her hold on his neck. As soon as she'd let go of him, he walked into the room. It looked like she was in the process of packing when he'd knocked on the door. It seemed she was in a hurry too.

"Going somewhere?"

Georgina looked around the room. More toys, all pink, were scattered everywhere. "Well, I thought I should go to the hospital and check on your baby. I heard she was taken there."

"How?"

"Joanie's neighbor works here as a housekeeper. I was organizing my things when she knocked to clean. I let her in, then she started talking about the Saint Claires. Someone from a local bar called her and you know how gossip travels. I guess everyone knows everybody's business in this town."

"So you heard that Sam almost died."

Georgina visibly paled. It took great effort not to raise his hand to her.

"No. I didn't hear that part. That's, that's awful. Well, I'll go back to our apartment since you're busy —"

"Busy saving my daughter's life."

"Oh, Julian. It must have been horrible. I'm so sorry. How is she? You said she almost died. So she's okay, right? She lived? Is Joanie with her right now?"

"Would you leave your daughter in the hospital after nearly losing her because someone mixed a can of cashew nuts and stuffed toys in the same bag?"

"No, of course not. Uhm, you...found the can?"

"Yes. With your name written all over it."

"Julian, what are you accusing me of? Hurting a child is, is..."

"A crime. An attempted murder. I almost lost my daughter because of you. You went to see Joanie not only to give back her mother's precious heirloom, which you broke in half, but also to get rid of Sam. You have no idea what you've done to her. She couldn't breathe, Georgina."

"Julian, listen. I —"

"I suggest you leave town now and don't you dare show up at my apartment. Call your lawyer. I swear next time you do your nails, it'll be in jail."

Before his eyes, Georgina's sweet face contorted in anger. He couldn't believe he'd lain with this woman.

She was nothing but a vile, evil thing. "You want that brat and her mother, huh? Asshole. You made me believe that you love me, that you would marry me. You are not fucking fair. What happened to your fucking promises? Huh? Does Joanie know your sweet words?"

"You forgot, it's been a month since you left. Whatever promises I gave you, you flushed them in the toilet when you walked away because you couldn't accept me for who I am."

"No. It was Rick's idea for me to move out. He said to play hard to get and you would come after me. It's his fault."

"No. He actually did me a big favor."

"Julian, please..."

"It's over, Georgina."

"Whatever. Fine, go to your wife and daughter. Don't come back to me when you find out your wife is nothing but a cold fish in bed."

"Is that why you think I'm staying here?" Julian questioned with amusement. "To find out if my wife is good in bed? Georgina, I've never met a more remarkable woman in my life than Joanie. She gave me her body because she loves me and expects nothing in return. Even after what I did to her, she took me into her house, fed me, and didn't deny me my right to know our child. Contrary to what you believe about her, she didn't sign the papers because of my money. In and out of bed, Georgina, Joanie is a simple woman with simple needs and a big heart. And she loves reading to my grandma."

"Julian, sweetheart —"

"Stop it. If it were up to me, I'd file murder charges against you. But I'll leave it up to Joanie to decide what to do with you. She has a heart of gold, but I tell you—if she saw you right now, she'd do more than cut your hair. You know how these wives are. And Joanie's no different. She would bite your head off."

Chapter Seventeen

Julian didn't mention the phone call from the real estate agent to Joanie. He'd wait until Sam was in bed for a nap, then they would talk. Oh, yeah. They would talk.

No one who saw Sam right now would believe that yesterday she'd been an inch away from death. His little girl was bending over peering down at a small puddle, hoping to see a tadpole or a crab. She was talking to Dolly, asking the doll if she had seen anything with scales. He laughed at that. Julian didn't think Sam would see one, but he told her that she might spot one later after she'd had her lunch. He looked at Joanie. His wife looked so tired he'd bet she'd fall over if she weren't leaning against the porch's post.

"Sam, hon, we need to go inside. We have to feed your little tummy. And Mama looks like she needs something to eat too."

"I don't want the one that made me sick. Ick."

"No, hon. Only good food this time. Let's go."

"Okay. I want cornflakes with milk and butter and sugar and a spoon."

"I think we have those." Julian picked up Sam and carried her on his shoulders. Joanie opened the front door for them, still not saying anything. He hated it.

He wished she would lash out at him, hit him, whatever. Not like this. Her silence was deafening. She probably wished he wasn't here with them, sharing lunch and talking to Sam. She had told him to leave, but because of what had happened he couldn't bring himself to get in his car and do just that.

He would talk to Joanie, and if she still wanted him out, then he'd leave.

Sam ate her sandwich and finished half a glass of orange juice before begging to leave the table to draw more butterflies.

"Sketchpad is on the table in the living room. Stay in there, okay, hon?"

"Okay, Daddy." With Dolly tucked beneath her armpit, Sam took off in a hurry.

He remained in his chair and watched Joanie clean the table.

"Are you tired of watching me yet? You've been doing that all night. When I opened my eyes this morning, you were staring at me. What, did I grow an extra head overnight?"

"You're finally talking to me?"

"Would you rather that I don't?"

"No, love. I don't mind hearing your voice morning, noon, and night. If I'd been offered the job of watching you all day and night, I'd gladly take it. I like looking at you. Watching you, Joanie, is like standing on the edge of a meadow filled with blooming flowers. So beautiful. So wonderful. So enchanting."

"Oh, dear. I am not a painting, Julian."

"You're better than a painting. You're warm, alive, and... I love you."

Joanie almost dropped the plate she was drying. Since yesterday, her nerves had been worse than when she'd started having labor pains. She had been able to hear her heart beat loud in her ears when Julian had left the hospital to get Sam's doll. It had taken him a long time and he hadn't returned until late. The whole time he'd been gone, she'd kept thinking what he was doing and where he was, if he was okay. She'd seen how distraught with grief he'd been from the moment they'd seen Sam lying on the floor. She hadn't been able to help but think that perhaps he was blaming himself for what had happened and had decided to stay away from them, to be alone, to think.

It had crossed her mind, too, that maybe he had left without saying goodbye. But when he'd shown up looking like he'd had a fight with himself, eyes red, holding a bouquet of flowers for Sam and her, balloons that the nurse had taken away because there were so many, and the biggest blowup butterfly she'd ever seen, she'd cried. Yes, his gesture was touching, but seeing him again was what had made her emotions open like the floodgates. She didn't want him to leave, but she was afraid to show what she truly felt.

Julian obviously loved his daughter and it was her fault that Sam had nearly died. If she hadn't been so hung up on her own hurt feelings, she would have watched Sam. All night, she'd believed that Julian saw her as an unfit mother. She couldn't cook, or clean, she danced erotically at the bar, and it looked like she'd failed as a mother as well. So why had he said what he'd just said?

"What did you say?" she asked.

"You heard me."

Joanie looked at the man she had never stopped loving sitting on the chair with his legs stretched in front of him, one ankle on top of another. His arms were crossed on his chest. He wasn't smiling.

"I think I heard you wrong."

"What did you hear?"

"You said, you said that… I didn't quite get it."

"I—love—you—Joanie. There. Is that clearer now?"

"But why? I am nothing but a twit and a mother who couldn't even take care of her own daughter. A mother who had to dance practically naked at the sleazy—"

"To put food on the table."

"I can't cook, that isn't—"

"You tried. And I love my food well done."

"I'm a horrible mother who plans to sell her daughter's precious woods."

"I am sure for a good reason. Joanie, I know you'll give your life for Sam and there's no way on earth that you'd hurt her on purpose. Now, tell me why you have to sell the woods."

"I need the money."

"We all do."

"You do?"

"Honey, even Bill Gates, founder of Microsoft, has bills to pay every month."

"Look around you, Julian. I am sure you noticed that this house is falling apart."

"I did notice, but when I met you, all thoughts about the mold, bowed porch, stained ceiling, and foggy windows disappeared. With you, in this house, everything looks wonderful, beautiful. No mansion or penthouse could beat this house. You made this place a home, a place where any man would want to come home to."

Joanie didn't know what to say to that. Julian grinned. Drat the man. He knew he rattled her senses and was now enjoying her discomfort.

"Well, that is surely the nicest thing anyone has said to me. Thank you, but the reality is I need to do something about this home. The carpenter told me that it's important that I replace the roof because it leaks, the windows because they can't stop the draft from coming in, and the ceiling—moldy from the water stains. Living around mold and drafty rooms is not good for Sam. I don't have money to spend on that. I closed my gallery when Dad died. I couldn't afford the rent. I owe the bank money from when Sam got sick last time. The only way to solve my problems is to sell the woods. I know Sam loves that place. But I love her, too, and her health is more important than anything. When you showed up I saw an opportunity to avoid selling the lot. Your money."

"Which you don't want anymore. You signed the forms in exchange for me leaving. You went ahead and contacted your agent to tell her that you changed your mind and want to sell the property to her client."

"Yes. How did you know about that?"

"Your Windermere agent called."

"Yeah?"

"Sam's Woods is sold. The buyer signed the papers today."

Wham! The news hit her so hard it paralyzed her. She heard the sound of her plate shattering as it hit the floor, but the sound seemed far away. Joanie groped for something to hold onto when the kitchen began to tilt.

Son of a bitch. Julian was on his feet right away when Joanie swayed like a tree. He barely managed to break her fall. "Hey, hey. It's okay." With Joanie in his arms, he sat back on the chair and set her on his lap. Joanie fought him, pushing his chest, urging him to release his hold on her. He didn't. Damn, he'd surprised her. He'd thought she was set on selling the property.

Julian pressed Joanie's head against his chest, planting kisses on her hair. Hot tears soaked his shirt, but he didn't care. More likely, he'd keep the shirt unwashed, to preserve her tears, her scent. "Honey, I'm sorry."

Joanie sighed and rubbed her nose on his shirt. "Sorry. Your shirt is —"

"Shhh... Don't worry about it." Man, she'd give him hell if he told her the truth of what had happened to the woods, of the deal he'd made without talking to her first. But buyers never talked to sellers. They both went through their agents.

"I'm sorry for breaking down like this. Normally, I am stronger and hardly cry."

Julian recalled calling her a cry-baby because she was a softy. "It's understandable. If I could hold you like this while you cry, I don't mind at all."

"I soaked your shirt."

"No problem, hon. You could wipe your nose with it too."

"Afraid I already did."

"I don't mind."

"Julian, the woods. Losing it is like losing Dad all over again. But I have to sell it, you understand? I'm not a bad mama."

"Of course you're not."

"Dad bought the property for Sam so she could run around there to find bugs. And he... He." Joanie swallowed. "He built the bridge for Sam so they could pretend to be fishing and to keep Sam's feet from having to cross the creek."

"Joanie, I have to tell you something." Julian tipped her chin up to look at her. Her eyes were red and her face blotchy. He'd never seen a more beautiful woman than her.

Without saying anything, he dipped his head for a kiss. Joanie met him more than halfway. He meant to give her a comforting kind of kiss, a quick touching of their lips, but the moment he felt her soft lips, his body came to life, especially the part directly beneath her bottom. He nipped her lower lip and she opened for him. Their tongues met, sharing an essence of taste that sent his senses spiraling down to the abyss of passion.

Joanie shifted and straddled him, her arms around his neck. Jesus, maybe he should hold off what he wanted to tell her. The moment was too good to ruin with his news. Just like their first kiss in his car, the magic curled around them but disappeared as soon as the damn headlights shined on them. Yeah, he'd tell her the news later.

He rubbed Joanie's back. Each stroke went closer and closer down to the round butt he was dying to cup right now.

He eased his hands inside her shirt, feeling her soft skin and the undersides of her breasts before cupping the mounds. His hips jerked up. Fuck, he was so hard his jeans felt tight and uncomfortable.

"Joanie, honey. I want you."

"Then take me." She nibbled on his jaw and ear while slowly grinding her hips.

"I want nothing but to take you. Here. Right now. But not while our daughter is in the living room and not in your state of vulnerability." Did he really say that? What had happened to I'll hold off on telling her the truth to avoid ruining the moment?

"Julian, I want you too. Been waiting for you for ages."

"You're not angry at me for bringing trouble to your home?"

"Trouble followed you. You didn't bring it. I will give my life for Sam in a heartbeat. But you, you'll keep her safe here and probably even in the afterlife. You love her too much to cause her trouble."

"You think highly of me."

"Since I was sixteen. I wanted you then and I still want you now."

"Oh, God, Joanie." He leaned his forehead against her collarbone. Sam had suffered because he'd fucked up. If he hadn't hooked up with Georgina, she wouldn't have come here to murder their little girl. Joanie must be told what Georgina had done. He hoped to God she'd forgive him. "Hear what I have to tell you first. Two important things. Then if you still want to continue this, say it."

Joanie moved a bit to look at him. Her brows arched high. "What?"

"First, when Georgina came to bring Sam toys, she stashed a can of nuts in one of the bags. Sam found it."

Raw hurt glittered in Joanie's eyes before they began to swell with tears. "She knew Sam's allergic to nuts?"

"Hon, I made a mistake of telling her. I never suspected she would —"

Joanie covered his mouth with her hand. "You trusted her. It's not your fault that she used the information against Sam, against us."

"I went to see her when I left you with Sam in the hospital. I made sure that she knows you will take action against her."

"I want her punished, Julian. Her waiting for a cop to knock on her door will have to suffice as punishment for now. We can talk about it later. Right now, I just want to enjoy the fact that Sam's okay. That's what matters most to me."

"You don't hate me for what happened?"

"No. You would never hurt our Sam. I know that."

"Thank God." He cupped her face and planted a long wet kiss on her lips.

"About your clip. Georgina must have searched my desk and found it. And when she did—"

"She broke it. While in the hospital, I figured everything out." She ran her fingers through his hair, massaging his scalp. "I remembered what you said about her not liking wives. Everything that she told me was a lie. Now what's the third thing you want to tell me?"

"I'm the one that bought Sam's Woods."

Joanie looked at him as if he had suddenly turned into a big slug or turd. She blinked fast, obviously thinking or absorbing what he had just said. "*You?* You bought the property. From who?"

"From Carmen. The Windermere agent. She called and I answered the phone. She told me to tell you that your buyer signed the papers. I couldn't let that stranger take our daughter's woods, Joanie. Our baby is crazy about the woods and her butterflies. No way am I going to let it go."

Tears bordered Joanie's eyes. Her chin trembled from biting her lips to control her sob. "You have no idea what this means to me."

"Oh, but, honey, I do. I saved the property not just for Sam. It's for both of you."

"I don't know what to say."

"Thank you, honey, is fine with me."

"Thank you."

"You're welcome. I'd give you the moon if I could afford it. I love you, Joanie."

"Why?"

"Why, why?"

"Why do you love me? I am the epitome of what you hate in a woman. You told me so the night you walked out on me."

Julian groaned and leaned his head on Joanie's shoulder. He couldn't believe how awful he had been to her. "I spoke in anger. No, that's not an excuse, and what I did is unforgivable. But, Joanie, hear this. Whenever I see a woman with the same color of your eyes, I think of you. When I see someone with hair that closely resembles the shade of your hair, I stare, thinking that it could be you. The women I...dated, none of them have chipped fingernail polish. But what do I see when I look at them? You. See, love? You were already embedded in my skin. I think you managed to do that when I used to watch you reading to Grandma. I didn't realize it until recently."

"Do you think that's the reason you didn't ask for a divorce right away?"

"Honestly, I really don't know the answer to that. One would think that would be the first thing I'd do, but I didn't." He rubbed her arms, feeling her smooth skin pucker.

"Until a few days ago."

"Yes."

"You still packed your clothes and were ready to go."

"For a totally different reason."

"Care to tell me?"

Julian leaned his forehead against Joanie's. "After what happened I thought you'd want to see me gone. So I packed my clothes. I'm ready to go."

"What happened made me see how much you really care for Sam. She cares for you too. She would hate for you to leave. I don't want you to leave, but you are free to go, you know. I signed the papers."

"Am I free? I thought I already spelled it out for you, Joanie. Maybe you'll understand me better if I quote Elizabeth Barrett Browning."

"You can quote Browning's poem?"

"Honey, you're not the only one who read to Grandma, you know. Let's see. Here we go. If I leave you both now, what will happen to me? Will I miss your cooking, your voice, our kisses, and Sam? Will I feel strange when I open my eyes and not see the stain on the ceiling and not find you in my arms? Will I be able to settle in a home other than this? No. No one can fill the space you and Sam occupy in my heart. No chubby arms can make..." Julian swallowed. His throat seemed to close up. "No chubby arms can make me feel loved and special. No Joanie to fold me in her wings of love. Without you and Sam, there won't be me." Hot tears rolled down his cheeks. He didn't care.

Joanie wiped his tears with the pads of her fingers. "That is beautiful. Not at all Browning's poem. It's way better. I love it."

"I know. Joanie, even if I go to the moon, you and Sam will still stay close to me. You can melt our ring and erase its existence, sign the divorce papers over and over, but I will never be free. How will I? You captured my heart, Joanie. Only death will set me free."

"Oh, God." Joanie wrapped her arms around him, her mouth on his neck. "I've waited for years to hear you say that."

"I'm sorry, baby. I'm blind and a big fat jerk." Julian kissed the top of her head.

Joanie looked at him and began tracing the shape of his eyebrows, nose, chin, and mouth. "I love you, too, but I will not beg you to stay."

"Why is that?"

"Because I love you that much. It'll kill me again to watch you walk out of my life, but if that's what you want, you won't hear me say 'Don't leave'."

"Not this time, honey. Leaving is not what I want. I'm staying for good. I love you."

Tears running down her cheeks, Joanie let out a short laugh followed by a deep sigh. "Sorry. I don't know why I cry so much. This is not me, okay. I'm not a— What's so funny?"

"Nothing, babe. Nothing. So you heard the two things I have to say. Now, what's your answer? Should we continue where we left off?"

"You mean this?" Joanie moved her hips in a thrusting motion, centering her heat on his already hardening shaft.

"Uh-huh?"

"Do you want to continue? I don't think you're..." Joanie wriggled her butt, "... getting excited."

"Minx. Want me to show you how excited I am right now?" His jeans were so tight he wouldn't be able to unbutton them right away.

"Hmm... That would be nice."

Julian cupped her face, smiled and pulled her close for a hot, hungry kiss. Their tongues danced with one another, dueling, plunging, and fighting for domination. Joanie was as hot and eager as he was.

Both of them burned from the fire he only knew one way how to douse.

"Kiss. Kiss. Kiss again," Sam said.

Joanie buried her face at the crook of Julian's neck, laughing.

"Our daughter has a penchant for showing up at inopportune moments," he whispered.

"God, you made me forget she's here. It's your fault," she whispered.

"Hey, Sam. Time for a nap, pancake."

"No, it isn't. I'm drawing."

"How about a bubble bath then a nap?"

"Yippee!"

"Thank God for small blessings."

Joanie laughed.

While tucking Sam in for her nap, Julian listened to the sound of the shower. He smiled in anticipation. He could hardly wait to have Joanie in his arms again.

Giving Sam one last look, he went downstairs and started making coffee. He was sitting on the chair looking at Sam's drawing when Joanie entered the kitchen.

He crooked his finger at her then patted his thigh.

Joanie raised a brow and chewed her lower lip. "What's on your mind? You're grinning. I don't trust that grin."

"You have to trust me, love. You're gonna like what I have in mind."

Once Joanie was close enough to him, he took her hand and urged her to straddle him. He lifted her shirt over her head and dropped it on the floor. Without bothering to unclasp her bra, he pulled the straps and lowered the bra to her stomach. Julian hissed at the sight. Joanie's breasts were enough to fill his hands. Without touching the sweet nipples, he lowered his head to suckle one while undoing the front of Joanie's pants. He slipped his hand inside and touched her heat. Hot damn, she was already damp. His middle finger slipped right in. Perfect. Just what he needed.

Joanie lifted her ass a bit to make room for his invading fingers. As he went in deeper, he smiled at the hungry look and anticipation on her face. "Baby, you're wet."

"Hmm..." was her only reply.

"You like that, huh?" He teased her nub with the pad of his thumb while his middle finger probed her deeper. Joanie moaned again when he squeezed her breast and sucked the other. His triple assault made her pant and grind her hips faster.

"More. More, Julian," she begged in her bedroom voice—sultry, soft, and erotic.

Harder, he sucked on her nipple imagining her clit in his mouth. He swirled his tongue around and around, tracing her areola, making her nipple move around. "Ah, babe. You are driving me crazy."

"Julian, I want you."

"The feeling is mutual, honey."

Joanie smiled lazily and got off his lap. She stood in front of him, yanking her pants and panties down to the floor. Naked, she crooked her fingers at him. He stood up at the invitation. "Take off your clothes."

Ah, his little wife wasn't shy anymore. Good. Because starting right now, he'd show her many ways to find pleasure in and out of bed. Because of his engorged dick, it took him longer to rid of his pants, but when he did, it sprang out and bobbed up and down. "I know what you want."

Joanie swallowed, her eyes focused on his cock. "You do?"

"Uh-huh." He knelt down and lifted her leg over his shoulder, exposing her already wet pussy. God, she was glistening and smelled good. He ran his fingers in between her folds, watching her center pulse. He drew his tongue along the inside of her thigh then repeated the process on the other one. Her flesh quivered.

"Julian, I can't wait anymore."

"Oh, yes, you can. You are so soft, honey. Soft all over." Cupping her bottom, he pulled her closer to kiss her mound. "Smell so good."

Joanie gripped his hair, urging him to press harder. "Now, please."

"So impatient."

As Joanie thrust her hips, trembling from the need he was sure paralleled his own, he tongued her. In an unhurried way, he licked her folds, savoring her taste, enjoying the sound of her erotic moaning. When he finally gave his attention to her distended nub, she cried her joy. Using his two fingers, he penetrated her sweet pussy. The slickness of her vagina nearly undid him. Damn, she was so tight and slick, he could do this all night. With a low growl, he trapped Joanie's clit in between his lips then sucked it hard. Ah, so fucking good.

Joanie's muscles contracted, squeezing his fingers. "Julian. Oh, God."

"You'll come, baby. We have the rest of our lives together. No need to rush."

"I don't have another minute to wait."

"Yes, you do." One harder suck and he let go of her clit.

"Julian."

"Shh… You'll wake our pancake up." Julian kissed Joanie, sharing with her the essence still lingering on his tongue and lips. "Good, huh?"

"Yes… This is so… Hmm…"

Julian chuckled. His wife was too hot and panting to form a coherent thought. Once again, he paid attention to her nipples, drawing out each one the way one would when sucking a lollipop, pulling at the same time. Fuck, he couldn't get enough of her. For the first time in his life, he wasn't in a hurry to find his own release. He wanted to please his wife—forever.

Gripping her hips, he turned Joanie around. "Put your hands on the edge of the chair."

"What?"

"Do it, Joanie."

"Like this?"

"Perfect. So beautiful." Joanie's ass was up in the air. He could see her plump lips wet and open. "Hang on, love." He gripped her hips tightly and aimed the tip of his cock at her entrance. "I love you," he said then drove home.

Joanie loved the position. Primitive yet sexually arousing. She could feel Julian rubbing the spot that raised her temperature to the max. Each time he drove into her, she moved her hips back meeting him, urging him to go in deeper. She cupped her breast and pulled her nipple, imaging Julian's hot mouth sucking it. "Julian, I love this. Don't stop."

"No fucking way, hon." Julian drove harder, ramming her with his long cock.

Just as she thought she'd die from intense pleasure, Julian slipped his hand around and touched her clit. "You coming, baby?"

"Oh, yes."

Julian surprised her when he pulled out swiftly, making her feel hollow. But a heartbeat after, he was licking her again, sucking her very center and rotating her clit at the same time.

"Julian, I'm coming. Oh... Oh... Julian."

It was the best orgasm she'd had in her life. Julian continued to suck her throbbing pussy. Before the pleasure ebbed away, he stood up and penetrated her again, triggering another orgasm.

"Now we fuck." Julian's hold on Joanie's hips was hard but his pounding was harder.

Their lovemaking became rough. And she loved it.

Julian was panting, chanting her name repeatedly. His sac slapping her clit titillated her and she could tell he was nearing his peak. Joanie reached down to massage him. That's when Julian let out a growl so long and low Joanie wanted to cry. She loved pleasuring him the same way she loved the idea that they were doing it because they loved each other.

"Oh, yeah. I'm coming, baby. Yes... Fucking good." Still joined, Julian kissed the column of her back. He helped her up then he maneuvered their bodies so he could sit on the chair while she sat on his lap.

"Should we go upstairs? You must be uncomfortable."

"Not when you're here with me. I want to stay like this forever."

"Me too." Julian pulled her even closer, his mouth hot against her neck. But something else was hot—his tears. She tried to turn around, but Julian only tightened his hold.

"What's wrong, Julian?"

"Nothing. I'm just so happy I feel I'm ready to burst. You're too wonderful, hon. I don't deserve you."

"Stop it. You're a good man, Julian. I think Dad knew it too. He wouldn't have led you back to our lives if he didn't believe that."

Julian sobbed on her neck, whispering, "I love you."

Chapter Eighteen

The front yard buzzed with little screaming and giggling voices. Kids took turns riding the elephant and bumblebee coin operated rides. A clown, armed with a bucket of bubble mix, walked around blowing bubbles on the kids while Animal Andy was busy making animals out of his tube balloons.

Parents hovered around the food table, busy serving their demanding kids with all kinds of treats consisting of animal shaped cookies, pies, hotdogs, and candies. In the middle of the table sat a pink butterfly cake from the bakery.

Under the huge cedar tree, separated from the crowd, Julian sat on the picnic chair savoring the excitement floating in the air, his can of Coors beer, and his friends who'd flown in last night.

"Man, it took you four long years before you found your dick. You have a lot of catching up to do. If I were you, I wouldn't let Joanie out of my sight. Damn, she's hot, isn't she?"

"Stop ogling my wife, Nolan. You're fucking engaged."

"Yeah, Nolan," Henry piped up. "Marry your girl and start making babies. Give Sam a playmate."

"I think someone already claimed Sam. See that little boy there?" Trey pointed at Marcus. "He's got the hots for Sam."

"The fuck, Trey. They're only four."

"Yeah, the same age you lost your virginity."

They all laughed, attracting attention from the grown-ups.

A pink balloon escaped from a little girl's grasp. It danced in the air, then floated away. The kids giggled and pointed at the balloon, making the girl cry. But all the attention was immediately diverted when Animal Andy popped a balloon.

Joanie grinned at something Dana had said. Julian stared at his wife sitting on the chair, her arm entwined with his grandma's. She swatted Mark's arm when he leaned in to say something that made his grandma shake her head.

He had flown his grandma in a few days ago to attend Sam's birthday party. She had cried her way to Oregon telling him, "I told you she's got a good heart," in between blowing her nose.

"You're one lucky son of a bitch, Julian. Joanie is a catch. If I marry, I want someone like her."

"Start looking, Henry. Marriage is not bad."

"Nah. I have to build my shipping empire first before I settle down. I'll just borrow Sam if I feel like stepping in mud puddles. Maybe I'll just borrow Joanie if I want to f —"

"Don't fucking say it or I'll kill you."

Henry hollered, "Anyone want another can?"

"Me." Trey answered.

"Be right back."

Julian stared at his wife. *His wife.* Joanie must have felt his stare and looked at him. He met her gaze.

Something invincible, maybe it was magic, connected them together. Julian felt a lump growing in his throat. He winked at his wife and laughed when she turned bright pink. He doubted his wife blushed because she was still shy around him, but because of what he'd done to her last night. The memory of their lovemaking had an immediate effect on him, especially the part that he knew he wouldn't be able to conceal if he didn't stop thinking about how Joanie had shattered in his arms.

Joanie must have read his mind, because she shook her head at him.

"What made your wife blush?"

"As if you don't know, Nolan."

"I swear I don't know. Couldn't be Julian's dick because his is just an inch long when it's hard."

Julian threw his empty can at Trey, hitting him on the side of his head.

"The fuck, man."

"Trey, catch." Henry tossed the can of beer. Trey caught it midair. "Whose dick is only an inch?"

"Yours," Henry, Nolan, and Julian said simultaneously.

He was still grinning when Sam came along, holding hands with her best friend Marcus. Her hairclip, a gold and emerald butterfly from Trey, was already dangling down by her ear. Julian wondered if Marcus would notice and fix it for her. To his surprise, Marcus stopped walking then pulled the clip off and hung onto it.

Julian shook his head, unable to believe what he'd just witnessed.

"Here come the young lovers," said Trey. "Hey, Sam. Having fun?"

"Yes, Uncle Trey. I like my clip," she touched her hair and pouted.

"Here." Marcus opened his tiny palm stained with dirt and grass.

"Can you hold it? Don't lose it or I'll punch you." Sam's brow furrowed just like Joanie's when she was mad.

Julian couldn't help it, he laughed.

"Daddy, Marcus said he wants to open the presents now and the big one over there."

Heart soaring whenever Sam called him Daddy, Julian picked up Sam and hugged her tight. "What about you, pancake? Do you want to see your presents now?"

"Uh-huh."

"All right, let's go."

"Presents, presents," Sam and Marcus chanted, drawing everyone's attention.

Parents and kids oohhed and ahhed at the presents, but he could tell everyone was anxious to see what was beneath the big white tarp. Finally, Sam opened her last present, a LeapFrog.

"The big one. Time for the big one, Daddy."

"Okay." Julian nodded at Mark, standing by the power generator. Mark smiled and turned on the generator. Popular music began to play.

Just as Julian had thought, the kids recognized the sound and screamed, "Carousel!" Between Julian, Mark and his friends, they pulled the tarp off and exposed the carousel. A frog, dolphin, turtle, unicorn, horse, elephant, pig, dragon, kangaroo, and, of course, a pink butterfly completed the whirligig.

Sam's squeal was the loudest when she saw the butterfly. She ran toward it, but Julian intercepted her. He tossed her high, hugged her tight. "Happy Birthday, Sam."

"Thank you, Daddy. I love you."

"I love you too."

"Can I go ride now?"

"Sure." He sat her on the butterfly and made a point of showing the kids that everyone riding must wear their seatbelts. Henry handled the line to avoid more tears, and Trey helped with the kids' seatbelts while charming their moms' pants off.

The kids took turns riding the animals, but Sam hogged the butterfly. No one complained. Julian watched his child, dressed in all pink, laughing and kicking her legs. He wondered if they'd be able to take her away from the carousel.

"She's a beauty, isn't she?" Mark handed him a can of cold Coors. "I bet she'll break many hearts someday."

"Good." He hoped to God she wouldn't fall for someone who'd only hurt her. He'd kill the guy or anyone who'd dare hurt his Sam. Julian snickered. Man, this must be how Saint Claire had thought about Joanie. Now he understood why the old man had gone as far as purchasing a gun to force him to marry his daughter.

"Joanie looks good. Better than ever, in fact. Although I noticed her yawning. I'd say she didn't get enough sleep last night."

"I can say the same thing about Dana. Thought I saw her wince when she sat down." He looked at Mark. They gazed at each other, then burst out laughing.

"Hey, I'm taking Marcus to see his grandma this weekend. Is it okay if I take Sam with us?"

"I have to ask Joanie first."

"Okay. Let me know. I can come and pick her up. Sam said Joanie's pancakes are brown now and not black. I want to see it for myself. And maybe have one too."

"You can also have her coffee."

"Really? Her coffee's not as black as tar anymore?"

"Oh, yeah. Still black, but it's the best coffee I've ever tasted."

Mark smacked him on the back, laughing his head off. "Man, you're doomed."

"What's so funny?" Dana stood in front of them with her arms akimbo.

"Hey, sweets. Julian just told me how much he loves Joanie."

"Well, what's funny about that?"

"Nothing. It's just a man thing."

Dana rolled her eyes at her husband, but Julian didn't miss the twinkle in her eyes. It was obvious the two were in love.

"Julian, I have something that belongs to Joanie. I think it's time she gets it back."

Dana opened her hand to show a simple gold band. He remembered asking Joanie what had happened to it, where it was. Her reply had been, "Somewhere."

"She gave you this?" he asked.

"No. She pawned it to me. I didn't want to take it, but she insisted. Mark and I offered to lend her money, but she wouldn't listen. She said she'd take it somewhere else. So I took it."

"How much?"

"Don't worry about it, Julian." Mark gave Julian a hard shove.

"Thanks, but no thanks. Joanie wouldn't like it. I'll pay you back. It's the least I could do for your help, for watching over my family."

"We love Joanie and Sam, and James too. Sad you didn't get to meet him without his gun pointing at you. James was a good father."

Julian looked at the couple who had given their friendship easily when he had finally convinced them of his intention. He couldn't ask for more. "I know. Thanks, you guys."

Pocketing the ring, he excused himself and walked toward Joanie. She was describing the carousel to his grandma when he stood in front of her. Without saying anything, he pulled her up to her feet. Right there, in front of Sam's guests, he kissed her. He heard a chuckle followed by giggles. Laughter and hoots echoed around them, but he didn't stop kissing his wife. He couldn't. His overflowing love for her had made him ignore the rest of the world.

When he was finally able to break his mouth away from Joanie's, he went down on his knees. Suddenly, all noise stopped except for the sound coming from the carousel.

"Julian, what are you doing?"

"Joanie Ravenwood, in front of Sam's friends and their parents, Grandma, and my friends, I promise to love you for all eternity. I dedicate my life, my soul, to you and Sam. I love you. Will you marry me – again?"

Joanie stared down at him with her eyes quickly filling with tears. "No," she said.

Gasps and groans were loud, but nothing compared to the blood pounding in his ears. "I understand."

"No, you don't. You see, we already had the best and most beautiful wedding. I don't want another.

Maybe someday, to celebrate our fiftieth, we could get married again. I love you, too, Julian."

Julian let out his breath. He grinned and kissed Joanie's hand before taking the ring out of his pocket. "In that case, Mrs Ravenwood, it's time you wear this."

The ring was a perfect fit. As perfect as his wife who couldn't cook, clean, or keep her hair tangle-free. He was about to get up from his position when he felt Sam's chubby arms wrap around his neck.

"I want another present."

Julian stood up with Sam on his back. He kept one hand beneath her bottom to keep her from falling. "What do you want, Sam?"

"A baby brother!"

Joanie groaned while everyone clapped.

Chapter Nineteen

Hours after the kids had left—some crying and most dragging their feet—Sam had insisted she continue to ride the butterfly. Julian occupied a lawn chair and sat in vigil watching his daughter wave at him each time the carousel went around. He thought if she hadn't been buckled in, she'd be on the ground by now. Her head had bobbed a couple of times, hitting her forehead on the pole, but she remained smiling. He'd bet it was to show him that she wasn't ready to go in yet.

Poor thing. I'll give her another minute then time to go night-night. His friends had hung around for a while before taking off to the Pink Mermaid. They had heard about the new blonde dancer who'd taken over Joanie's job and wanted to see her dance with a snake draped around her neck. Dana and Mark had stayed to help clean up, thank goodness, because the whole yard looked like Hurricane Katrina had come for a visit.

The carousel went around one more time. He waved back at Sam who hugged the pole as if it were the most precious thing in the world. Maybe he should unplug the generator. She wouldn't hate him, would she?

He was contemplating doing just that when he felt a familiar touch on his shoulder. Julian leaned his head to nuzzle Joanie's hand. God, how he loved this woman.

"She'll still love you even if you tell her it is time to stop."

"You sure?"

"I'm sure, Daddy. Come on, you spent enough time with her."

"Jealous?" Julian pulled her on his lap.

Joanie giggled when his hand began to wander. "No. I know I will always have my special time with you."

"Better believe it," he grinned. He cupped Joanie's face and gave her a long, wet kiss guaranteed to keep her hot and panting until she got her special time with him. "I'll bring Sam inside." His hand wandered toward to the part he planned to taste, feel, and fill all night, but Joanie gripped his wrist, stopping him from getting even closer.

"Little bug will fall asleep sitting on Flitter if you don't bring her in now."

"Flitter?"

"Uh-huh. She named all of the animals. You'll have to ask her tomorrow because I can't remember which one is which."

"All right. I'll bring her in. Warm up the bed for me, love."

After planting a kiss on his lips, Joanie stood up and left, leaving him hard and feverish from anticipation.

* * * *

Sam was out even before her head touched the pillow. He tucked her and Dolly in, sang *You Are My Sunshine* then kissed her baby lips. Like always, she smelled of soap.

He was already at the door when he heard Sam mumble something about flying and zoo and butterflies. Smiling, he left the room and went into the bedroom where his wife waited.

Joanie stood by the dresser combing her hair. She wore the pink negligee Sam had picked for her. "She had a great time. You didn't have to buy her the carousel. It must have cost you a fortune."

"I'd buy her the moon if it was for sale, Joanie. I love her that much."

"You're spoiling her."

"That's their prerogative as kids. Like it's my wife's prerogative to be pleasured in bed." Julian heard a catch in her breath. "You look great in your gown."

"Thank you," she said above a whisper.

"Now take it off." He shut the bedroom door quietly.

"I just put it on."

"Okay, but now I want you to take it off again. Or shall I do it for you? I can't promise you that I'll be careful, though."

When Joanie made a move to remove her gown, he shucked his cargo pants. His shirt joined them on the floor seconds later. Joanie's eyes were riveted to his bulging jockey briefs.

"Good God."

Slowly, he walked toward her. He stopped to grab her arm then he resumed walking until they were inside the bathroom. He turned on the shower.

"I already showered."

"Good. Now you're getting another one, Mrs Ravenwood." He swatted Joanie's butt.

"Julian," she said indignantly but did what she'd been told.

Happy, rock hard, and so much in love, he rubbed soap all over Joanie. He lingered on her breasts, enjoying their smooth feel before sliding the soap down until he reached her warm heat. Slowly, he moved the soap back and forth between her legs.

"Julian."

"What, Joanie?" Julian smiled and kissed her.

"I want you."

His temperature was near to boiling point. He placed the soap back in the holder so he could cup Joanie's sweet ass. "I'm here." He plunged his tongue inside her mouth the same time he eased two fingers inside her. She moaned while rocking her hips, urging him to go deeper.

He suckled her lower lip then her chin. He bit her shoulder without breaking her skin before bending down to lap on her nipple. Like a starving man, he sucked her hard. Joanie's juice pooled and wet his fingers. He kneeled in front of her. "I want to taste you again, love." He anchored her leg over his shoulder, spread her folds, then he began to feast.

Fuck, he almost ejaculated. He was ready to explode, but he wanted to taste his wife's cum first and to hear her scream. He trapped her clit in between his tongue and the roof of his mouth, pulling it out of its nest.

Joanie moved her hips, fucking his mouth. "Julian, Julian..."

"Yes, baby." Using his two fingers, he penetrated her.

Sweet, erotic whimpers urged him to pump his fingers faster and hard. Simultaneously, he finger fucked and sucked Joanie's clit until her muscles contracted. Giving Joanie one more languorous lick, he stood up and turned off the faucet. "Open your eyes, love. Don't fall asleep on me. We're just starting."

"God have mercy on my lusty husband."

Laughing, he wrapped a towel around her and hugged her tight. "Have I told you that I love you today?"

"Many times. But I don't mind you saying it over and over."

"I love you, Joanie."

"And I love you, Julian."

Julian led Joanie back in the bedroom. He could feel his control slipping and his pre-cum welling up and beading on the head of his cock. But he'd wait. He removed Joanie's towel, picked her up then laid her on bed. His body followed. "God, you're so beautiful." He showered Joanie's face with kisses before lying on his back. "Ride me, Joanie."

"I will." But she positioned herself between Julian's legs instead. Smiling, she wrapped her slender fingers around his shaft. "My turn to taste you, love." And she did.

Julian's toes curled from the sheer pleasure of her timid licking. "Good God, Joanie." He let his wife have her fun and watched his cock disappear inside her mouth. If he let this go on another second, he'd ejaculate while her mouth was wrapped around his hard shaft. Gritting his teeth, he pulled her on top of him.

"Take me now, baby. Now. Take me in. Yes, that's— fuck..."

Joanie slowly took his whole cock inside her dripping pussy. "Ohhh." She began to rock back and forth.

Julian reached down to touch her clit. "Yeah, baby. Fuck it. Come on. You're still tight."

Joanie's wet hair dripped water. She looked down at their joined bodies, licking her lips. Ah, his little wife would probably enjoy looking at herself in the mirror while he fucked her. Next time. For now, he'd give her what he could. He surged his hips upward to meet her. Without missing a beat, he helped her come.

"Julian, oh my God." She lifted her breasts, rolling her nipples in between her thumbs and forefingers. "I want your mouth on my breasts, Julian."

"Sure, baby," he placed his hands just below her armpits and pulled her closer so he could suckle her.

Joanie moaned and rocked her hips faster.

As soon as she gasped his name passionately, he flipped her on the bed so he was on top, their bodies still joined. "I love you." He surged deep and hard into her pussy.

His release shook him to the core. Exhausted, he collapsed on top of her, quickly rolled on the side, and pulled Joanie against him.

"I love you," he repeated then closed his eyes.

"I love you more."

Those were the last words he heard before he finally let sleep win.

Chapter Twenty

Rays of sunshine streamed through the canopies of cedar that were scattered around the cemetery. Birds flitted around the paths, perching on the grass where the headstones lay. Julian watched Sam riding her tricycle, her basket full of flowers they had collected from Joanie's garden.

Joanie hadn't told Sam the truth about her papa. Someday, Sam would know about him. Right now, Joanie wanted Sam to keep thinking about her papa still living, only sailing.

Sam stopped, turned around to smile at Julian, then waved before resuming her task of scaring the birds away. Joanie explained that Sam used to do that with her papa, to see if he was still behind, following her. Julian told her, unlike her papa, he would follow Sam until she was old enough to make a decision for herself.

Julian looked at the woman walking beside him. She looked so fresh and breathtaking in her white spaghetti strap dress. Her hair, tied in a bun, sagged, but she still managed to look sexy. Joanie oozed sex appeal without even trying. Tonight, he'd show her again how she affected him. Julian grinned at the thought.

"What's funny?"

"You really want to know?"

"With that grin? Yeah."

"How about if I just show you what I am thinking later?" He waggled his eyebrows.

"God, you're insatiable."

"You didn't complain last night or the night before or the night before that." He wrapped his arm around Joanie's waist and pulled her close.

"I'm not complaining."

"Good, because I know more positions to show you."

"Lord save me from my horny husband."

Julian kissed his wife. She tasted like morning sun and something uniquely Joanie. "I love you."

"I love you too."

Holding hands, they reached Saint Claire's resting place. A simple headstone with his name, birth date and the date of his death carved on the front. Beneath it, he read the words, "Here lies Sam's Papa and Joanie's Dad. The world will never be the same without you."

Joanie kneeled in front of the stone and called out, "Sam, bring your flowers here, please."

Sam brought the flowers then dropped them on Joanie's lap. "A picnic."

"No, bug. We are here to visit Papa. He's here resting."

Sam's little pink lips puckered. "Why? This is not his bedroom."

"I know, bug. But this is where he's going to stay forever."

Julian heard Joanie's voice shake. He moved away from his wife and daughter to give them privacy. From a short distance, he watched them. Sam was arranging the flowers while Joanie remained on her spot, her head bowed, without a doubt praying for her departed father.

He smiled, watching Sam tuck flowers in Joanie's hair. She threw the rest of the flowers in the air, then ran back to her tricycle. He'd bet Sam didn't understand anything about her papa sleeping there.

Joanie stood up and followed Sam.

Julian took the opportunity to visit Saint Claire. It was hard to believe that the man who had left a dark bruise on his rib when he had poked him with his gun now rested beneath the earth. He could still see Saint Claire's eyes full of hate and something akin to disappointment and sadness. Saint Claire had threatened to haul his ass to court if he didn't marry Joanie, but it was his words that had made him show up at the church.

'*Marry my daughter, Ravenwood. That's all I ask from you. She's a good kid and a gem. Look harder, you'll know what I am talking about.*'

He was right. Joanie was a priceless gem. Julian stared at Saint Claire's name. "It may be too late, but I still want to thank you for giving me Joanie and for trusting me with Sam. I promise you I will take care of them to the best of my ability. I love them as much as you loved them. If you are listening, please forgive me for all the heartaches I've caused you."

The wind picked up, disturbing the fallen leaves scattered around. Somehow, Julian knew Saint Claire was there to see his family, and hopefully, to forgive him. "Rest in peace, Dad."

Sam called his name. He turned around to see his daughter running toward him with Joanie a few feet behind her. He caught her in time before she head butted his crotch. "Hey, there."

"I want to go home and ride Flitter."

"Okay. How about you, Mama? Are you going to do some—?

"Julian."

"What?"

"Nothing. Let's go."

"All right." With Sam on his shoulders and Joanie walking beside him, his arm wrapped around her waist, he turned around to look at the grave again. It must have been his imagination but he thought he saw someone wave at him, then within a blink of his eye, the image was gone. *Thanks, Dad.* "Who wants a hot fudge sundae?"

"Me!" Sam kicked her legs and wrapped her arms around his head.

"Mama? How about you?"

"I'm gonna be fat before the month is over. Okay, I'll have one too."

"Good, Mama."

"Don't you miss Manhattan, Julian?"

"No, babe. I love it here. After all, this is where my heart is." Joanie smiled up at him, squeezing his side. He leaned down for a quick kiss making Sam squeal.

"Kiss, kiss, kiss!"

Yup, he loved it here.

About the Author

Tierney O'Malley began writing her first book when her youngest was in fifth grade. Now she is a multi-published author of erotic and paranormal romance. Her books appeared on KOBO, Bookstrand, and other third party bestsellers list. Ms. O'Malley lives with her husband and children in Seattle Washington, and is currently working on a new novel and sets of series she recently sold.

Tierney O'Malley loves to hear from readers. You can find her contact information, website details and author profile page at http://www.totallybound.com.

Totally Bound Publishing

Home of Erotic Romance

www.ingramcontent.com/pod-product-compliance
Lightning Source LLC
Chambersburg PA
CBHW021519240626
47154CB00002B/693